BIRTHRIGHT

DEUCES WILD™ BOOK FOUR

ELL LEIGH CLARKE

MICHAEL ANDERLE

BIRTHRIGHT TEAM

Thanks to the JIT Readers

Nicole Emens
Kelly O'Donnell
John Ashmore
Peter Manis
Mary Morris
Daniel Weigert
Larry Omans
Micky Cocker
Paul Westman

If I've missed anyone, please let me know!

Editor
Lynne Stiegler

CHAPTER ONE

**<u>Unmapped Location, Aboard the *Penitent Granddaughter*,
Bridge</u>**

Nickie took her feet off the console and sat up to glare at the empty space around the *Granddaughter* on the screen. "Where the fuck did he go?"

Adelaide gave Nickie an apologetic glance from the nav console. "He just vanished. There's nothing to show where the *Briar Rose* went."

"A whole fucking ship can't just disappear into thin-fucking-air." Nickie got up to pace while she bitched. "I know he doesn't have Gate technology."

Grim turned from his station. "This is why we should have traveled *with* John instead of tracking him from a distance." He ignored Nickie's icy stare. "Then we wouldn't be here—wherever here is."

Keen wore a frown. "Where exactly are we?"

"Dunno." Nickie shrugged. "The ass-end of nowhere?

There's fuck-all around by the looks of it. Meredith, where did Prince Precious go?"

There was a barely noticeable delay before Meredith answered through the intercom. "Oh, this is new. He has passed through the interdiction."

"Interdiction? Why aren't we following?" Nickie demanded. "That word sounds familiar…" The ship shuddered. "Meredith, what's going on?"

"How much do you actually *want* to follow the prince?" Meredith asked. "This could become somewhat awkward for you."

Nickie glared at the speaker. "We wouldn't be all the way out here in the first place if I didn't want to know what he was up to. Just follow him, Meredith. I don't care where you have to go."

"Which is what I thought you would say. We can go around…I think. Meredith came back a few seconds later. "Yes, we can. I'm correcting our course."

"Go around *what*?" Nickie demanded. "Will you quit being so fucking mysterious?"

Meredith sniffed. "The planet's defenses. Unless, of course, you want to go through Federation checkpoints?"

Nickie dragged a hand down her face. Of *course*, it was Federation space. She should have known it was too much to hope, to avoid it forever. "As *if*. I might as well turn up waving a fucking banner to announce my arrival."

Grim chuckled. "I wonder how that would go down?"

Nickie pulled a face at him. "It wouldn't, because it's not going to happen. Meredith, our route?"

Meredith sounded smug. "Luckily for you, I have an

idea where we are, which tells me where John is headed. We'll arrive shortly after he does."

Nickie looked around at the others. "Yeah, but where is he going?"

Neither Adelaide, Durq, nor Keen had the faintest idea.

Grim gave her a look but just lifted a shoulder in reply to Nickie's questioning glare. "I know nothing. But you want to find John? Just go with it."

Nickie sat back down in her captain's chair with a heavy sigh. "Whatever. Mere, just get us to wherever he's going."

"That's the plan," Meredith chirped.

Nickie frowned and got back to work. She had a sinking feeling that whatever Meredith knew was going to piss all over her already-less-than-stellar mood.

However, her mind was stuck on the same track it had been on since she'd accepted that she had a crew. Especially now that the first few days had passed, and everyone had begun to fall into a comfortable routine.

Nickie ate and worked with the others, and she had even stayed behind in the mess after dinner a couple of times. She knew that fully immersing herself in the easy camaraderie was going to take a little longer, though.

The others respected Nickie's need for space as much as any group living aboard a ship could. She still spent most of her free time alone, and when being around the others became too much, she went down to the training hold and worked her frustrations out on her bag.

Her *punching* bag.

It wasn't just the adjustment to her living situation, though. John had gotten her back up in more ways than one. She was still more than a little uncomfortable with the breezy way he'd sailed into her life and straight back out of it again, trailing his assumptions about her behind him like a judgmental fucking bridal veil.

Nickie still wasn't sure she even *liked* him. While she might have been willing to overlook his…quirks for the sake of a wild night or two, boyish charm was only charming for so long before it began to wear on her.

Sure, he was hot, but he had that relentless naivety that she loved to hate. Nickie didn't want to admit to herself that part of the reason she was keeping her distance was that she didn't want to find out if the attraction between them during the volcano mission remained now that the danger had passed.

Nickie was well aware of how emotions got ramped up when lives were on the line, and how easily the relief of survival turned into the urge to grab the nearest warm body. Shit, she'd picked up her last lover that way.

The memory cut her for a second, but she shook it off. That was the past. Prince Pretty should have taken her up on her offer while she was feeling generous, but he'd missed his chance. Nickie was back to thinking of him as an annoyance, albeit a reasonably interesting one.

What Nickie *really* wanted was to find out what John's secretive behavior was covering.

They'd followed him to Zuifra and waited just outside the planet's detection capabilities while he'd delivered the plant that would save his father's life. Nickie had intended to hail him once he'd taken care of his family business, but the prince had all but snuck away from his home planet afterward—which set off alarm bells with the whole crew.

Nickie's instincts had told her to follow John and remain hidden. The others had agreed at the time, despite Grim's current stance on the effectiveness of their surveillance now that the *Briar Rose* appeared to have vanished.

Nickie found the situation confusing. John had been pretty forthright during the volcano mission. Almost too open, if she were honest. In fact, if she were *completely* honest, there was no "almost" about it. Whether or not he'd meant to affect her that way, her conversations with him had forced her to examine some hard truths about herself.

Consequently, John's sudden vagueness about his destination after he'd taken the plant back to his planet had tickled her curiosity.

Some things just don't change.

Nickie scowled mentally at Meredith's intrusion. *What do you know?*

I know you, Meredith replied.

Yeah, well, then you know to leave me alone unless you're going to stop being a pain in my ass. What's going on here, Mere?

You know what's going on. We're following your prince.

He's not my *fucking prince,* she grumbled. *How long until we get around this interdiction?*

A few hours.

The bridge was companionably silent while Meredith took care of the ship. Nickie alternated between brooding in her chair and pacing the bridge while she waited for the EI to announce that they'd reached their destination.

A short time later, Grim took Durq with him to get a start on dinner. Keen sat back in his chair and practiced the ancient military art of sleeping while there was a minute, and Adelaide did what Adelaide always did when she wasn't fixing things: she read up on how to fix things.

Eventually, Nickie gave up pacing and flopped into her chair to take a leaf out of Keen's book. Just as she felt herself begin to drift off, the ship ground to a halt.

She opened one eye when she felt the almost imperceptible change. "Meredith, why have we stopped?"

"We've reached the planet," Meredith replied. "We've stopped because we *don't* want to get caught in that shielding."

Nickie's heart sank. "It's an outpost? Shit. Well, take us into the dock as quietly as you can. We might be able to sneak in and out without anyone noticing."

"It's a little late for that," Meredith told her. "We're being hailed."

Nickie sat up and narrowed her eyes. "Who's hailing us? Put them onscreen."

A man in a familiar uniform appeared on the screen. "Skaine ship captain, identify yourself and your purpose… Oh, you're not a Skaine."

Nickie scowled at the Guardian as she sent the ship's registration over. "It's pretty fucking obvious I'm not a Skaine. We can dispense with the niceties. Which outpost is this?"

The Guardian looked at her as though she'd hit her head. "You don't know where you are?"

Nickie rolled her eyes. "Would I be asking if I did? I've been away for a while."

"Must have been a long while," he replied.

"You could say that," Nickie deadpanned. "So, are you going to let us in?"

"I don't know. Wait a minute." The Guardian held up a finger and reached down to pick up a handset. He half-turned while he waited for an answer.

"Get me Jennifer or Charles. Yes, it's urgent. There's a Skaine ship here with a human captain who wants to know where she is." A pause while the person on the other end spoke. "The *Penitent Granddaughter*," he replied. There was a longer pause. "No, they don't know where they are, but they have Federation verification. I know that's weird. Yes, ma'am. Of course."

He hung up the handset and turned back to Nickie. "This is High Tortuga, ma'am. You have clearance to land just as soon as someone gets there to confirm your identity."

"Oh, fuck my *life*," Nickie groaned.

The Guardian smiled. "Welcome back to the fold, ma'am."

He cut the connection before Nickie could tell him to fuck off, which she appreciated since she was making an effort to be pleasant to people unless they deserved differently. It wasn't the Guardian's fault she'd ended up in the very place she'd been avoiding like a Baka avoided soap and water. She would save it for John. He was the one who had enticed her into coming here. *The fucker.*

The screen returned to showing the planet, and the ship resumed its usual thrumming as the engines kicked in again.

"I've received a course for safe passage through the defenses," Meredith announced. "We've been instructed to dock at the platform over the southern continent. Last chance to turn back, Nickie."

Nickie considered it for a moment. There was a chance that some of her family were here. She was surprised to find she could admit she cared. Could she face them? She wasn't sure.

She had changed for the better—that much she knew. That she still had so far to go was arbitrary. She had hit rock bottom and was clawing her way back up one good deed at a time. That had to be worth *something*.

She was torn for a moment. The urge to run was strong, but something in her refused to back down to her fears. She was Nickie-fucking-*Grimes*, for fuck's sake.

She *never* backed down.

"Take us in, Meredith. It's about time I stopped running."

"As you wish."

The *Granddaughter* jerked as Meredith turned the ship to follow the path through the deadly satellites to the platform in high orbit above the planet. The ship came to a stop again when they reached the dock, and the majesty of High Tortuga slowly revealed itself.

Keen and Adelaide drank it in. They were awed by the shining cities stretching from one end of the northern continent to the other, and then again by the sharp contrast when the wilderness of the southern continent came into view a short time later.

Adelaide tilted her head. "This planet is beautiful!"

Nickie put her head in her hands and silently cursed the day she'd met John-of-fucking-Reinek. "This place has my aunt's size seven footprints all over it."

"I didn't know your Aunt Tabitha wore size sevens," Grim commented as he arrived on the bridge with Durq.

Nickie scowled. "Not *that* aunt."

"Just how many aunts do you have?" Adelaide teased.

"Enough to make war on the entire galaxy," Nickie shot back. "Right now I'm talking about my aunt who is the former Empress." She winked at Adelaide's shocked expression.

Adelaide recovered quickly. "The *Empress*? Do you think she's here?"

Nickie grimaced. "Fuck, I hope not. Otherwise, Meredith's prediction about this being awkward might be a little bit of an understatement."

"We have visitors," Meredith cut in. "Shall I allow them to board?"

High Tortuga, Above the Southern Continent, Aboard the *Penitent Granddaughter*

Nickie stomped through the ship's corridors to meet the Guardians at the airlock. She had swung by her quarters on the way, and the boarding party was annoyed by the delay. That was okay, *she* was annoyed by having to divert to the southern continent just so they could verify her identity.

Nickie? The Guardians won't wait forever. They are Wechselbalg, remember. They're not famed for their patience.

Nickie slowed her pace. *I'll be there in a minute; they can wait that long. I have a bone to pick with you.* She was tempted to refuse to allow them onto her ship, but they had already docked and were requesting entry.

A bone?

Yeah. You knew all along where we were headed.

I had an idea when we came across the shielding at New Devon. You were more interested in finding Prince John, so—

Nickie cut her off as she turned into the corridor that led to the airlock the Guardians had docked at. *Don't give me that shit. You could have told me we were headed right for Federation space. You've wanted me back in their clutches ever since I reactivated you.*

Meredith sniffed. *This isn't exactly Federation space. And this isn't exactly a Federation planet, either.*

If they bow to my aunt, then it's a fucking Federation planet no matter what they dress it up like. I bet there's Coke in every bar, a huge cemetery, and a suspiciously low crime rate planet-wide.

Um...

Nickie hit the wall next to the airlock. *Just fucking let them in already.*

Okay, but let's not break too much of the ship in the meantime.

Shut it, Meredith.

The airlock completed its cycle and disgorged a quartet of Bethany Anne's finest onto the *Penitent Granddaughter.*

Nickie looked them over as they filed aboard—three men and a woman. The woman was clearly in charge. She returned Nickie's appraisal with a cool smile and produced a small device. "Hello, Captain—"

"Grimes," Nickie supplied. "Guardian?"

"Lakshmi," the woman supplied. She held out a hand, which Nickie looked at for a moment before turning her attention to the other three Guardians. Guardian Lakshmi stowed her hand, and her cheery tone dropped a touch. "Nice name to have, Captain Grimes."

Nickie lifted a shoulder. "It's just a name. Don't Guardians usually come in threes?"

"Not this time." She held out the device. "Place your right thumb here, please, Captain. As soon as we confirm your identity, we'll be on our way."

Nickie snickered. "Yeah, I don't think so." She held up the Ranger badge she'd snagged from her quarters. "This is all the ID I need."

Guardian Lakshmi's eyes bulged. "Where did you get that badge? You *do* know it's an offense to pose as a Ranger?"

Nickie tucked the badge away. "Who says I'm posing as anything? It's *my* badge, and it proves my identity."

The Guardian gave Nickie a hard stare. "I know Tabitha, and *you* are not her." She held out a hand. "Give me the badge."

Nickie made a show of checking her own ass out as she replaced the badge in her pocket. "Yeah, you've got me there. Was it my ass that gave it away? I am a little lacking in the badonkadonk department compared to my aunt."

"Your aunt, sure." The Guardian's frown deepened. "The badge, Captain."

Nickie shook her head. "Not happening."

Guardian Lakshmi turned to the other three Guardians and pointed at Nickie. "Arrest her."

The ship speaker system crackled. "Nickie, just identify yourself. This woman is only doing her job."

The Guardians halted in their tracks at Meredith's interjection.

"Meredith?" one of the men asked in confusion. He looked at Nickie. "Who *are* you?"

Nickie sighed and grabbed the woman's device. "Oh, for fuck's sake. Here." She jammed her thumb onto the device's pad and waited for the burn. Once it had taken a DNA sample from her, she tossed it back to the Guardian and crossed her arms. "You go away for a few years, and all of a sudden nobody knows who you are when you turn up without telling anyone and try to bypass security."

The device beeped.

"Oh," was all the Guardian managed when she looked at the screen.

Nickie's smirk returned. "Oh? Is that all? Not 'Sorry, Nickie?' 'Welcome back, Nickie?'"

One of the other Guardians blurted in a near-whisper, "Oh, shit! I know who she is! She's John's granddaughter. The one the Queen exiled."

Nickie thought about objecting that she hadn't been exiled, but it wasn't any of their business, so fuck them. "Are you satisfied?" she asked Guardian Lakshmi.

Lakshmi nodded. "Yes. You're cleared to go down to the planet, Captain Grimes." She tapped her wrist holo a couple of times. "I've sent Meredith coordinates for landing. How is she here? So far from the *Meredith Reynolds*?"

Nickie tapped the side of her nose. "That would be telling."

The Guardians all nodded as though Nickie's answer was to be expected. "It was good to hear her voice. You can keep the badge," she added.

Nickie broke into a full laugh. "I fucking *know* I can. The only way anyone gets this badge from me is to pry it from my cold, dead fingers."

The man who'd recognized her snickered. "Better you

than us when you have to answer for using it, Grimes or not."

Nickie gestured toward the airlock. "If we're all done? I have places to be. Say bye to the nice Guardians, Meredith."

Meredith opened the airlock. "I wish you all a pleasant journey."

The woman looked back. "Funny, I don't remember Meredith being so snarky."

"And I don't remember Guardians being so stuffy," Meredith replied airily.

Nickie snorted. The woman *was* a bit stuffy. It didn't mean she forgave Meredith, though.

The Guardians left, and Nickie made her way back to the bridge. The others were all elsewhere for the moment, which meant that Nickie was left alone with her thoughts whether she wanted to be or not.

She slouched in her chair and sighed. She wasn't ready for this, not yet. She had about a year to go before she was expected to appear before her aunt. She still hadn't decided if she would go back or if she would just keep moving forever.

What's the matter, Nickie?

Nickie tsked. *Why do you want to know? So you can trick me again?*

I didn't trick you, Nickie. Meredith feigned sounding hurt. *I just know better than to argue with you when you're focused like that. Would you have given up if I'd told you?*

Nickie huffed. *No.*

There you go, then. Besides, we're here now.

Because you lied to me, Nickie pointed out.

I didn't lie, Meredith corrected. *I can't lie.*

That was a fucking lie right there, Nickie told her. *Where exactly is 'here?' I've never heard of High Tortuga, but I can tell before we even go planetside that this place is important to Aunt Bethany Anne. The security here is fucking ridiculous.*

I don't know a lot about the planet yet, Meredith informed her. *Just what I've gotten from the public information systems. I was a little reluctant to connect with the planet's EIs since you were already upset about being here, and revealing my presence would reveal yours.*

Nickie snickered. *Yeah, well, it's probably for the best. You never know what nasty virus you'll catch from hooking up to a strange network. What do you have?*

Where would you like to begin?

Nickie hesitated when Meredith brought up the aforementioned system menus in her HUD. She scrolled past the first sections of video feeds, which were labeled "Justice System" and "Libraries." High Tortuga looked to be a hub for…what, she wasn't sure. It was only just outside the Federation, or at least a good percentage of the available maps agreed that it was.

Meredith, these maps have been tampered with.

Ah, yes. The location of High Tortuga is need-to-know. Your Aunt Bethany Anne commandeered the planet during her Baba Yaga phase.

Nickie frowned. *You know about this place?*

I know a little, Meredith confirmed. *Baba Yaga locked this planet down a short time before the end of the Empire. It was to be her safe haven after the Federation was formed.*

Nickie laughed. *You mean after the rest of the galaxy'd had enough of being terrorized by her and demanded she step down?*

Meredith's tone became a little cooler. *My Queen stepped*

down because she wanted to. Visiting High Tortuga was impossible last I knew. Consequently, I am rather surprised that Prince John was aware the planet existed. Even more so that he knew the route to get here. Things have changed.

Nickie's heart flipped in her chest. Maybe Tabitha was here. *And there was me thinking you were on my side. Is Aunt Bethany Anne here now?*

I do not believe so, Meredith told her. *Or at least I have not been contacted by ADAM, which is as good as the same thing. You know that I am on your side, Nickie, but you cannot expect me to badmouth my mother. You should be glad you have me and not a copy of ADAM. He would have given you a little zap for speaking about Bethany Anne that way and called it a kindness.*

Nickie snorted. *Fuck that—although it's not as bad as you threatening to wear me like a meatsack. So, if Bethany Anne isn't here, what about Aunt Tabitha?* She almost didn't want the answer. *Actually, don't tell me. No, tell me.*

I can't tell you anything except that we're almost at the coordinates Guardian Lakshmi provided.

Who? Oh, the stuffy woman. Sure. She sat in silence for a few moments. *Mere?*

Yes?

What if Tabitha is here? What if she doesn't want to see me?

Why would she not want to see you?

Nickie shrugged. *I dunno.*

Tabitha loves you, Nickie. All of your family love you.

Nickie snorted. *They have a funny fucking way of showing it. I feel so damn loved out here on my own, just like I felt fucking swamped in that shit after they all fucked off and left my mom and me behind.*

Meredith's tone was hopeful. *Are you ready to talk*

about that?

She shrugged again. *No. But I suppose it would make me feel better or some stupid shit like that, so go ahead.*

They do *love you, Nickie, but you can't see that, can you?*

Nickie bit back a laugh. *No, Mere, I can't. All I can see is that everyone I love leaves me—or makes* me *leave because they can't handle me.*

You are rather intense, but that's standard for your genetic line.

Thanks. Nice to know the rejection is because of something I didn't choose.

It isn't why people move on, Nickie. Life happens, and they move with it or get sucked under.

Nickie frowned and squirmed to adjust her position in her chair. *What do you know about it?*

I've had two hundred or so years between iterations to observe humans and learn how they work. You wouldn't have entertained this conversation just a few months ago, and now look at you. You should feel good about the progress you've made.

Nickie's first reaction was to tell Meredith that nothing had changed, but it had—and she *did* feel good about where she was now. It sure as fuck beat the anger and hurt she'd lived with for the majority of her sabbatical.

Meredith continued, *Do you still want to push everyone away? How about the crew?*

Well...no. I do kind of like having them around. Grim is good. He gets me. Durq is Durq, and I have to work not to scare him, but he's not too jumpy these days. I'm kind of getting used to having Adelaide and Keen around. I like Addie. She reminds me a little of my Grandma Jean.

Their heuristics are markedly similar in areas. Have you

noticed a difference in the way the crew reacts to you compared to others?

I...um.

They appreciate that you care about them, and they show it in return.

Nickie found that a stretch. *I wouldn't go that far. They like that I provided a way off the colony.*

I hope you realize that isn't true. What about Grim? He could have gone anywhere, but he chose to stay with you.

Nickie smiled. *Grim is...my friend. But don't tell him I said that.*

Why not?

She didn't answer.

You believe he will leave if you show your affection for him?

Everyone leaves, Meredith. Everyone. Nickie sighed.

You left, Meredith reminded her gently.

Yeah, because my aunt made me. It wasn't like I had a choice.

I meant before that. You left the Meredith Reynolds. *Your mother.*

She didn't want me around! What was I supposed to do, hang around and wait for her to drop me a few crumbs whenever she pulled herself from her work? She banged her hand on the armrest of her chair. *All I wanted was to be a Ranger like my Aunt Tabitha, and even she didn't want me enough to fight for me when it came down to it.*

Meredith chuckled softly. *You think Tabitha didn't want you? I thought you blamed your grandfather for her absence.*

Yeah, well. I've had a few experiences lately that made me see he might not be completely to blame for Tabitha leaving.

So you have shifted your hard feelings to your aunt?

No! I'd never blame her. She's a Ranger, and she had a duty to uphold. *She had to do what she had to do, regardless of how I felt about it. I suppose my grandfather had to make the same kind of hard decisions when the Empire broke up, but my mom... well. She could have come here with everyone else and started a new life on High Tortuga. She chose to separate us from the rest of our family.*

Meredith was quiet for a moment. *I think you are getting closer to the truth.*

What more truth do I need? I could have grown up here with my aunt and been a Ranger, but instead, I spent a miserable childhood alone on the Meredith Reynolds *while my mom buried herself in work. Then, when I had issues, she was more than happy to wash her hands of me.*

You weren't an easy teenager to raise, Meredith pointed out. *It couldn't have been easy for her when you started abusing every substance known to man, woman, and alien.*

It wasn't easy for me, either! Nickie didn't want to cry. She'd cried enough as a kid to make her want to hit things instead of feeling—things like bars, clubs, and anywhere else the music was loud enough that she didn't have to think. *Why do you think I did all the drugs in the first place? What, does everyone think that teenage me just decided one day to get high for the fun of it? They fucked me up, Mere.* She scrubbed her sleeve across her eyes to stop the stinging. *Fuck, I should* blame *my mom for all of this! I'm fucking glad I left!*

Meredith made a soothing sound as Nickie's tears flowed. *It's okay, Nickie. I know. And you are past that now, because you are stronger than any pain or any drug. You have me, and I will never leave.*

I know, Mere, she sobbed. *I know.*

CHAPTER TWO

**<u>High Tortuga, Northern Continent, Space Fleet Base,
Hangar 126</u>**

John was slightly unnerved by the single robed figure waiting for him when he disembarked from the *Briar Rose*.

There was nobody else there. No welcoming parade, no banners. It was a touch disconcerting since his father had told him to prepare for both. However, he was pleased to avoid the usual rigmarole associated with a royal visit. Maybe he could get his father to drop some of the traditions once he got back home.

He ducked back inside the ship to dump his regalia, squared his shoulders, and paced down the ramp toward the solitary figure with what he thought was a princely enough smile.

John held out a hand. "You must be Barnabas."

Barnabas shook the offered hand. "And you are John of Reinek. Follow me, please." He led John to a buggy and drove them off the base. "Your father just called a short time ago to ask if you had made the journey safely."

John chuckled uneasily. "I almost didn't."

Barnabas gave him a questioning look. "Do tell."

John shrugged, a little embarrassed. "Devon. It's a little crazy there. I ran into a little trouble in the bazaar during the stopover. I was lucky there were some friendly humans nearby."

Barnabas' mouth twitched. "Rather. Well, you are here now, and in one piece, as it were. I was delighted to hear your father is recovering from his sickness. It cannot have been easy for your mother to believe he was going to die."

"How did you know about that?" Only John's immediate family had known how close his father had come to death.

Barnabas inclined his head to hide his smile as he made a turn. "It is my job to know these things."

John had to school his face as the city opened up before them. He'd seen the city from orbit, but it was a different beast entirely now he was on the ground. High Tortuga was a far cry from Zuifra. In fact, it outclassed most other places he'd visited outside the heart of the Federation. He leaned his head against the frame of the buggy and soaked it all in while Barnabas drove in silence.

Tall, dark buildings made of glass hemmed them in on all sides, making John feel like he was traveling a mirrored walkway rather than the wide, perfectly maintained road they were on.

John saw that the packed sidewalks were split into lanes. The people on the outside were mostly just everyday citizens going about their day, but the inner lane drew his eye. He wondered why the glazed-eyed people walking there didn't cause accidents since they were all immersed in their holos.

A closer look when a gap formed showed him that they followed guidelines painted on the ground. He supposed that allowed everyone to go about their day in studied ignorance of everyone else around them.

John had a sudden surge of homesickness. He wanted to be back by the river on Zuifra, having a picnic with the sun on his skin. Maybe after he picked this device up, he could go back to Themis and invite Nickie to come with him. He looked at Barnabas as the older man made a turn. "Where are we going?"

Barnabas didn't take his eyes from the road. "To the biosphere research center."

John nodded, a little put out by his guide's short replies.

Barnabas smiled. "There will be plenty of time to talk once we are in a secure location. Patience is a virtue, young man."

John did a double-take and twisted in his seat to face Barnabas. "Did you just read my mind?"

Barnabas sniffed. "It hardly counts as an intrusion when you broadcast your thoughts so loudly." He reaffirmed his grip on the buggy's steering and continued to stare nonchalantly at the road ahead.

John leaned against the frame of the buggy again and went back to watching the city. He tried to keep his thoughts to himself as they traveled, however someone was supposed to do that. High Tortuga didn't *quite* feel like a Federation planet, although John's experience so far had taught him that outside of the official boundaries things tended to run a little differently.

Devon had been a prime example of that. He was glad to have moved on from that wild place. In contrast, so far High Tortuga was like an ultra-organized ants' nest compared to the spread-out frontier he'd had to pass through to get here.

Barnabas stopped the buggy at an intersection while a long maglev train thundered by. The block they'd stopped at was given over to rolling grass and trees, all a little purpler than John was used to. His planet's ecology was closer to Earth's. John's gaze lingered on the extensive landscaping, the sculptures that dotted the open park, and the well-dressed families taking time together within.

This place had wealth. *Lots* of wealth.

John was in awe of the casual use of advanced technology wherever he looked. Even the smallest personal transports zipping along the shipping lanes in the upper stratosphere put his ship to shame, and the people clearly had the means to pursue fashion and art. Some of the children in the park had toys that John as a grown man would love to play with.

In fact, if he had been brought here on the royal transport as his father had almost forced him to instead of flying himself, he would have been hard-pressed to believe he was anywhere other than the center of the old Empire. John didn't actually care. He was here to pick up the device for his father, and then he was heading straight back to Zuifra before the disease the device would prevent hit his planet.

"You're impressed?" Barnabas asked.

John nodded. "It's hard not to be. This place is amazing —but I suppose that was the point of this?" He waved a finger to encompass the fleet of tiny *ArchAngels* and the holonannies that shepherded the children playing in the park, the luxury vehicles on the road around them, and the drones that moved overhead.

Barnabas snickered. "Not really. I just wanted to drive." The last carriages of the train flashed by, and Barnabas continued on through the city. He turned again, taking the buggy into the barely visible side entrance of an imposing onyx building.

There was a brief moment of darkness, and then they came back into the light as Barnabas took the buggy down a spiral ramp. "We have no need to impress anyone. You are here for our help, after all."

John felt his cheeks warm with embarrassment. "I'm sorry, I just assumed…"

Barnabas pulled into a parking spot by a large set of doors on the third level below ground. He waved John off and headed for the doors. "It is no matter." He pressed his thumb to the keylock on the doors and waited for them to be admitted.

The light turned green, and the door clicked open. John followed Barnabas out of the dimly-lit parking lot into the research facility.

"I understand that you are in need of protection against the Vlargian rot?" Barnabas inquired as they walked. "When I spoke to your father, he was extremely concerned for your people."

John nodded solemnly. "The Zuifran people are at risk of starving if the rot hits. It's struck on four planets in the

Rebus Quadrant already, and our crops have no immunity. It's a pretty tense situation. Our only hope is to get the technology you offered us up and running before it reaches us."

Barnabas looked suitably concerned. "Well, this intervention should be enough to prevent any of that from happening."

John screwed his face up. "I hope so. To be honest, I'm a little unsure how we can reprogram our entire biosphere without causing devastation to the ecosystem."

Barnabas grinned. "That's why you're here asking for our help instead of fixing the issue by yourselves." His grin widened at John's blank expression. "Don't worry about it, I have no idea how it works, either. I leave the tech to those who understand it, like Tabitha."

John furrowed his brow at the familiar name. "Tabitha?"

"The programmer for this," Barnabas told him as if that explained it all perfectly. "It would have been better if she could have been here to talk you through it, but we will have to muddle along without her, I'm afraid."

John was about to press for more information when Barnabas' expression became unfocused.

He recognized that look. Barnabas had an onboard EI?

Nickie had an onboard EI.

He kind of missed her, although maybe it was the sense of danger he felt when he was near her that he really missed. He loved a challenge, but that woman was like a lit powder keg wrapped in a nest of spitting cobras. Thrilling, but not survivable in the long term.

He caught himself smiling and snorted at the searching

look Barnabas gave him. He'd forgotten the man could read his mind.

High Tortuga, Northern Continent, Biosphere R&D Lab

Barnabas bent down to the low cabinet and peered inside to locate the device John had come to collect. While he hadn't expected his niece to follow the prince to High Tortuga, it was no accident that *he* was here.

On intercepting the message from John to his parents, Tabitha had made it Barnabas' business to discover everything he could about the man who had designs on their niece.

Barnabas was dubious, and protective too. His checks had revealed the prince's wanderlust, which was not something they wanted to encourage in Nickie since they all wanted her home as soon as she could be persuaded.

With Shinigami's help, the vigilante had poked around and discovered that John's home planet was in danger from a virulent spaceborne fungus. The contact with John's parents couldn't have come at a better time. Offering to help Zuifra had been the right thing to do, but it also gave him a reason to investigate the prince further. The opportunity to bring Meredith Nicole a step closer to home was icing on the cake.

Barnabas had to repress a chuckle at the combination of attraction and fear he felt from the prince as his niece passed through John's thoughts. He certainly knew Nickie well enough, although he seemed unaware of Barnabas' relation to her.

Barnabas didn't think this pampered and idealistic

prince would last two minutes with the nuclear Nickie he remembered, but he would love to be wrong. From what he'd seen in John's memory his niece had softened somewhat in her time away, just as they had all hoped she would when Bethany Anne had made her ruling.

The young man should still watch his step, though. That kind of fire didn't just disappear overnight.

Shinigami interrupted his musings.

Barnabas, there is someone in orbit presenting herself as Ranger Two.

Oh? Interesting. He knew that there was only one person who would dare turn up at High Tortuga and disregard the law. *Is it Merry?*

The Guardians who went to verify the captain's identity appear to believe so. She had Tabitha's badge.

The corner of the former Ranger's mouth quirked. *We must do something about that. It's not an entirely acceptable title these days.*

Shinigami snorted. *Like Nickie cares. What are you going to do about* him? *He let her follow him. What if it had been someone else?*

What do you suggest I do to him?

I don't know. Maybe just a little light torture?

Barnabas sighed. *You know that's not going to happen. Where is Nickie's ship docking?*

Back at the base, Hangar 003.

Then we'd better get over there before she starts a fight with the ground crew. He turned to John, who was thinking about his niece right at that moment. "You allowed yourself to be followed."

John's face dropped. "I did not!"

Barnabas shook his head. "Then please tell me why the *Penitent Granddaughter* is coming in to dock? I know my niece would not be here voluntarily."

"Nickie is here…" John's voice trailed off. "And she's your niece? That must mean you're *the* Barnabas. Shit, she was telling the truth about her family. You're a Nacht, and that's how you can read my mind." John paled.

Barnabas sighed the sigh of the eternally put-upon and handed the young man the device he'd come for. "Indeed. I'm going to meet her at the dock now. Keep up, or you will have to find your own way back to your ship."

He left the lab with a swish of his robe.

John hurried after Barnabas with a slightly glazed expression.

CHAPTER THREE

High Tortuga, Northern Continent, Space Fleet Base, Hangar 003

Nickie burst onto the ramp, impatient to find John and get the fuck off High Tortuga before any of her family realized she was there. It was a small hope and one that proved fruitless when she saw who was waiting to meet her. "Uncle Barnabas."

"Merry," he returned. "Will your crew be joining us?"

"Some." Nickie glared and pointed to the ground crew who were hurrying to take care of the *Granddaughter*. "I have a Skaine onboard. Anyone who hurts him will die, and it will be a painful fucking end. Am I clear?"

Her uncle looked a little bit too pleased for her liking. "Of course, your Skaine is safe," he assured her.

The ground crew all nodded and got to work.

"Good." Nickie turned and waved to her people. Grim, Adelaide, and Keen exited the ship.

Barnabas tilted his head at them and smiled. "Pleasure to see you again, Grim'zee."

"You too, Barnabas. It's been a while." Grim leaned down to speak into Nickie's ear when he reached her. "Durq doesn't want to leave the ship."

Nickie turned and stalked back up the ramp. She remembered to calm her body language before she reached the door, so she didn't scare the timid Skaine any more than he already was.

She found him hanging onto the rail by the door. He was shaking so badly she almost wanted to pick him up to comfort him. "Durq, you don't have to leave the ship if you don't want to."

Durq looked up at her with wet eyes. "I want to go with you."

Nickie raised an eyebrow. He clearly didn't. She spotted Brandy at the end of the hall, which gave her an idea. She laid a hand on his shoulder. "Durq, I'm sorry, but I really need you to stay here and ride herd on the house bots. There are still repairs to take care of, and they've all been acting screwy since we left the colony."

"Really?" Durq's skinny shoulders sagged in relief. "I mean, if that's what's best."

Nickie smiled fondly at the little Skaine and shooed him toward Brandy. "It is. Off you go, then."

Keep him busy, Meredith. I don't like leaving him when he's this afraid.

There's plenty for him to occupy himself with while you're gone, Meredith assured her. *I've given the house bots a good long list of repairs that Durq can handle with their help. He'll be fine.*

She headed back down the ramp to where her crew waited with Barnabas and his companion, who Grim appeared to know already if the animated way the two were talking was an indication. Looked like she had found her missing prince.

She walked over and slapped them both on the back. "Why am I not surprised that you two rekindled the bromance the minute I turn my back?"

"Nice to see you again, too," John replied.

"I didn't say it was nice." Nickie grinned. "What are you even doing here?"

John's smile faded. "My planet is in trouble."

Nickie snorted. "Again? Didn't you just have a disaster? You should probably start looking to move planets. Zuifra doesn't sound like the best place your family could have chosen."

Barnabas shook his head at Nickie's teasing. "Just as one matures out of it, another is dropped in my lap. When will the universe decide enough is enough and leave an old man to go and wreak vengeance in peace?" He sighed and waved for the five of them to follow him out of the hangar. "This way, all of you."

They left the hangar and took a short flight of stairs to the ground floor level, then Barnabas led them through the base.

Nickie walked with her uncle while the others followed a short distance behind. She glanced back to make sure none of them were wandering.

"You take good care of them," Barnabas remarked.

"Don't look so surprised," Nickie replied offhandedly.

"They're my crew. If I don't take care of them, my ship doesn't run."

Barnabas chose not to comment.

Nickie appreciated that he didn't press further. "So this is where everyone ended up? Meredith told me Aunt Bethany Anne took over."

Barnabas chucked dryly. "Not quite. This planet belongs to Baba Yaga."

Nickie gave him a look. "Really?"

"Ask anyone, and they will tell you all about the Mistress. We're set up to run the whole planet from the base," he told Nickie. "The governance system we've developed has been more than successful."

"What's that—do as you're told or die?"

Barnabas sighed. "Not quite, my dear. Maybe in the early days when crime was still rampant here. Your aunt wanted crime to be the less attractive option. This place was the original Devon, in case you didn't know."

"*I* didn't know," John chipped in.

"You weren't supposed to," Barnabas returned in a cool tone. He turned back to Nickie. "Anyway, Baba Yaga cleared out the more unsavory elements and turned the others to her purpose, then Bethany Anne made the adjustments necessary to the infrastructure and provided education and healthcare for the masses. Now the planet is thriving, and the people are mostly content."

"It sounds like a great idea," John enthused. "Mostly content is about the best you can hope for as a ruler. How does it work? Maybe some of it would be useful for Zuifra."

Barnabas launched into an explanation of the libraries,

the rollout of universal medical care planetwide, and the support system for those who struggled to live by someone else's rules.

"So that's why Devon resembles feeding time at the zoo," John marveled. "What if the new planet revolts? You put that many rabble-rousers together, there's bound to be trouble at some point."

Nickie snorted. "Then Baba Yaga will probably turn up in the mood for a fight."

Barnabas shrugged. "I'd argue that, but I would be lying if I said it's not how it would go down. However, there are measures in place to ensure that the people of Devon do not revolt." He turned to John. "I believe you met some of them."

John frowned. "I did?"

Barnabas smiled. "Your rescue in the bazaar? That was more than likely undercover Guardians."

Now John was impressed. "That's... The Empress is too smart."

Barnabas snickered. "She knows."

Nickie kept her reactions to herself, but the others had no issues with pointing out all the interesting features they passed as they followed Barnabas through the base.

She dismissed the technology that fascinated Adelaide, was unimpressed by the detailed attention paid to the décor, which drew Grim in, and was as far from Keen's total awe at the sheer scale of the place as it was possible to be. Even John paused with the others to watch a troop of Guardians training in an open courtyard they passed.

Nickie had seen it all before. "Hey," she called. All but John turned to look at her. "You can stay and watch if you like. Just ask the base EI where to find me when you're done."

Keen and Adelaide high-fived and went back to watching the sparring Guardians. Grim tilted his head in a question but turned back to cheer along with the others when she nodded to confirm.

Nickie rolled her eyes at their overexuberance and picked up her pace to match her uncle's.

High Tortuga, Northern Continent, Space Fleet Base

Barnabas gave Nickie a half-smile when she fell into step beside him on the stairs. "You are somewhat mellower than the last time we met, my dear."

Nickie returned his smile. "I've had some time to chill. Doesn't mean I'm going to take any shit from anyone."

"So it would seem." They walked in silence for a while before Barnabas spoke again. "How have you been?"

Nickie waved a hand. "Oh, you know. Mostly high." She scowled when she didn't get the reaction she wanted.

"Meredith tells Shinigami differently." His tone was gentle. "You have been doing some good work recently."

"Meredith is a fucking snitch." Nickie shrugged, a small smile escaping her as she spoke. "But yeah, I've been helping out at this colony. They were fish in a barrel for whatever asshole came through there to take advantage of them." She grimaced at Barnabas' questioning gaze. "Fucking Skaine. Don't worry, they're dead now."

Barnabas smiled. "So you have ceased to fight your nature? We were never close, but it hurt us all to see you on such a destructive path."

Nickie looked away. "There comes a point where poker and drugs just don't do it anymore. I had to grow up sometime." She didn't flinch from the comforting hand Barnabas laid on her shoulder.

"That is a relief to hear. Perhaps you may not need your final year after all. It would be good to have you home, my dear. When you are ready," he added quickly as Nickie stiffened, then changed the subject. "You will have to tell me how you ended up with a Skaine on your crew. I saw how kindly you treated it."

"Him. How I treated *him*." Nickie hadn't been aware that Barnabas had watched her interaction with Durq. Seeing her be nice to a Skaine must have confused the hell out of him. She snickered internally. Let him wonder. Serve him right for being nosey. "Maybe," she hedged.

The silence grew heavy between them as they walked. Finally, she relented. "So, where are we going? Are you taking me to my aunt?"

Barnabas gave her a sympathetic glance. "None of your aunts are here right now."

"But *you're* here."

Barnabas chuckled. "Yes, Merry. I am. I have my own mission in these parts."

Nickie locked her emotions down, feeling her uncle's scrutiny. "None of them?"

Barnabas shook his head. "There was a matter that needed Bethany Anne's...*personal* attention. They will be back. At some point."

Nickie shrugged. "Whatever. I was here to find Prince Pretty Boy anyway. I'm a little surprised he's here, to be honest."

"His planet is facing a crisis."

Nickie snorted. "You have to wonder why they settled that planet in the first place."

Barnabas nodded sagely. "I believe the original colony was founded in somewhat of a hurry to avoid a civil war." He pulled the stairwell door open and gestured for Nickie to go through.

"Well, that explains some of it. I'm more curious about High Tortuga, to be honest." Nickie waited for Barnabas at the top of the stairs. "Why here? Why this planet? Why not settle somewhere inside the Federation?"

"Many reasons," Barnabas told her. "Not least of which is that Bethany Anne and Michael have chosen to raise their family here."

Nickie's mouth fell open. "Bethany Anne had *kids?*" She had never thought to hear that her whirlwind aunt would settle long enough to raise a family. "You have to be lying. You're serious?"

Barnabas broke into a grin and pulled a tablet from his robes. "Would you like to see proof?" He showed her his screensaver, a photo of two mischievous-looking identically grinning children with Bethany Anne and a man Nickie assumed must be the infamous Michael. "Alexis is the girl, Gabriel is the boy."

Nickie peered at the photo and searched for the appropriate thing to say. "They're...small. Very nice. Michael wasn't dead, then?"

"Not exactly. He was scattered in Myst form across the Etheric for a hundred years or so. He had recovered by the time Bethany Anne found a way to repair the Gate and went back to Earth to rescue him."

"They got the Gate to work?" Nickie asked. "Fuck. I didn't think even BMW could get it done this century. Is the Gate still active?"

"The way is closed," Barnabas commiserated. "The Gate had to be hidden since we are definitely not supposed to have it."

"Shame. I always wanted to see where my Grandma Jean came from." Nickie took a closer look at the photo. "I get why Bethany Anne was so cut up. Dude's still pretty hot for a guy from the Stone Age."

Barnabas gave her a stern look and put the tablet back in his pocket. "If you say so. We have company." He tucked his hands into his sleeves and nodded toward the stairwell they'd just left.

Nickie huffed when Barnabas halted. "Great."

"You don't like the prince?" Barnabas asked. "I assumed you two were involved."

Nickie glowered. "You're not reading me? It's not like you to respect boundaries. He's a pain in my ass."

Barnabas chuckled and held up his hands. "I won't ask. In fact, I'll give you two a minute." He slipped through the door at the bottom of the stairs, leaving Nickie to wait for John.

John was panting slightly when he burst through the door, but he ran down the stairs to where Nickie stood impatiently. "Thanks for waiting." He flashed his dimple at her. "So...you couldn't resist following me."

"It wasn't too difficult." Nickie grabbed the door handle. "You shouldn't have made it so easy to tail you if you didn't want to be caught." She flounced through the door and took the stairs two at a time until she caught up to Barnabas.

Barnabas turned when he heard her approach. "Merry."

"You can just call me Nickie like everyone else." She heard John clattering down the stairs after them. "Where are we going?"

"You're hungry," Barnabas told her, "and I would like to discuss a certain matter with you. We can do it over a meal."

Nickie was about to protest when her stomach growled.

Barnabas smiled knowingly. "Come, my dear. Let's get you fed." He waved a hand in John's direction when the prince appeared behind Nickie. "You, too."

High Tortuga, Northern Continent, Space Fleet Base, Rec Room Theta

Barnabas listened to Nickie and John snarking at each other over their food at a table in the corner of the small rec room while he waited for something to eat.

He absently watched his food being printed on the tray behind the hatch, his mind on his niece and her unexpected return.

Nickie's sabbatical appeared to be having the desired effect. Barnabas had scanned her mind before she'd even exited the ship. He had been pleasantly surprised to find she was no longer the unpredictable ball of anger who had caused so much trouble in her younger years, although she was still troubled deep below the surface.

When Bethany Anne had sent her away, some of the family had disagreed with such strong measures. Barnabas had not been one of them. His own road to perdition back on Earth long ago came to mind. Sometimes the only way to break through to the light was to fall all the way into darkness.

I like her, Shinigami told him.

I am not surprised. You are drawn to chaos, and she is a long way from still waters. However, I will be glad to report to Bethany Anne that our niece is on the road to recovery.

She reminds me of Tabitha. You know, if Tabitha was likely to break your face at any moment. You could use her in that situation with The Six.

Maybe that is not such a bad idea. Her training is impeccable, and it would be an opportunity to allow her some contact without pushing her into rejoining us too soon.

You want to ease her in.

Yes. As gently as possible. Nickie will run like the wind if we overwhelm her. The food replicator blinked to tell Barnabas his food was ready, and he took his tray over to the table.

Nickie and John paused their bickering when he sat across from them and sighed pointedly at the painfulness of their youth.

"What's up, Uncle B?" Nickie asked brightly.

"Nothing in particular," he replied, wrinkling his nose at the nickname. "I have a situation that needs to be taken care of."

"Why would you involve me?" she retorted. "I've fuck-all to do with this place."

"I was unsure whether to involve you at all, but you might be the best person for the job." Barnabas paused with his fork halfway to his mouth. "You were claiming to be a Ranger, were you not?"

Nickie shrugged. "So what if I was? Aunt Tabitha left that badge for me to use."

Barnabas shook his head. "Tabitha left that badge to remind you of who you are. The Rangers have been outlawed, Nickie."

Nickie narrowed her eyes. "If the Rangers were outlawed then how the fuck do you have a 'situation?'"

Barnabas gave her a solemn look. "The Rangers may have been disbanded, but my need to see Justice brought wherever it is needed is not that easily quashed. I could not allow injustice to continue unchecked, so I became an outlaw. Or rather, a vigilante."

"Vigilante?" Nickie snickered. "You mean you want to tear shit up and have a reason for it. You're just the same as me."

Barnabas' eyebrow twitched. "We are all the same at heart, but yes. I see the vigilante spirit in you. Which makes me wonder if you might be interested in assisting me with my situation."

Nickie gave her uncle a hard look and pointed her fork at him. "Look, I already told you I want nothing to do with High Tortuga. I'm not going to involve myself or my crew in your drama, because the next thing I know you'll have sucked us in with no escape."

"I promise that is not the case at all. I was asked by Lance to take care of a certain obstacle to a system joining the Federation."

"That sounds a little assassin-y," Nickie cut in.

"It does," John agreed.

Barnabas inclined his head a touch. "It could very well be. However, I am a little busy taking care of this planet at the moment. It makes things difficult since the system is not close enough for me to return to High Tortuga quickly should trouble arise."

John frowned. "So why are you asking Nickie? She's not an assassin."

Nickie glared daggers at John. "What is it you need me to do?" she asked Barnabas.

Barnabas placed his fork on the table. "The system in question is called 'The Six.' It has, funnily enough, six planets, all of which want to join the Federation."

Nickie shrugged. "So what's the problem? Sign them up."

"It's not that simple, unfortunately. The Six must be brought in together, as per the trade agreements that have already been negotiated. The issue is the internal politics of the first planet, Vietania, which Lance cannot be seen to interfere with."

John's head snapped up. "That name sounds familiar."

Barnabas looked at the prince as though he were a child who had just sat on the potty for the first time. "Very good. Your people came from there originally."

"Must have been a *long* time ago," John remarked.

Barnabas smiled. "Yes, I suppose for you it would be."

Nickie hated all that committee shit. Action was how she dealt with problems, which was one of the reasons she'd held herself apart from colony life back on Themis. Leave that to the people who loved to talk shit all day and night. When they needed something punched, then she would show some interest. That was her political stance. "What's the problem with the first planet?"

"There's a dispute about the line of succession, which could topple the monarchy of the planet."

"I know all about them," John chipped in.

Barnabas frowned at the interruption. "Yes, well, *you* should be getting back to resolve your own planet's issue."

John lifted a shoulder. "I will, once you finish explaining the situation Nickie is walking into."

Nickie glared at him. "Why? You barely know me."

John gave her that maddening grin. "You wound me. I thought we were friends, Nickie?"

She narrowed her eyes at him and turned to Barnabas. "Just get it over with so Prince Prissypants here will fuck off home."

Barnabas looked from Nickie to John, who was a little too happy to have gotten under Nickie's skin. The silly boy might as well have pulled her hair, and Barnabas remembered how upset Lillian had been by what Nickie had done to the last boy who'd done *that*.

However, the prince was still in possession of all his teeth, so maybe the teasing wasn't too unwelcome. Young love had changed much since he had last courted a lady. "As you wish. The dispute involves the line of succession, as I said, and who is the true heir to the throne. The council of the Six has been unable to resolve the dispute, and until they do, they cannot join the Federation since all six planets need to sign to complete the process. To separate them would unsettle their delicate ecology of trade agreements and currency balance."

"So you want me to go in and knock some heads together?"

Barnabas shook his head. "No, I want subtlety on this. It

is imperative this situation is quickly and quietly resolved in a way that leaves the rightful monarch in charge. The means don't matter, only the resolution."

"Isn't that a little drastic?" John challenged. "I mean, it sounds like you want Nickie to go in there and murder someone."

Barnabas gave the young prince a hard stare. "And if that is the solution, then that is what it is. One day you will be responsible for your people. You will learn that ruling is not all largesse and parades."

John looked away. "I didn't think that it was," he grumbled.

"What is in the people's best interest is sometimes not pleasant for the individual. This is an extreme case. The Six are interdependent. They share overall leadership, and their economies are inextricably linked. Without intervention, the entire social structure of the system will come crashing down. The fate of the Six and their place within the Federation depends on the ability to make hard decisions. Nickie is more than capable of these choices."

Nickie warmed a little at the praise, but she didn't like it. "My days of taking Federation orders are done."

Barnabas turned his gaze on her. "You are not listening. This has nothing to do with the Federation. They have to be completely in the clear in case any investigation occurs afterward. You, my dear, will be a vigilante. A lone wolf acting on her own agenda." He winked at her. "What fault could lie with the Federation if a rogue element stepped in to remove an obstacle to peace?"

"Yeah, I get it, but why would I want to put my neck on

the line? Never mind my crew's. They've done nothing to deserve getting caught up in Federation fuckery."

Barnabas spread his hands wide. "Fuckery aside, I know you care. These people need help, Nickie." He shrugged and picked up his cutlery to continue eating. "Think about it before you reject the mission out of hand."

Nickie ate her dinner in silence. She ignored John's attempts to draw her into conversation, too wrapped up in the decision Barnabas had presented her with. He soon gave up and turned his annoyingness on her uncle. *Ha.*

What the fuck was she supposed to do about her dilemma? The last thing she wanted was to be pulled back in. But the people... She was torn.

Meredith? No answer. *Meredith? Where have you gone?*

I haven't gone anywhere, Meredith replied. *I was avoiding your wrath.*

What wrath? Nickie complained. *I am an absolute fucking delight and don't you forget it. You, however, are a snitch. The least you can do is help me with this decision after you sang to Shinigami.*

What is there to say? The people need help, and you can help them. I'm not going to tell you to absolve yourself of your sense of responsibility. How would that help?

Nickie had hoped that was exactly what Meredith would do. *I don't want to deal with this right now.*

Take your time. I know you'll make the right decision. In the meantime, another of your Aunt Tabitha's diary entries has become available.

Mere, you are forgiven. Nickie pushed her tray away and stood up to stretch. "I'm beat to hell, Uncle B." She let out a huge yawn to emphasize her point. "Can I sleep on it and give you my decision tomorrow?"

Barnabas smiled. "Of course. We'll pick up your crew on the way to the guest quarters I had prepared for you all."

Nickie balked. "Quarters? I'm fine on my ship, thanks."

Barnabas folded his arms. "Nonsense. You will be my guests, and nobody will know you were here. I insist."

Nickie sighed, too conflicted to argue any further. "Whatever. I just want a bed."

CHAPTER FOUR

High Tortuga, Northern Continent, Space Fleet Base, Guest Suite

Barnabas left, having shown them all to their room for the night, a self-contained apartment on a corridor near the rec room they'd eaten in.

Adelaide, Grim, and Keen were still bubbling about the base. Nickie joined them in the kitchen to hear about it all. She badly wanted to read her aunt's diary entry, but she decided a few minutes with them wouldn't make a difference.

John had disappeared into one of the bedrooms off the communal area as soon as they'd arrived. Nickie listened to Adelaide's recounting of their tour for a little while, and then made her excuses and headed for bed.

She chose the nearest bedroom, which happened to be the one next to John's. The bed inside called to her, singing a sweet song of comfort and coziness. She looked at the adjoining door to John's room, which called to her for other reasons.

Are you ready for me to open the diary entry? Meredith asked.

Nickie halted mid-step toward the door. *Wow, Mere. Just as I was about to get some.*

Meredith snickered. *I have no idea what you are referring to.*

You know exactly what I'm talking about. A ride on the bone rollercoaster, a meat injection. You get me yet? I was about to climb aboard the vagina miner—

Stop, Meredith pleaded. *You go too far.*

Apparently not far enough. Otherwise, I'd be getting into a different bed right now. Nickie kicked off her boots and shrugged out of her overalls. She dived into the bed and snuggled into the duvet. *Open it, then. Cock will have to wait. Some things are far more important.*

She looked at the door again.

For now.

She settled back to read and almost cried out when she saw the first page.

It was a note from her Aunt Tabitha, and the timestamp matched today's date.

Hey, Trouble!

So, you made it to High Tortuga!

I wish I could have been there to see you, but duty comes first and I'm up to my eyeballs in *that* these days. I haven't forgotten my duty to you, though.

Barnabas told me that you are healing. I'm so proud of you! Of course, *I* knew you just needed to burn off a little steam, and you would be fine.

You've been on my mind the whole time you've been gone, but even more since you started to make your way back to us. I want you home! You've been out there alone for too long, my *pobrecita*.

Let's see if I can help you get here sooner.

I can't help remembering my Merry, the little girl who used to follow me around with my badge around her neck. Do you remember those days?

QBBS *Meredith Reynolds*, Grimes Family Quarters

Tabitha threw the chopped vegetables into the pan with a scowl.

Jean noticed her expression and snickered. "What is it with you all? You can face off against the biggest bad but you see a vegetable, and it's the end of the *Gott Verdammt* world!" She passed Tabitha a bunch of carroty-looking things.

Tabitha took the kitchen knife to them. "It's not that I don't like veggies. I just don't like *these*."

"They're modified so that everyone finds them delicious. What's not to like?"

Tabitha pointed at the veggie pile with her knife. "Veggies

are not supposed to taste delicious, not without all the seasonings and butter. I want to know I'm getting the goodness. How am I supposed to know if they all taste so...wrong?"

"Wrong?"

"You know," Tabitha frowned and cleaved a carrot in two, "*nice.*"

Jean raised an eyebrow. "I've seen some of the things you're willing to eat. A few modded vegetables should not be an issue for you. Besides," she waved over the pan, "this is something I'm making to freeze for Merry. We've been looking after her a lot lately, so I wanted to make sure she's eating properly when it's just her and John. We have steak and greens for dinner."

John appeared in the doorway. "You're making me eat greens *again?*"

Jean turned and smiled knowingly at him. "No, you can have the kiddie veggies."

He grinned. "Thanks, babe. Lillian just called. She's still at work, so she asked if we could pick Merry up from daycare."

"Is Merry staying the night?"

"Uh-huh. Lillian's pretty pissed about missing family time. She only got her delivery an hour ago, so she's going to be working through the night. Apparently some issue with her components supplier on Yoll?"

"Again?" Jean frowned. "I offered to step in and find a more reliable company aboard the *Meredith,* but you know how hard-headed our daughter is. She has to do everything by herself."

John chuckled. "Just like her mother."

Jean pointed her spoon at him. "You're just happy you get out of date night at the theater."

John came over and nuzzled Jean's cheek. "I was glad of the time together. It didn't matter what we planned."

Jean turned into him and sighed. "I know, but we have to support Lillian."

"That we do. We're all so lucky to have you."

"And as long as you make sure I know it we're golden, you big lug. C'mere." Jean kissed him soundly.

Tabitha made a gagging sound. "Ew! Get a room, you guys!"

"We *have* a room," John deadpanned. "You're standing in it."

Tabitha rolled her eyes. "Very funny, John. Have you ever considered switching to a career as a stand-up comedian?" She dumped the carrots in with the rest. "I can watch Merry while you two have your date night." She smirked at John. She knew as well as Jean that he didn't want to sit through the Torcellan opera that Jean had been going bananas over for the last month.

"That would be great!" Jean squeezed John to her. "Go collect Merry, and we can still eat together before we leave for the theater."

John narrowed his eyes at Tabitha, who stuck her tongue out at him. "Sure thing, babe. I'll be back soon."

Jean let go of John and shooed him toward the door. "Just don't take too long or dinner will be ruined."

John returned with Meredith Nicole just as Jean and Tabitha were putting the food on the table. "Hey, Grandma Jean, look who I brought with me."

Merry squirmed in his arms. "Let me *down*, Granddad!" She ran straight past Jean to Tabitha. "*Aunt Tabbiiiiie!*"

Tabitha held out her arms to catch the blond-curled whirlwind and spin her around in a circle. "My Merry! Did my little angel have a good day?"

Merry scowled. "No! I got in trouble! Stinky Ms. Daniels gave me a timeout. I *hate* her!"

Tabitha and Jean looked at John for an explanation.

John shrugged. "She busted some kid's nose. He's a Wechselbalg, so it wasn't too serious an injury."

Jean frowned lightly. "Why would you do that, sweetheart?"

Merry's face was thunderous. "Stupid Kevin. He took Lacey's snack, so he deserved it! Meredith said not to, but it wasn't *his* snack, and Lacey cried, so I socked him a good one."

Tabitha snorted. "You are definitely *my* niece."

Jean gave Tabitha a pointed look, then returned her attention to Merry. "Okay, sweetheart. I get that you didn't like that Kevin upset your friend, but did you need to hurt him?"

"Of course I did." Merry broke into a proud grin. "I got Lacey's snack back."

John ruffled her curls. "You're my little hero for standing up for your classmate, but when Meredith tells you not to do something you should listen to her. She's there to guide you."

Merry stuck her tongue out at her grandfather. "I'm not little! I'm…" She counted on her fingers and held up a chubby hand to show them. "Nearly three! I'm a *big* girl, Granddad. I fighted in Justice!"

That brought a chuckle from the three adults.

Jean held out her arms to take Merry from Tabitha. "Come on, my little Justice warrior. Let's get you cleaned up for dinner."

Tabitha smiled fondly at Merry's chatter as Jean carried her off to the bathroom.

"Grandma? When is Mommy coming?"

"She has to stay at work tonight, sweetheart," Jean told her. "You get to stay here with me and Granddad, and Aunt Tabbie."

Merry blew a raspberry. "I hate work. Mommy *always* has to be there. When I grow up, I'm not going to go to work. I'm going to be a Ranger like Aunt Tabbie and do fighting instead..."

"Oh, yeah?"

"Yeah! And if anyone tries to make me, I'll sock them just like I did to Kevin!"

Dinner was over, and Jean and John had left for their date an hour ago.

Merry was bathed and sweet-smelling. Tabitha had helped her into her footie pajamas, and they were playing before bedtime.

"Ready or not, here I come!" Tabitha wandered through the house on her tiptoes, the seeker to Merry's hider.

She heard a giggle from the closet.

Tabitha opened the closet door and scooped up her niece before she fell off the box she'd pushed over and climbed up on to try to reach Tabitha's gun belt from the hook inside the door. "Oh, no, Merry. Aunt Tabitha's weapons are not for little hands like yours."

"Want them. I like the pretty guns. *Pew-pew!*"

Tabitha grinned. "That's why Grandma Jean made you your own. Would you like to wear my badge instead?"

"Yes! Yes! Badge!" Merry waved her tiny hands in a "gimme" motion for the badge.

Tabitha put Merry down and took her Ranger badge from around her neck. She shortened the chain and slipped it over her niece's head. "You look just like a Ranger now, Merry!"

"Can we play Ranger?"

"Of course we can, *nene.*"

Merry's eyes unfocused for a second while she conferred with her onboard EI. "Hey! I'm not a baby!"

Tabitha ruffled her curls. "Of course not, sweet thing. You're Ranger Two; your badge says so."

Merry made her best approximation of a scowl. "That's right! I'm Ranger Two, and *you* are a naughty Skaine. You better run, 'cuz I'm gonna get you!"

Merry grabbed her toy pistols from the toybox, and the two ran around the house some more.

The child was fast since her natural enhancement gave her better control over her motor functions than an unenhanced human. Tabitha also knew that Merry had some other advantages waiting to be switched on when she was older.

She would hate to be the bad guy her niece came across once *those* were fully activated.

Merry made her *pew-pew* noises while firing bubbles at

Tabitha, who ran and ducked, and dived theatrically to avoid getting hit by the soapy bubbles.

"You won't get my treasure!" Merry yelled. She jumped onto the couch and fired two streams of bubbles down the back of it, where Tabitha was hiding.

"Oh, noooo," Tabitha moaned. She stood and clutched her chest. "You got me, Ranger Two! No more being a naughty Skaine for me!" She fell onto the couch with another groan, and Merry dived on her. "Mercy, Ranger Two!"

"*Neverrrrr!*" Merry yelled, brandishing the tiny bubble-pistols Jean had made her. "I'm Ranger Two, and I *always* get the baddie!"

Tabitha grabbed her and tickled her. "Then I'll have to fight back!"

Merry giggled. "Aunt Tabitha, stop! Skaines don't tickle!"

Tabitha let go of Merry, and she scrambled to her feet. "Silly Tabbie!"

Tabitha did her best not to choke on the stream of bubbles that hit her in the face. She fell backward with her arms spread wide and played dead.

Merry laughed. "Ranger Merry! *Pew-pew*! No escape! I get the baddies just like you, Aunt Tabbie!"

Tabitha tucked Merry into bed a short time later with a kiss to the forehead. "Sweet dreams, my angel."

Merry yawned and rubbed her eyes. "Not an angel. I'm a big scary Ranger."

Tabitha smiled as she turned out the light. "Yes, you are, my sweet."

CHAPTER FIVE

QBBS *Meredith Reynolds*, Open Court, Ashley's Leather Emporium

Tabitha held up the tiny coat to inspect it. "Tell Tiera that it's totally perfect. Merry is going to *love* it. I just hope she doesn't grow too much before I get to give it to her."

Ashley grinned, her curly topknot bobbing as she nodded along with Tabitha. "Is it everything you wanted? Tiera asked me to tell you that she'll make any alterations you need if it's not a perfect fit."

"Her birthday is soon, so I think we'll be good. Unless she has another growth spurt." She stroked the butter-soft leather lovingly. "Tell her I said thanks, though."

"Anything for our best customer." Ashley cooed over the coat. "Merry is going to look *just* like a mini-Ranger! You are a wonderful aunt, Tabitha."

"Thanks to yours and Tiera's expert work," Tabitha told her. "Just look at this stitching and the cut! You're both so talented! I wouldn't go anywhere else for something this special."

Ashley blushed. "You're too kind." She sighed. "But I should probably tell you that Tiera won't be around as much. You might want to find somewhere else soon."

"Are you closing the store?" Tabitha's heart dropped. She got a lot of her work gear from Ashley's. Some of Peter's favorite date-night outfits had been made by Ashley and Tiera, too. He would be disappointed.

Ashley shook her head. "No, but I know that it's Tiera's work that you really love, and I just can't afford to keep her on full time."

"You're going to fire her?" Tabitha was shocked. "But she has a son to support."

Ashley nodded glumly. "I know, which is why I've kept her on despite the business' struggles. She's already taken on another job to make up for her short hours here. There's just not much I can do if we aren't getting the commissions. At least this way she's been free to find a better-paying job to make up for the loss of income."

Tabitha screwed up her nose. "Let me see what I can do to help. In the meantime, I can always use some more pants...ooh, and a coat to match Merry's exactly. I'd get that just to see her face."

Ashley tilted her head. "Sourcing the cowhide for that is going to be expensive. Are you okay with that?"

"Like it's not worth it for quality work like this? Besides, bistok leather is nowhere near as supple as this. It's worth paying extra for the cow." Tabitha handed little Merry's birthday gift back to Ashley to be wrapped. "You have my measurements, so you can get started on the coat whenever you like. Just charge my account for materials."

Ashley placed the tissue-wrapped coat in a gift bag and wiped a tear away. "Thank you, Tabitha. This means a lot."

Tabitha waved her off as she headed for the door. "I know how challenging it can be to run a small business. I'll help however I can. I have to get going, but I'll be in touch to give you the rest of my order."

Tabitha really felt for Ashley and Tiera. She opened a link to Peter as she left the busy shopping court.

Hey, you busy?

Peter came back a split second later. *Never too busy for you, babe. What's up?*

Ashley's business is struggling. Any ideas on how I can help?

Ashley who does the amazing leatherwork?

Uh-huh. She skirted a group of Yollins and broke from the crowd to head for the elevators. *I'm concerned for her and Tiera. Remember I told you about her kid, the one who got a place at the Academy two years early?*

Yeah, I think so. He's great with electronics or something?

That's the one. Ashley told me she might have to let her go. I don't want to interfere, but...

You really *want to interfere, right?*

Totally. But should I*? I mean, I'm just a customer, really. We're not exactly friends.*

I dunno, babe. Do you care about them?

Well, duh, of course! Otherwise, I wouldn't be bugging you in the middle of the day to talk about it, would I?

Peter chuckled. *Then go stick that pretty nose of yours in and find out what you can do to help them.*

Aw, you think my nose is pretty?

I think all of you is pretty, babe. Your nose, your eyes... his inner voice became dreamy, *that little heart-shaped birthmark on your sweet, sweet ass...*

Tabitha laughed. *Suck-up. What are you after?*

What else could I possibly need when I have you? You know that you—

Tabitha knew what was coming. *Don't do it, Pete.*

Complete—

I told you!

Me. Peter laughed.

Asshole. You had to ruin the moment. I hate that movie.

Love you, babe. Good luck helping your friend. I'll catch you for dinner later if you're free.

Love you, too, she grumped. *I'll catch you later.* The elevator arrived, and she stepped in.

"Where to, Ranger Tabitha?" Meredith asked.

"I'm looking for Tiera McCormack. Do you know where she is right now?"

"She is at the main APA."

Tabitha frowned. "What is she doing *there?* Never mind, let's just go."

"Of course, Tabitha."

"Thanks, Meredith."

<hr>

She left the elevator and headed for the APA.

Tabitha stopped to read the sign taped to the doors. The APA was closed to the general public for station security training exercises. That explained why Tiera was here; this must be her second job.

Her supposition was correct.

Inside, the APA had been reconfigured to mock up the various areas around the *Meredith Reynolds* where trouble was most likely to occur. She spotted Tiera over in the AGB scenario, where she looked a little out of place and all too uncomfortable in the station security uniform.

Her group was running barfight drills under the watchful eyes of Rickie Escobar and Matthew Tseng.

Tiera didn't see Tabitha, but Rickie did.

He waved her over, flashing her his trademark stupid grin. "Hey, Tabbie. What are you doing here?"

Tabitha punched his arm. "That's *Ranger Tabitha* to you," she teased. "I came to find Tiera." She nodded to the woman, who was currently getting her ass handed to her by another female Tabitha didn't recognize. "She's working as station security?"

"Yeah." Rickie made a face. "To be honest, I don't know if she's the best fit. Her combat skills aren't the strongest."

Tabitha nodded as she watched Tiera get up and square off again. "She's determined, though."

Rickie nodded. "You know that I don't normally accept unenhanced humans onto the teams unless they just came out of the military, but the woman would not take no for an answer."

Tabitha snickered. "What woman worth her salt would?"

Rickie chuckled. "This one is made from a mountain of the stuff if that's the case."

The drill came to an end, and Rickie returned to the group to move them on to the next scenario. Tabitha stayed to see how Tiera did. The scoreboard that the

Guardians usually used to tally their wins and losses had been appropriated to score the individuals in each test.

Tabitha ran her eyes down the list of names and there was Tiera, three spaces below the red cutoff line. She wasn't going to make the cut, and Tabitha could tell that she knew it.

But still, Tiera didn't give up. She did a little better at spotting the "shoplifters," and she worked well with her partner, which got her moved up a spot. However, her failure to arrest her target got her bumped down again.

Achronyx?

Yes, Tabitha.

I want to know why Tiera is so determined to do this job when she's clearly not suited to it. She lacks the aggression the rest of her group have.

I would think that was obvious. Station security is one of the higher-paying jobs. It makes sense that she would look for something to supplement the job she loves that does not pay enough to support her and her son.

Hmmm... There has to be something I can do about that.

Rickie called a break, and Tabitha made her way over to the hydration station where Tiera sat against the wall to find out from the woman herself.

Tiera looked up when Tabitha's shadow fell across her. "Hey, Tabitha! I didn't expect to see you here. Is there a problem with Merry's coat?"

Tabitha grinned. "The coat is perfect. That's not why I came to find you."

Tiera got to her feet. "Oh? Then why?"

Tabitha didn't want to offend the woman. "I wanted to

know what the hell you were doing here. You're a seam-stress, not a fighter."

Tiera bristled slightly. "Not you, too. Did you speak to Ashley or something? Look, I needed another job, and this is a *good* one."

"You couldn't find something more suited to your skills?"

Tiera sighed wearily. "I'm sick of having to go hungry whenever Sebastian needs something for school, and I refuse to rely on the kindness of others to provide for him when Ashley can't give me enough work. With this job plus whatever hours Ashley has for me, I can take care of all of that. Who cares if I don't enjoy it if it puts food on the table and clothing on my son's back?"

Tabitha's mouth curled down, and she blew her breath out as she considered the situation. "What about if you get hurt and you can't take care of him at all? What if you damage your hands? I know you love your art."

Tiera shrugged. "That's a risk I'm just going to have to take. There's just no option but to work two jobs."

"Three jobs."

Tiera frowned. "Three? No, just this one, and my work for Ashley."

Tabitha smiled. "And being a mother. Especially the kind of mother you are. Look, I want to help if you'll let me."

Tiera shook her head. "No. I'm doing this by myself. I appreciate that you care, but I have to show my son that we can earn our own comfort. If I take every helping hand that's offered, then what am I teaching him?"

Tabitha placed a hand on Tiera's shoulder. "That people who stand together are stronger for it?"

Tiera shrugged her off. "No. I'm not going to teach Sebastian that we can only get by on handouts from others. Thanks, but no thanks."

Tabitha's hand dropped to her side. "I respect that. Really. But I'm sure we can find a different job that pays as well without risking you, Tiera."

"I'm fine with this job! Security personnel are always needed around here. I'll keep working at my fighting skills until I get them, and we'll do just fine.

Tabitha narrowed her eyes at Rickie, who was making a "see?" gesture behind Tiera's back. She couldn't and wouldn't force Tiera to accept her help, but maybe she could do something to help her keep this job and remain intact. An idea occurred. "What if I set you up with some tutoring?"

Tiera frowned. "Tutoring? In what?"

Tabitha grinned. "In combat skills, of course. What, you thought I meant accounting or something? In that outfit?" She nodded at Tiera's flak vest, blue fatigues, and boots. "It wouldn't be a problem. I know a former Guardian who specializes in this sort of thing."

Tiera looked interested for the first time since Tabitha had begun the conversation. "I don't know. Who is it?"

Tabitha sent her the details for Pete's old student, a teacher himself now that he'd retired from active duty. "His name is Maxim. I just sent you the contact. Just promise me you'll go, for Sebastian's sake if you won't do it for yourself."

Rickie called the teams in, and Tiera dropped her towel and water bottle by the wall. "I'll think about it."

Tabitha nodded. "That's all I ask. I know we don't know each other all that well, but I hate to see you going through this by yourself."

"Well, we wouldn't have had to if my asshole husband hadn't run away with that young thing. I hope she gave him super space crabs."

Tabitha cracked up. "You'll have to tell me about that sometime. Dude pissed you off that much, I can always have a bounty put out on him. You want him back?"

Tiera snorted. "Hell, no!"

Tabitha raised an eyebrow. "How about I have him sent back in a body bag?" Tiera burst out laughing. "What? I'm just sayin,' I can make it happen." She grinned and winked.

Tiera's laughter subsided into snickers. "You say the funniest things, Tabitha. I better get back." She turned and jogged over to her group, who all started questioning her about why she'd had a visit from a Ranger.

Tabitha shrugged as she left the APA. *I don't know what's so funny. Anyone who would leave a family like that behind to chase tail deserves everything they get.*

You're not really going to have the husband who absconded killed, are you?

Tabitha tsked. *Of course not. It wouldn't be very Rangerly of me to murder a man just because he can only think with his trouser-brain, would it? If I did that there'd be a total shortage of men, and then where would the human race be?*

Heaven forbid.

Achronyx, you're very snarky today. Did I do something to upset you?

I'm bored. We have been here for months now. When will you take another mission?

As soon as Barnabas has something for us.

Can't you make him have something?

You want me to make a crime happen just so you can get off the Meredith Reynolds?

When you put it that way...

I am putting it that way. Cheer up. We won't be here long. There's always some asshole out there who needs correction.

I suppose so.

You're just going to have to keep yourself entertained aboard the station for now. I thought you would be glad of some time with ADAM?

Do you know how slowly time runs for me?

Tabitha shrugged. *I just assumed you hibernated when things get boring.* She checked the time, and it was getting close to dinner o'clock. *I need to speak to Maxim before I meet up with Pete. Don't want Tiera to show up and he has no clue she is coming.*

Achronyx huffed. *So you get a life, and I get to hibernate? Seems fair. I want a body.*

Tabitha snorted. *Don't we all? Oh, you mean like Eve?*

No. A real body.

Really? Now I know you've been spending too much time with ADAM.

I won't bother to share if you're just going to be rude about it.

I definitely don't want to share your body, Achronyx. This one suits me just fine.

If you're not going to take me seriously, I'm not going to talk to you.

Tabitha winced as he left her mind with the mental equivalent of a slammed door. "Oops." *Sorry, Achronyx.*

Silence.

Will you at least tell me where Maxim is?

More silence. Tabitha rolled her eyes. Moody EIs were no fun. "Meredith?"

"Yes, Tabitha?"

Meredith sounded a little cooler than usual, but Tabitha knew better than to piss off the EI who controlled everything on the station. She did not want her shower to be cold that night, and neither did she want to get "stuck" in an elevator—again. "Can you tell me where Maxim is, please?"

"He is in the Guardian's rec room."

"Thank you, Meredith."

She made her way to the Guardian's rec room and went inside to search out Maxim. She found him at the weight bench spotting a Yollin she didn't know. She leaned against the wall and waited for them to finish the set.

Maxim looked up when she cleared her throat and tapped the Yollin's shoulder. "Hang fire a minute, Drk, we've got company."

Drk racked his weights, and he and Maxim came over.

Maxim gave her a charming smile. "What can we do for you, Ranger Tabitha?"

Tabitha returned his smile. "You can drop the formality, for a start. I have a favor to ask. There's a woman I know, standard unenhanced human. She needs training."

"Oh, yeah? For anything in particular, or just in general?"

"So she doesn't get killed on the job." Tabitha frowned.

"She's taken a security position, but her combat skills are below standard. She has a kid, and I'm worried she's going to leave him orphaned if I don't get her some training."

Maxim's eyebrows went up. "Really? I'm a little surprised Rickie allowed her on the team if that's the case."

Tabitha smirked. "She's got balls. She didn't really give him a choice."

The Yollin, Drk, laughed and elbowed Maxim in the ribs. "I know a few women like that. Your wife, for one."

"Don't I know it," Maxim agreed fondly. He turned to Tabitha. "I can fit her in. Just send her over."

Tabitha winked at him. "I knew you would. I already gave her your contact info, and she'll be in touch." She checked the time again. "Dammit, I'm late. I have to run. Thanks, guys."

QBBS *Meredith Reynolds*, NS Squared

Tabitha slipped into the dim booth on the far left and Peter pushed a glass of warm, rapidly flattening beer over to her.

She looked at the beer skeptically. "I'm not *that* late."

"You're late enough that your beer went warm." Peter drained his beer and picked desultorily at the platter of nachos in the middle of the table.

She kind of wished she hadn't outgrown kicking him under the table, but he would have just moved anyway. "I went to see Maxim about Tiera."

Peter was confused. "What does Maxim have to do with Tiera?"

"Nothing just yet, but she's going to train with him so she doesn't lose her job."

She took sips from her glass and stole nachos from his plate while she told him what she'd turned up when she'd found the seamstress earlier that day. "When you said dinner, I imagined candles and something actually cooked."

Peter shrugged. "I just wanted to come here."

Tabitha knew that look. "Tough day?"

"New recruits."

She put her hands over his. "You miss him."

Peter nodded, looking down at their clasped hands on the table. "Uh-huh."

She didn't need him to explain further. New recruits were something he and Todd had always taken care of together. "Give me a minute."

She went over to the bar. She was about to order a couple of shots but thought better of it and just pointed at the bottles on the mirrored back wall.

The bartender was new. He gave her a look, and she jerked a thumb over her shoulder toward Peter. "My man has had the worst day. Find me something that will get a Pricolici and a vampire drunk and give me two clean glasses."

The bartender's hand hovered over the rows of bottles as he searched for something that would fit the bill. He selected a dusty, dark bottle with a toxic warning on the label. "Hmmmm. There's this from Bad Company? There are instructions for it. Oh, they're from Pearl…" He blew the dust away and squinted to read the handwritten warning in the low light. "180 Proof. Emergencies only. Not for human consumption."

Tabitha grinned and held her hand out for the bottle. "Sounds like exactly what I need."

The bartender looked at the Joneses at the other end of the bar for permission. The Weres looked at Tabitha, who tilted her head toward the booth where Peter sat with a long face. They nodded to the bartender.

She took the bottle and the glasses from the bartender. "Can you fix us up with something real to eat? The nachos aren't gonna cut it if we're drinking this."

The bartender nodded, and she took her haul back to the booth and plonked it all on the table.

Peter snapped out of his brooding. "What's that?"

Tabitha poured them both a short measure and grinned when the fumes stung her eyes. "No idea. Let's find out while you get today off your chest."

They touched glasses and nervously knocked the mystery drink back. It had the desired effect since Peter was too busy choking to think about his grief for the moment.

Tabitha's eyes nearly burst out of her skull, and she wheezed along with Peter. "*Whooooo!*"

"*Fuuuck!*" he exclaimed throatily. "What's *in* that?"

Tabitha wiped away the tears that flowed freely down her face. "I dunno," she gasped. "It's effective, though."

Peter grabbed the bottle. "Shit. Toxic to humans?"

"That's what nanos are for," she told him as she poured them another. "Drink up, and spill."

"If I survive another I'll tell you anything you want to know."

Tabitha smirked. "Bottoms up!"

Peter laughed. "What, here?"

This time she did kick him under the table.

"What was that for?"

Tabitha winked. "Call it foreplay."

They went through another minute of coughing and spluttering as the alcohol burned its way into their systems.

When they were done and Peter looked a little more relaxed, she sat back and gave him a searching look. "Now, what happened today?"

Peter's sadness returned from just beneath the surface, where it had simmered since Todd's death. "It was just… We always broke the recruits in together, you know? I kept turning to make our usual jokes, and he wasn't there." He shrugged. "I don't know how to get past it. I think I've dealt with his loss, and then some random occurrence reminds me of him, and it's all fresh again."

Tabitha held out her glass and Peter topped her off before refilling his own with a slightly shaky hand.

"Don't spill it, Pete. It's too good to waste." She couldn't remember the last time she'd gotten this drunk, and they'd barely made a dent in the bottle. "Truth? I don't know how to get over it, except to live as hard and as well as we can. To honor him and Shin, we carry on fighting the good fight in their memory."

The bartender came over with a fresh platter, this one stacked with a Pricolici-sized mixed grill. "You two are still alive. Good. Ruben sent this over."

They thanked him, and he returned to the bar while they got stuck in.

Tabitha snagged a chop from the top of the pile and dipped it into the accompanying gravy before tearing off a bite. She could have kissed the bar's chef, only she didn't actually trust her legs to carry her to the kitchen until her nanocytes had processed some of the alcohol in her system. "Mffff… Pete, you have to try this." She held it out so he could take a bite, and immediately regretted it when he demolished two-thirds of it with a single chomp.

"Pete!"

Peter grinned and dug out another chop for her from the mountain of meat on the plate. "Sorry, babe."

She took the peace offering and bit down delicately. "As long as you replaced it," she told him through her mouthful as she pointed with her fork. "There's a nice bit of steak there. You can have that."

High Tortuga, Northern Continent, Space Fleet Base, Guest Quarters

Nickie awoke from a night of fractured dreams with her mind made up. Tiera's story had cut way too close to the bone, and Sebastian's even more so. She hadn't ever considered that her mom worked so much because she had to. All she'd seen was that she wasn't there.

Nickie felt raw inside. She grabbed her gear and left the bedroom, sending Barnabas a message as she walked. She kept her head down as she passed through the communal area to the shower, avoiding eye contact and any conversation she came across on her way.

The shower helped her feel halfway human again, and by the time she joined the others at the breakfast table the cup of coffee she'd gulped had dragged her the rest of the way.

Grim was first to test the waters. "Morning, boss. How did the visit with your uncle go?"

"It wasn't exactly a normal family reunion," John cut in before Nickie could answer.

"How would you know how my family operates?" Nickie shot back. "It went okay," she told Grim. "We have a mission."

"You're going to do it?" John asked in disbelief.

Nickie ignored him. "We have not one, but six planets to save. Grim, I need you in fighter mode for this one. It could be tricky."

Grim chuckled. "You know I'm more of a lover than a fighter, but whatever you need."

John wasn't going to be ignored forever. "I'm coming with you," he announced.

Nickie fixed him with a stare. "Why the fuck would you want to do that? I thought you had to save your own planet?"

Adelaide was instantly concerned. "Zuifra's in trouble? Is Themis okay?"

"As far as I know," he told her. "There's a nasty space-borne fungus going around the quadrant, but all of Themis's agriculture is inside the biomes, so it should be unaffected." He hesitated for a moment. "I'm coming with you. I have time; a few more days isn't going to make a difference. Besides, I want to know more about this system."

"What about your dad?" Nickie pressed. "Doesn't he need you?"

John shook his head. "Docs say he'll be fine until I get there. You could use me on this, don't deny it."

Nickie sighed. She probably could, since he would know how to deal with royals without pissing them off too much. "Ugh, whatever. Just don't get in the way if things get messy."

She received a message from Barnabas apologizing for his absence and instructing her to take her crew to be briefed. "Breakfast is over, and we have a briefing in fifteen minutes." She stood up from the table and grabbed her coffee mug to refill it for the walk over to the meeting room.

There was a familiar face waiting for them in the meeting room. It was the Guardian who had hailed the *Granddaughter* when they'd arrived in-system. He grinned and indicated the empty chairs around the table. "If it isn't the Last Ranger." He chuckled as the rest of the crew and John shuffled in behind Nickie. "They don't really fit my recollection of the Tontos, though."

Nickie glared at the Guardian. "My crew is just fine, thanks."

He held his hands up and smiled disarmingly. "I don't disagree. Let's get on with the briefing." He pressed a button on his wrist holo, and they all received an information packet. "This is from Barnabas. He told me it contains everything you need to get started. He also asked me to provide you with cover IDs." He smirked while he typed. "You are now the…Silver Line Trading Company."

"Why do we need a cover?" Adelaide asked.

The Guardian looked up from his holo. "The details are in the packet, but you're going to use the trader cover to access the palace. We're going to provide some attractive tech that will ensure you get in to meet with the targets. The meetings will give you the opportunity to assess the situation and act accordingly; and the cover will make it possible to get the meetings in the first place."

Nickie snorted. "You mean it will help the Federation avoid the backlash if it all goes tits-up."

The Guardian gave her a double finger-gun salute. "Got it in one." He stood to leave. "I have to run, but if you need any help getting to requisitions then just call for the base EI, CEREBRO. I wish you all luck with this."

Nickie watched the door until the Guardian left, then turned to the others. "Read your packets. We don't have to take this assignment," she told them. "We can walk away right now if we're not all comfortable with the orders."

"I'm not comfortable with the orders," John grumped.

Nickie gave him a bright smile. "You're free to leave whenever you like. I was offering *my crew* a choice. Speaking of which, Meredith, send everything my uncle gave us over to Durq. He gets a choice, too."

Already done, Meredith replied. *And well done. I knew you would make the right decision.*

High Tortuga, Northern Continent, Space Fleet Base, Requisitions

Nickie had finally found something to be impressed with.

She led the crew into the requisitions warehouse, which stretched back farther than Nickie could see. It was broken up into long vision-distorting rows by floor-to-ceiling racks filled with crates, boxes, and weapons cases.

Nickie recognized the stamp on many of the crates. She was too caught up in what cool shit of her Grandma Jean's she was going to scam out of the armory to see who was manning the desk.

Quartermaster Sofia Gutierrez was over the moon to see Nickie. "Nickie, let me see you, child!" She rushed around her desk to take Nickie by the shoulders and inspect her. "You are looking *healthy!*" she declared. "If your grandma was here to see you she would be happy."

Nickie's face burned with embarrassment, but she allowed her old babysitter to turn her from side to side. "How did you end up here, Sofia?"

"I came out here to work with Jean on some stuff." Sofia released her and took a step back to cast an eye over the others. "You're lucky you caught me before I left. Jean's away at the moment with Bethany Anne and the others, so I'm taking the opportunity to do a full inventory on the base while it's quiet."

Nickie felt her heart constrict in her chest. "It's really good to see you, Sofia." She didn't care if the others saw her admit it or what they thought when she hugged Sofia back. Sofia had always been good to her, and up until she'd hit rock bottom, she had been careful to show respect to the woman who had been there with a sandwich and a shoulder whenever Nickie needed it.

Sofia peered around Nickie's hug. "Who are your friends? And what can I help you with?"

Nickie didn't blame Sofia for her slightly mistrustful tone. "Not just my friends, my crew." She showed Sofia the requisitions list from Barnabas. "See, we're legit…ish."

Sofia looked it over and smiled. "This is beyond good to know." Her eyes shone a little as she spoke. "I was worried about you every day, Nickie. I'm so happy you are on the right path again." She turned toward the aisles. "Let's get you geared up in style, shall we?"

Nickie grinned. "That would be awesome."

Sofia led them on a complicated route through the maze of racks, stopping every now and then to take down one of the smaller boxes that surrounded the larger crates.

John pointed out one of the large crates while Sofia was exchanging Nickie's old JD Specials for a more up-to-date set. "What's in these?"

Sofia winked at him. "I *could* tell you, but then you'd have to stay here forever. Your choice."

John took a step away from the crate. "It's cool. I don't need to know."

She continued to lead them on their twisting journey, loading the crew for pretty much everything they might come across on the mission as they went up and down the aisles.

"What's this?" Nickie asked, holding up a heavy crate Sofia had instructed her to take from the rack.

"It's a bolt-on for standard ore extraction equipment that improves efficiency by around thirty-five percent. It's the thing that's going to get you into the palace. You turn up with this, and they'll bite your hand off as soon as kiss your ass to get hold of it."

Keen frowned. "If it's so good, why are you giving it to us?"

Sofia grinned. "I said *they* would want it. That's an outmoded version, and I have a whole warehouse full of them just gathering dust. You can take as many as you can fit in your ship. It sounds like the system will be joining the Federation anyway so we can give them a production boost with no problem." She looked at their ears. "How are you communicating during missions? You've been out there a while. Do your crew have comm chips?"

Nickie shrugged. "We get by."

"Wait here." Sofia gave her a knowing glance and hurried off. She returned a few minutes later with the smallest box yet. It wasn't the most aesthetic thing, which let Nickie know it was something from BMW rather than her Grandma Jean.

"Etheric comm," Sofia explained as she handed the box to Nickie. "But they weren't on the list, so I did not give them to you, and you return them when the mission has been completed."

Nickie touched the side of her nose and winked. "Don't worry, I totally stole them while your back was turned."

Sofia nodded once and turned to Grim. "Now, do I have something for *you*! Follow me, my good Yollin. All of you follow me."

They left a short time later, completely weighed down by all the goodies Sofia had tricked them out with. Sofia had also extracted the promise of a return visit from Nickie while she fitted the crew for new armor.

Durq was ecstatic to see them return to the *Penitent Granddaughter*. He skipped down the entrance ramp with the house bots following in a line behind him, looking for all the world like a mother hen with a brood of bulky metal chicks. He made a beeline for the antigrav pallets. "What's all this?"

Nickie grinned. "Our gear for the mission, all of it."

Grim hopped from one foot to another in impatience as the ramp to the cargo bays descended. "Let's get it all inside, and then you can see it all instead of just hearing about it."

They got the pallets aboard and started to unpack and organize. The floor of the cargo bay they were using as an ad hoc armory was soon strewn with empty weapons crates and packing materials. The house bots had been sent to unload the ore extractor tech into the next bay. They had been helping the crew, but then Bradley had tried to "tidy up" a box of grenades and nearly blown them all up.

Grim laughed. "It's like Exodus morning!"

Nickie gave him a puzzled look. "You celebrate Exodus Day?"

Grim shrugged. "Why not? Some Yollin families celebrate from Exodus Day to Revolution Day."

"Revolution Day?" Durq asked.

Grim nodded. "The day Bethany Anne killed the asshole Kurtherian who had enslaved the Yollins without us even realizing." He opened the first crate on the armor pallet. "I think we should move our base out here just for the tech, Nickie. I can't believe Sofia found almost the exact same armor that I came to the Empire wearing."

Nickie snickered, enjoying her friend's joy. "Just how old are you, Grimmie?"

"Old enough to know better," he joked. He became more serious when he lifted out his armor to mount it. "Old enough to remember the first Revolution day."

"Were you involved?" Keen asked.

Grim nodded. "I'm ashamed to say I fought against the

Empress, or at least I did until I was set straight. Youth is blind until its eyes are opened." He craned to see what Keen was unpacking at that moment. "Oh my, that is something else that has improved."

Keen couldn't get over the flexible skin-tone armor plates. "They just *stick*?" He almost tripped over the pallet behind him, he was so engrossed. "Don't they fall off when you sweat?"

Adelaide had other concerns. "Doesn't the glue damage your skin?"

"No, it's a specially developed adhesive," Nickie informed them. "It stays in place until you take it off without doing any more damage than a band-aid would cause."

Grim strutted over. He walked a little stiffly, weighed down by the bulkiness of his upgraded armor. "What about you? I see that the quartermaster changed out your JD Specials."

Nickie grinned and patted the reassuring weight at her hips. "That she did. I even have real ammo now." She felt good. They were about to embark on a new adventure, one that would benefit others. That Barnabas trusted her with the real thing, not the restricted pistols she'd been issued before her exile, meant a hell of a lot.

She took one from its holster to examine it for the sixteenth time.

Keen let out a low whistle when she ejected the magazine to inspect the load they carried. "Your old ones were pretty damn amazing, but those are just—"

"Special?" Nickie supplied.

Keen chuckled. "Yeah."

Durq returned with the house bots, and the crew got to work sorting through their newly issued gear.

Nickie came across an extra crate that wasn't on the manifest. She was about to open it when she saw her name stamped below her grandmother's chop. There was only one thing that came in a crate this size and shape with her Grandma Jean's mark.

"Great work, everyone," Nickie praised them. "Keep it up, I'm gonna head up to the bridge and take us out of here. I want to get there before John." She raised a fist as she exited the bay. "We've got a mission, *woooot!*"

CHAPTER SEVEN

<u>System of the Six, Planet Vietania, Plomerilia, Shipyard</u>

The *Granddaughter* arrived just before the *Briar Rose*, which pleased Nickie as much as she was certain it pissed John off.

It was Nickie who was left steaming when John exited his ship with his usual easygoing grin. "So, this is Vietania."

Use the comm, Nickie told him. *All you have to do is think of the person you want to speak to.*

Got it, John replied.

What about the rest of you?

Easy, Grim replied.

This is weird as hell, Keen chipped in.

Just remember to keep it on the comm, Nickie reaffirmed. *And don't forget to listen for your cover names like we practiced on the way over here.*

Nickie was going to have to work on Durq's agoraphobia while the others were away gathering intel. He hadn't even come to the ramp to say goodbye to Grim,

Addie, and Keen because he was too afraid to show himself on a human planet.

They looked around the open shipyard, which was pretty standard as shipyards went. It was packed with vessels from all over the system. Some were in the middle of repairs, others were being loaded or unloaded by groups of uniformed dockworkers.

Nickie noticed the drones overhead, and the IDs everyone around them wore around their necks. One of the dark spheres dropped to hover above Nickie.

"Credentials, please," the drone chirped.

Nickie produced their cover credentials, and the drone dropped printed IDs like everyone else's into her waiting hands.

It whirred. "Reason for visiting?"

Nickie gave the drone the spiel she'd prepared. "We have an exciting opportunity that has the potential to change the face of commerce on this planet. How do I get an audience with the monarch here?"

"All requests for an audience must be routed through the bursar's office at the palace," the drone replied. "Appointments are to be booked six calendar months in advance. Would you like to request an appointment now?"

John paled at the information. "I can't hang around that long. Maybe you should make the appointment, and we'll come back in six months."

"Fuck *that*," Nickie grumped. *Meredith, can you hack this thing and get us in sooner?*

Of course. When would you like me to fit you in?

Nickie considered going straight there but saw an

advantage to getting the feel of the place first. *Tomorrow will do.*

Easy as pie.

The drone dipped, and Nickie received a ping on her holo. "You have been allocated an audience with Her Highness tomorrow afternoon. In the meantime, enjoy your time on Vietania, Captain Dakkar."

The drone zipped off as quickly as it had arrived, leaving Nickie to put her newly formed plan into action. She turned to the others with a grin. "Get unloaded. We're going into the city."

System of the Six, Planet Vietania, Plomerilia

Nickie had the crew fan out and filter into the city streets. She walked them to the entrance and stopped at a street vendor to buy a hot drink as a reason for hanging around the shipyard entrance while she watched them go off in their pairs.

How are we all doing? she asked over the comm as soon as they were out of sight. *Everyone good with their objectives?*

Sure, Adelaide replied. *We're just a pair of traders taking some downtime to see the sights.*

Nothing as fun as John and Grim, Keen grizzled.

Bar crawls are hard work, I'll have you know, John snarked. *We're making this sacrifice, so you don't have to.*

Grim chuckled. *Someone had to take one for the team. It just happened to be us this time.*

I never told you to go on a bar crawl, Nickie objected.

Grim's reply was a little smug. *Ah, but when you told us to take note of public opinion, that's what I heard. What better way to find out what people really think about the heirs?*

And I agreed with him, John chipped in.

Just don't get into any fights, Nickie warned. *I don't want to have to bail your asses out because you pissed off an angry drunk.*

Grim affected a scandalized tone. *Would I do that?*

Would I warn you if I didn't think it was a possibility? Nickie countered. *No fights. I'll be here, hacking my way into the municipal networks. One way or another, we'll get to the bottom of this.*

CHAPTER EIGHT

Adelaide looked around in wonder as she and Keen made their way through the city. It wasn't anywhere near as advanced as High Tortuga, but Plomerilia had a certain charm all of its own. It reminded Adelaide a little of the settings of the grand romances her mother loved, the only difference being that the genteel facades of the buildings were plastered with screens and advertising holos.

They strolled through a market they came across, chatting about nothing over the comm while listening to the conversation around them for any talk about the current political situation.

Adelaide accepted a flower from a vendor who was giving them out in hopes of making a bigger sale. *Do you think John came along because of the monarchy thing or just to spend time with Nickie?*

Keen snorted. *I'm staying right out of that disaster-waiting-to-happen.*

Adelaide gave him a puzzled glance. *Really? I was hoping*

they would get together. She sniffed the flower and smiled. "This is beautiful. So sweet! I'll take a half-dozen."

Oh, God, I hope not. They don't even like each other. What are you going to do with those?

I'm going to put them in my quarters to brighten the place up a bit. Adelaide smirked. *They* do *like each other, can't you tell?*

I can't see it, Keen admitted. *Then again, I'm not the best judge of these things.*

I don't even remember you having a relationship.

Keen's smile softened into something sadder. *I was married once.*

I'm sorry, Adelaide soothed. *I didn't mean to bring up something painful.* She linked her arm through Keen's. "It's a beautiful city."

"That it is, lass," Keen replied heartily, his usual affable expression returning. "What do you say we get out of this sun and find a place to get a cold drink and a bite to eat?"

Adelaide grinned and squeezed his arm tightly. "I think that's a fine idea."

They found a quaint café on the corner of a narrow side street and slipped inside to escape the rapidly mounting heat of the day. Nickie would have called it a vision from a frilly royalist hellscape, but Adelaide found the place completely charming.

She let go of Keen's arm when they went into the busy tearoom and headed straight to the wall of framed photographs at the back. "You order? You know what I like. I just want to look for a minute."

Keen's eyes twinkled fondly. "Something hot and caffeinated and the biggest slice of cake I see?"

Adelaide grinned. "You're the best!"

"Coming right up. Don't be too long, Addie." He winked at her and went to find them a table.

Adelaide scrutinized the photos. The most recent ones were of a tall, haunted-looking woman with high cheekbones and a halo of dark hair. Others were of a man with similar features and a tiny woman with a crown woven into her blonde ringlets. Above all of these was a single tiny oil painting. It was no more than cameo-sized, but it was positioned so there was no doubt that it was the most important image in the collection.

"You like my shrine?"

Adelaide turned to see a rosy woman whose smile stretched from dimple to dimple. "Hi! Um, yeah. I'm not from around here, so would you tell me about them?"

The woman beamed. "It would be my pleasure. This is Jolie, the rightful heir to the throne. These two are the dearly departed king and his…consort."

Adelaide heard the distaste the woman tried to cover in her tone. Second marriage, maybe? That wouldn't go down well with everyone. She pointed to the oil cameo. "What about this one? Was she the queen?"

The woman clasped her hands together. "No, more's the pity. This is Braella, Jolie's sainted mother. She was spurned by the king for her common blood, and she still gave her life to helping those in need."

"So Jolie is the queen?"

The woman shook her head sadly. "She is the *rightful* queen, but her sister is legitimate, so Jolie's is seen as the contentious claim. She is her mother's daughter and the heart of the people, but the law says Cynthia's legitimacy tops Jolie's firstborn status, so we're stuck with that spoiled brat."

Adelaide thanked the woman for her time and made her way over to where Keen sat with their meal. "I just had an interesting conversation," she told him.

"Me too," he replied. "You first."

Adelaide ran through it quickly for him while they ate. "So the obstacle to this planet's stability might not be so simple to remove as the brief we were given suggested."

Keen laughed and slapped his leg. "They never are, kiddo. You learn that along the way." He picked up his glass and drained it in one. "There's a rally or something happening in the city square. We should get over there and see if we can't work this out."

System of the Six, Planet Vietania, Plomerilia, Ugh Bar

I think it's a stupid name for a bar.

Grim sighed internally at the thirtieth unasked-for opinion from John in half a minute. He'd had no success at all in blocking his personal thoughts from their Etheric comm channel, and the constant onslaught of vacuity was getting to be a little much.

He must be really attractive on a human scale, Grim had decided. Otherwise, he couldn't think why Nickie hadn't lost her temper and spaced him already. She was usually much less patient than Grim when it came to inane chatter.

They made their way through the patrons to the main room, which had couches and coffee tables on one side and rows of desks with interactive screens on the other.

John looked at the patrons, who were all staring at the screens with the glazed eyes of the engrossed. *Hey, maybe we can find out something there?* The prince rushed straight over to the person standing by the nearest screen and began to pepper them with questions.

Grim left him to it, glad of the reprieve. He went to the bar and ordered himself a double measure of good Yollin whiskey, then sat at the bar for a moment to sip it in silence. The first measure was to offset the headache that was beginning to form. The second one was for Nickie, but since she wasn't there, Grim would make sure it didn't go to waste.

John plonked himself on the barstool beside Grim's and waved to catch the bartender's attention. He pointed at Grim's glass, and the bartender grabbed the bottle and a glass for John and came over.

John nodded and swiped his wrist holo to pay. "Can I get some time on the 'net?"

The bartender held out the holopoint again. "It's extra for off-worlders."

John shrugged and swiped his holo again. "Thanks."

"Screen eleven," the bartender told him.

John grabbed his whiskey and motioned for Grim to follow him. "You've got to see this."

Grim picked up his glass and followed John to the screen. "See what?"

John waved a hand excitedly. "It's like a planet-wide diary, here on their 'net for everyone to see."

Grim frowned. "What do you mean?"

John swiped the screen and clicked a brightly-colored icon. "They write down every detail of their lives, take photos and video of every moment, and store it in the public archives."

Grim snickered. "You mean they have social media?"

Huh? John's attention was on the screen. "What is social media?"

"Zuifra doesn't have anything like this? It's pretty common."

John shook his head. "No, not really. We have media, obviously, but it's mostly for public service announcements." He turned back to the screen, speaking over the comm to avoid drawing attention with his rant. *Look at this, it's ridiculous. These people are ranked in order of their popularity. Look at this—it gets worse.* He selected the photo of a carefree young man. *He's groomed to within an inch of his life. All of his archived entries have to do with one party or another, what woman he's dating, or his latest purchase. I get no sense that he does anything for anyone other than himself.*

Grim had seen it all before. He even recalled his own time of idealistic outrage, although his had been beaten out of him in training after Nickie's grandfather had shown the adolescent him mercy on Revolution Day. "They do appear to be singularly focused on the pursuit of pleasure."

"I don't get it." John frowned. "How they can party like there's no tomorrow while their whole world is hurting? I know I'm a little spoiled, but I recognize that I have a responsibility to others. Wealth is power, and those with power shouldn't waste it on frivolity like this." John's agitation grew with each profile he looked at, and he was beginning to draw attention to them.

Grim laid a hand on John's shoulder. "Let it go. We're not here to pass judgment on the nobility's children.

Search for the queen, and then we can get back to Nickie and the others and get on with this mission."

John made a small sound of consternation when he found the queen's profile. He stood up and pointed at the screen. "She's the worst of them all!"

The man at the next screen took exception to that. He stood up without warning and shoved John off his stool. "You shut your filthy mouth!" He waited for John to get to his feet and lunged at him again.

Grim caught the guy's hand mid-punch. "Sorry, can't allow any damage to the prince."

The disturbance caught the attention of a nearby table full of rowdy young men and women. "What's this?" one called.

Grim let the man go. "Just a misunderstanding, nothing to be concerned about."

"What misunderstanding?" the man demanded. "He fucking insulted Queen Cynthia!"

The reception to that was mixed. The twenty-somethings at the table all got up and began shouting at John, but the older patrons jumped to John's defense.

Pretty soon the bar was in an uproar as the two sides edged closer to physical violence. Grim rubbed his temples to ease the deep throbbing in his skull. "John, just apologize so we can get out of here."

"I'm not going to apologize for speaking the truth!" John shouted over the racket.

"Then you can get the fuck out of here!" someone yelled.

"How about you do the same?" another returned snappily.

"Yeah," a woman sneered. "Take your pampered queen with you! We want Jolie!"

Grim raised an eyebrow at the last. He saw this descending into the worst kind of fight of all: the one where both sides totally believed that they were right. Grim didn't know who was right and who was wrong. He just knew he didn't want to be in the bar when the fight broke out.

The drunken woman threw her glass at the queen's supporters, and it smashed at the feet of the closest one. As if it were the cue for a brawl to begin, the two sides launched themselves at each other.

Grim grabbed John by the back of his shirt and dragged him out of the melee. John twisted out of Grim's grip and jumped straight back in.

Grim stood to the side and waited for John to work the frustration out of his system. Unfortunately, the prince was knocked out cold before that happened, and Grim decided that enough was enough. He shouldered his way over to John and picked him up off the floor.

He draped the unconscious human over his armored shoulder and shoved toward the bar exit. A pair of bulky humans blocked his way, security guards for one of the noble kids, maybe.

Grim didn't care.

He strode out of the security-guard-shaped hole in the bar door a few seconds later and hailed a cab to take them back to the *Granddaughter*.

John came to in the back of the cab and stared groggily at Grim as his senses returned. "What happened? Did I win?"

"Yeah, sure. You okay?" Grim asked.

John nodded and winced. "Yeah. This place, though—definitely not okay. Barnabas was right. This society is going to crumble if this isn't resolved soon." He lay back against the seat and closed his eyes.

Grim checked John's pulse to make sure that he had just fallen asleep, then sat back to think about what they'd discovered. This planet was a hot mess. A disaster waiting to erupt. Grim had to wonder if his mother would ever see her favorite son again if Nickie took any more missions like this.

CHAPTER NINE

<u>System of the Six, Planet Vietania, Plomerilia, City Square</u>

Addie and Keen moved with the current of the crowds. The city square was jam-packed with thousands of protesters, all present to support the illegitimate princess speaking on their behalf there today.

The buzz over the square was one of anger mixed with hope. Adelaide was concerned by the snatches of conversations they overheard as they worked their way to the center of the square where Jolie was slated to speak.

There was a disturbance in the crowd to the far left of them. The woman herself had arrived, but not in the center of an entourage as Keen had told Adelaide to expect.

Adelaide craned to see. "Keen, let me up on your shoulders!"

Keen bent so she could scramble up, and she relayed what she saw to him.

"The crowd is moving to let someone through. It must be Jolie! She's so beautiful, Keen. She's stopping; they all want to speak to her."

Jolie slowly crossed the distance to the stage. She kissed every proffered infant and hugged every man and woman who stepped forward to thank her. There was one person with her, a small, wiry woman with a recording device. She stayed at an exact ten-foot distance at all times and kept her camera drones on Jolie.

Adelaide climbed down when every screen around the square suddenly came to life with the woman's drone footage. They watched the screens in silence.

Jolie eventually took the stage, to rapturous applause. She waved it down immediately and leaned over to speak into the microphone on the podium. "Save that for yourselves," she began. Silence fell across the square at her first word. "Thanks to the hard work and sacrifice of everyone here today, we have cut childhood fatalities from preventable diseases globally by more than we could ever have hoped possible. Today, thanks to the credits raised, the hours and goods donated, and the sheer damn relentlessness of everyone who got involved in the campaign, we are closer than ever to realizing our goal of ensuring adequate health care for everyone on this planet."

She gave the audience a bright smile. "A society which denies resources based on social status will always fail in the end. The imbalance in the system only damages us as a people. A healthy society is a happy and productive one. A society that works to lift everyone is a society that will be welcomed into the Federation."

The crowds cheered wildly.

Jolie raised her hands for quiet. "Which is why I'm so happy to make this announcement today!" She stepped back from the podium and gestured around. "Thanks to the hard work of everyone here and everyone watching, construction on the Plomerilia children's hospital will begin next week!"

The crowd erupted again. This time Jolie waited for the cheers to die down before speaking. "I would like to add my personal thanks to the good ministers who assisted the project during the planning stage. Without them, this hospital would not have been approved so quickly."

The camera feed switched to a still image of Jolie shaking hands with a series of people in ceremonial robes.

"We are better than we have become. As long as we work together, we have a chance to be a part of something much bigger than ourselves. The Federation represents much more than the trade deals and technological advantages the Council of the Six have negotiated." Her voice rose with passion. "They are the shining example of what working for a common cause can achieve, and *they want us to join them!*"

They love her, Adelaide remarked over their comm link. *Hell, I love her!*

Keen nodded without taking it in, too enchanted by Jolie.

Adelaide shook her head. *This just got waaay more complicated than court politics.*

· · ·

<u>System of the Six, Planet Vietania, Plomerilia, Shipyard, Aboard the *Penitent Granddaughter*</u>

Nickie sat back from the screen and rubbed her eyes. *Fuck my life! This shit's complicated. So, the older one was raised as the heir apparent until King Dad married Blondie and produced the younger one?*

Pretty much.

That kind of sucks. So when Dad and the step-monster died, the sisters went at it?

Not exactly, Meredith told her. *Jolie—*

That's the older one, right?

Yes. She's the one who works on behalf of others. She has no desire to oust her sister. By all accounts, her motivations lie in taking care of the people.

But the younger one, whatshername—Cynthia. She just wants to party hard and leaves everything to whoever is around to pick up the pieces? What about the council or whatever? They can't resolve it?

It isn't that simple. The council is split on who should lead.

Huh. Politics are some seriously headache-inducing shit.

You can take a break from it, but I can't promise it will be a welcome one.

Why?

Grim just arrived back at the ship. He is sort of carrying John.

Sort of? Nickie spun her captain's chair to face the bridge door. "Well, well, well, what do we have here?" she snarked when they came through it a few minutes later.

Grim looked miserable, and John looked to have had seven shades of shit beaten out of him.

She gave the two of them a stern look. "Fuck. What did I tell you two about getting into fights?"

"Do it if I'm defending my honor?" John slurred around his split lip.

Nickie got up and came over to poke at his swollen left eye. "Yeah, go and get some first aid. Meredith, call Durq to take care of him."

"I'm fine!" John protested. "It's just a couple of bruises." He staggered a little as he spoke.

Nickie and Grim each grabbed an arm and steered him toward the nearest chair. Nickie checked him over for injuries and found a fair few bruises and lumps. "Did he get hit a lot?"

Grim nodded. "I pulled him out once, and he jumped straight back in. After that, I just waited until he got knocked out and threw him over my shoulder."

Nickie sighed at John. "This is the last time I allow you to go to a bar. Seriously, I can't take you anywhere."

Durq arrived with Bradley and Lefty, and between them all, they got John up onto the gurney the house bots had brought. Durq instructed them to take the prince to the infirmary on the *Briar Rose* since it had the best tech.

"I should have thought about that," Grim admitted glumly. "I was too wrapped up in what we saw today."

"It's been a little weird here too, I won't lie." Nickie flopped back into her chair and put her feet up in their usual place on the console. "What did you guys find out?"

Grim dropped into his chair and sighed. "It's madness out there." He rubbed his temples. "The fight would have happened whether or not John opened his mouth."

Nickie raised an eyebrow. "So he *did* start it."

Grim ignored her accusation. "This is going to be harder than we thought. The people are split on which sister they want on the throne."

"So we need to remove the opposition." Nickie shrugged. "No rival, no unrest."

"It's not going to be that simple."

Nickie glanced up as Adelaide strode purposefully onto the bridge. Keen followed her a moment later, looking similarly fired-up. "What's got you two so worked up?"

Addie stopped by Nickie's chair and bent to type on her console. "This. Jolie isn't the one we should be removing. Cynthia is." She punched a final key, and the video from Jolie's speech played for Nickie and Grim.

"See?" Adelaide exclaimed when it was over. "She's the one who cares about the people."

"We spoke to a lot of people at that rally," Keen added. "They all agreed that Cynthia is a terrible leader."

Nickie shrugged. "It's nothing to do with us. All we're here for is to remove the obstacle to this place joining the Federation."

Grim gave her a thoughtful glance. "This woman might not be the legal heir, but she behaves in a more queenly fashion than the woman John and I saw plastered all over this planet's social media."

Nickie wrinkled her nose in thought. "We need to meet them both before deciding which to take out. We'll start with Cynthia since we have an audience tomorrow. In the meantime, everyone should hit the sack and get some rest."

Nickie crawled into her bed a short time later.

She was just drifting off to sleep when Meredith woke her.

Nickie? The next entry of your aunt's diary has just become available. It can wait until morning.

Nickie lay on her back and folded her arms behind her head. *No way, Mere. Sleep can wait. Show me the diary.*

CHAPTER TEN

QBBS *Meredith Reynolds*, Rangers' Offices, One Week Later

Tabitha flounced into Barnabas' office and dropped into the chair in front of his desk. "You wanted to see me? Please tell me you have a mission for me. I feel like I want to go to work just to get a break."

Barnabas raised an eyebrow when she didn't put her feet on his desk. "Are you feeling okay?"

Tabitha shrugged. "Yeah, I've just got some things on my mind. Why?"

"You have been here for two whole minutes, and you haven't been even a bit disrespectful." He continued to eye her with mild concern. "I have to say it's a little disconcerting, Tabitha."

Tabitha shrugged. "I just don't have the motivation. I'm trying to work out how to help someone who doesn't want to be helped, and I miss my Tontos. They've been gone so long I've almost forgotten what they look like. I can make an effort to sass you if it would make you feel better?"

Barnabas appeared to actually consider that. "You know, I think it would. But don't. We have business to take care of." He smiled. "If it makes you feel better, your Tontos will be back tomorrow. I recalled them from Zaphod a couple of days ago."

Tabitha grinned. "That's fantastic!"

Barnabas "Why didn't you go with them?"

"Lillian is going through it at the moment. I've been helping Jean and John out a lot with Merry. I didn't want to leave the munchkin for weeks unless it was necessary." Tabitha smiled, remembering how sweet Merry had been at bedtime last night.

She had read almost every story on Merry's bedside bookshelf, giving in each time to her pleas for "Just one more!" Tabitha had kept reading even after Merry had dozed off with a sleepy smile on her face.

Tabitha didn't consider herself mother material, but this child had stolen her heart when she came into the world and used her first breath to rage about it. Tabitha would have read her a thousand bedtime stories just to see that smile. "Don't tell anyone, but that kid is my favorite kid ever. I'd have stayed behind even if it had been a trip to Larkatia on offer. Besides, the guys are enough to help Abbot Scroat around their contemplation. They didn't need me for this visit."

"The abbot will have been sorry you did not visit this time. I know he looks forward to the rare opportunities the two of you have to spend time together."

Tabitha tilted her head and pointed at Barnabas. "Are

you reading my mind?"

The corner of Barnabas' mouth quirked slightly. "No, just my communications from the abbot."

Tabitha wondered when that had started happening.

"We've been in contact for the last thirty years or so—since his father passed away and he was voted in by the rest of the order." He grinned when she narrowed her eyes at him. "Okay, *that* time I was reading your mind."

"I knew it." Tabitha sat back and folded her hands behind her head. "I can go to Zaphod next time. Lillian needs support more than I need a vacation."

Barnabas nodded. "That young woman has been through so much these last few years. It's so sad how resilient she has had to become."

"How do you know?" Tabitha demanded. "Did you read *her* mind?"

Barnabas reddened slightly. "Only out of a desire to make sure she was okay."

"Do you know who Merry's dad is?" Tabitha chuckled when Barnabas reddened further. "Of course, you do. I don't even know half of what she's been through. She doesn't talk about it to anyone."

Barnabas sighed. "Maybe one day she will, but it's not our place to open old wounds before she is ready to deal with them."

Tabitha didn't have to like what Barnabas was saying to know it was the truth. "I know. All I can do is be there for her and Merry. So, what business do we have?"

Barnabas brightened. "Your wish is my command. I have a mission for you."

Tabitha grinned. "Achronyx will be pleased."

Barnabas tilted his head and did that annoying thing where he put his hands together wisely. "He's still not talking to you?"

Tabitha shrugged. "He'll be fine once I get us off-station. He's bored."

"He won't be bored for long."

She leaned in and paid attention. "Where are you sending us?"

Barnabas's demeanor became serious. "There's a colony group in the Arista system in need of Ranger assistance."

Tabitha searched her memory for the name. "That place way out past the Torcellan quadrant?"

Barnabas nodded. "This is going to be a tough one, Tabitha. They've been taken over by a gang of criminals. The despicable bastards have hooked their children on some kind of drug and are using the children's addiction to coerce their parents into working for them."

Tabitha couldn't believe what she was hearing. "For real?"

Barnabas nodded sadly. "Unfortunately, yes. The information I received was a little bit vague, but that's the gist of it. You get your whole team for this since the problem has spread across four planets in the system."

Tabitha sneered in disgust. "Just point me at the *hijos de folladores de cerdo*. It won't take me but a minute to shoot some sense into them."

The corner of Barnabas' mouth twitched. "I don't doubt it for a second. However, the people you are going to assist are already more than capable of 'shooting sense' into the gang. Your mission is to discover and eliminate the gang leadership, then bring our people and their children back to the *Meredith Reynolds* for rehabilitation and counseling."

Tabitha almost knocked her chair over in her rush to get going. "Send me the details. I'll round up the Tontos as soon as they get here. They've had enough R&R."

Barnabas stayed her with a hand. "You leave in two days. Rushing in unprepared puts the children's lives at risk."

Tabitha stopped, sighed, and sat down again. "Oh. Yeah. Definitely don't want that." She thought for a moment, her eyes drifting up to the ceiling as she got her thoughts in order. "I'll get with Jean tonight when I go to babysit Merry. She told me she had some new toys, so they might be helpful."

Barnabas pursed his lips. "Good idea." He noticed she still hadn't placed her feet on his desk.

He might need to give her busywork next time—something that would drop her down to Yoll for a couple of days. *Keep your friends close, your enemies closer, and Tabitha the closest of all.*

He finished, "I want you to do your research before you jump in feet-first. This situation is volatile. Nobody is more unpredictable than a parent whose child is in danger, except maybe the people who were heartless enough to get their children addicted to drugs in the first place."

Tabitha nodded. "I'm pretty sure people like that are completely predictable. They'll want to stay in control no matter what." She stood to leave. "It's gonna suck to be them when I get hold of them."

. . .

QBBS *Meredith Reynolds*, Grimes Family Quarters, Later that Night

Tabitha sat on the couch with her feet curled under her, watching John and Merry wrestle on the rug while she talked Jean through her upcoming mission.

She sipped the tea Jean had made to help her calm down, keeping her voice low so little Merry couldn't hear the conversation.

"So the a-s-s-h-o-l-e-s have taken over and are using the kids to force the parents into working for them. It's like, the worst situation. I can't just blast my way in because I don't know where their headquarters are."

Jean scrolled through her inventory list. "You have someone to meet you on the ground?"

Tabitha shook her head. "No, the situation is too precarious. I'm going to have to stay dark if I can. Should we go into another room? It can't be good for Merry to hear this."

Jean waved her off. "Oh, it's fine. I asked Meredith to filter us out. She can't overhear us."

Tabitha raised an eyebrow. "Huh, I never considered that you could use Meredith that way."

Jean grinned. "Oh, hell yeah. Meredith is there to protect Merry, whatever that means at the moment. Right now it's making sure her innocent mind isn't disturbed by the details of your mission. Sometimes it's making sure she doesn't hear the nighttime activities from mine and John's room." She winked at Tabitha and got up to pick up some of Merry's discarded toys. "So you need all the best cloaking tech. The *Achronyx* is fine, but your transport

Pods need to have some installed. I'll get someone over there."

"That would be great." Tabitha looked at her niece, who was hanging on to John's neck gamely while he gave her a bumpy horsey-ride around the living room. "I just don't get how anyone could use a child in that way. The parents —I understand why they've done whatever the kidnappers wanted. I won't even bring charges against them. I mean, what if it were Merry on drugs? What *wouldn't* you do to get her back?"

Jean's face hardened. "There is *nothing* I wouldn't do." She looked at her granddaughter, her lips pressing together. "That girl is my life."

"Exactly." Tabitha made a face. "I could do with some advantages, Jean. I won't lie, this isn't going to be an easy mission. This *gang* has resources, and they have four planets locked down."

"Sure, just tell me what else you need. We can go through my inventory tomorrow morning while my people are refitting your Pods."

"I'm thinking I'll get Achronyx to help me get in, posing as a buyer to get the lay of the place, then when I find whoever is running it all, I introduce them to the hot end of my JDs."

"Well, if it ain't broken…" Jean snickered. "I love that I'm part of every bit of Justice you and the others bring. It gives me immense satisfaction to know that every day people sleep safely in their beds because of the work you do."

Tabitha grinned. "We couldn't do it without you. Are you sure it will only take a day to refit the Pods?"

Jean gave her an incredulous look. "Who do you think you're talking to? I already have a team on their way to the *Achronyx*."

Tabitha cracked up at that. "Jean, my friend, you are a *total* legend."

Jean wagged a finger. "No, I work for an Empress who would have expected this done *yesterday*." She shrugged. "It's just the way I work."

Tabitha wouldn't accept that. "Nope. You are the best, and that is decided. No arguments. Now…" She was about to get back to finding out what goodies Jean had when she received a ping from Maxim asking her to come down to the Guardians' rec room. "Oh, this is important." She looked up. "I've gotta run," she apologized.

Jean waved her apology away. "Come see me in the morning, and bring the Tontos. I'll make sure you're all loaded for scumbag before you leave."

Tabitha grinned. "You're fabulous." She untucked her legs and shook her feet to get the feeling back into them before getting up to say goodbye to Merry.

Merry looked up from where she was busily destroying one army with another outside her toy castle. "You're going?"

Tabitha smiled and ruffled her curls. "Duty calls, precious. I'll see you again tomorrow, and I'll be back as soon as I can. I wouldn't want to miss your special day, would I?"

Merry's perfect face was marred momentarily by her frown of concentration. "It's twenty-nine sleeps until my birthday, Aunt Tabbie. Will you be gone that long?"

Tabitha held out her hands, and Merry jumped up to

wrap her arms around her aunt's legs. "I might be. Some children need my help. But if I don't make it back in time for your birthday, then I promise that you and I will have a special day all our own, okay?"

Merry looked up with a fierce expression. "Okay. You get the bad guys, Aunt Tabbie! Make them sorry, and *then* come home for my day!"

Tabitha grinned and leaned down to kiss Merry's forehead. "Of course I will. I love you, Merry."

Merry squeezed tight. "I love you too, Aunt Tabbie!"

QBBS *Meredith Reynolds*, Guardians' Rec Room

Tabitha made her way through the lounge area and the changing room to the workout area in back where Maxim was running Tiera through a simple kata.

She spotted Sebastian and Maxim's granddaughter, Elena, who were engrossed in their homework on one of the benches over by the far wall. Tabitha went across to visit with them while the adults trained and looked over their shoulders, not sure what they had in front of them. "Hey, kids. What are we studying?"

The teens looked up at her and Elena grinned.

"Hi, Tabitha!"

"We're looking at the history of micro- and nano-fabrication," Sebastian told her, "with a view to understanding how applications have changed over the centuries." He blushed, embarrassed by his enthusiasm for the subject.

Tabitha nodded. She knew a little about this inasmuch as it had pertained to her previous life as a hacker, before she'd taken on the mantle of the person whose name made hardened criminals run crying to their mommies. "Sounds fascinating."

Not really.

Elena held up her Academy tablet to show Tabitha. "It's really very interesting. We have been learning about the manufacturing techniques available back in the twenty-first century and how they affected the composition and shape of the mechanisms we have developed since leaving Earth."

Tabitha took Elena's tablet and skimmed through the reading material. "This *is* interesting!" Perhaps she had judged a bit too quickly. "Maybe I wouldn't have turned to hacking if I'd had a stimulating curriculum like this when I was at school."

Sebastian blushed again. "But then we wouldn't have the galaxy's best hacker, would we?"

Tabitha chuckled. "I think that title goes to ADAM, with Achronyx a close second. I'll admit to best *organic* hacker."

What, acknowledgment? Achronyx snarked in the back of her mind.

Tabitha was so happy to hear from him she almost squealed out loud. *Achronyx! Where have you been?*

I have a life as well, you know. I've been working on something with Meredith to pass the time.

It's good to have you back. We're heading out on a mission tomorrow.

I know. That's why I'm here.

Tabitha handed Elena's tablet back with a smile and a wink. "Keep up the hard work."

She left them to their homework, sitting down on the next bench to wait for Tiera to complete her kata.

Maxim sent her to hydrate and walked over to Tabitha. "You made it. Good. I wanted you to see that Tiera is advancing. She's not so bad at this now that she's feeling more confident in herself."

"My mom's a total badass," Sebastian chipped in, glancing at his mom to make sure she hadn't heard him cursing. "There was no way she wouldn't improve if she set her mind to it."

Maxim grinned. "That she is, Kiddo. But if I hear that kind of language out of you again, I'm going to give you push-ups."

Sebastian frowned. "For cursing?"

Elena snickered. "For *unoriginal* cursing. It's a Guardian thing."

Tabitha raised a finger. "Actually, it's an Empress Bethany Anne thing."

Maxim shrugged. "We're her Guardians, and it doesn't matter who is standing on your back when you're doing them."

Tabitha knew better. "You'd feel differently if your drill instructor was wearing six-inch stilettos instead of combat boots."

He started shaking his head. "Can't see Peter rocking the high-heeled look," Maxim teased.

Tabitha snickered. "Not with those calf muscles."

Tiera joined them. "What's that about stilettos?"

"Tabitha was just telling us how the Empress punishes—"

"Corrects," Tabitha modified.

Maxim inclined his head. "My apologies, Ranger. *Corrects* poor cursing with the help of her more-than-impressive shoe collection."

Tiera tilted her head. "What do you know about shoes?"

Maxim shook his head. "Too much. More than almost any man wants to."

Elena giggled. "Nannie doesn't really give you a choice, *dedushka*."

Tiera grinned. "It's too easy to get caught up in the design. I should know."

Tabitha smirked. *Finally, an idea worth two additional seconds of consideration. Or a month.* "It was great to see you're doing so much better, Tiera. I'm away on Ranger business for the next couple of weeks, but when I get back, I have something I'd like to discuss."

She stood up, tossing them all a smile and a wave of her hand as she left the group without another word.

CHAPTER ELEVEN

QBBS *Meredith Reynolds*, Grimes Family Quarters, Living Room

The four women and one tiny child sat around the coffee table while Merry solemnly poured the imaginary tea from her teapot into Lillian's cup. "Careful, Mommy. It's still hot."

Lillian blew on the toy cup before taking a careful sip. "Mmmm. Yummy! Thank you, Twinkle."

Merry's tinkling laugh filled the room. "You next, Grandma!" She leaned over and did the same for Jean, then for Tabitha and Gabrielle, chattering the whole time. When she was satisfied that every person, doll, and stuffed toy around the table had a cup of tea, she sat down and picked up her own teacup.

Tabitha made the appropriate slurping noises. "Tea parties are the best."

Lillian nodded. "They are." She smiled at Merry, who

was rubbing her sleepy eyes. "And so is being home for bedtime. Come along, Twinkle Star, time for your bath."

Merry squirmed in her chair and pouted. "But I don't wanna bath! I'm not sleepy, Mommy!"

Jean tsked disapprovingly. "You mind your mother now, Merry."

Merry scowled at her grandma's stern tone. "Won't, Grandma!" Her cheeks got redder by the second and her chubby hands clenched in frustration as she tried to stay in control of the tears forming in her eyes.

Tabitha and Gabrielle stayed out of it, knowing full well that they did not want to be the ones who set off Mount Meredith Nicole.

Lillian scowled at Jean. "I've got this, Mom." She smiled at Merry and held up her hands in a show of unconcern. "We could skip bedtime if you like. No big deal. But then you'll miss out on stories…and your surprise."

"Surprise?" Merry brightened instantly. "What surprise?"

Lillian winked. "To find out, you need to say goodnight to Grandma and your aunts and get ready for bed."

Merry scrambled out of her seat and flew around the room to give everyone a quick hug. "G'night, Grandma, night, Aunt Tabbie, night, Aunt Gabby." She ran to Lillian and tugged her hand. "C'mon, Mommy. Let's go already!"

Impending eruption diverted, Lillian allowed Merry to pull her from the room.

Gabrielle let go of the breath she'd been holding. "Nice save. I wonder what gadget Lillian built for Merry this time?"

"I think she built her a projector." Jean got up to put the

toys away. "Lillian's really good at diverting the Grimes temper. I didn't master that until Lillian left home, and she was nowhere near as much like John as Merry is. My daughter has her hands full." She shoved the toy box into the corner cupboard and headed to the kitchen.

Tabitha got up to give Jean a hand. "Let's be honest, she's never going to have it easy. Raising children is hard enough when it's a regular child. Raising a full-on Grimes by herself? It's a good thing she has us all to lean on."

Jean made a noise of agreement as she rummaged in the kitchen cupboards for plates and glasses. "Even better is that she's realized it's not a weakness to lean on us when she needs to."

She fished around in the fridge and came out with a bottle of wine. She put it on the counter next to the plates and went back to the fridge for a stack of resealable containers, which she put into the closest thing in her kitchen that worked like an old microwave to heat things up. "John and I are just glad she agreed to move them both back in here until she's gotten the business off the ground."

"It makes sense when you think about it." Tabitha collected the plates and glasses and took them to the living room, and she and Jean set everything out on the dining room table. "Plus, it's better for Merry to know where she's sleeping every night."

Jean came in with the food and smirked as she opened the tubs. "That was what made Lillian decide to take us up on our offer in the end. Merry's staying here a lot at the moment, so it just made sense. Lillian has kept her own place, but she's letting it out for a little income boost while she's here."

The aromas coming from the Chinese food were maddening to Tabitha. She hovered over the table in hopes of an opportunity to grab a nibble before dinner, but Jean fended her off with her serving spoon while she scooped the contents of the tubs onto serving plates.

"One little bite isn't going to hurt!" Tabitha complained, rubbing her knuckles where Jean had rapped them soundly when she tried to swipe a spring roll.

Jean chuckled evilly. "It'll hurt *you* if you keep trying. Wait for Lillian; she'll be done putting Merry to bed in a few minutes. I want her to have a nice family dinner for a change. She spends so many hours in that office of hers, it's the least I can do when she emerges."

Tabitha grabbed a breadstick and sat down to nibble that instead. "That's nice of you." She used the bread to point to a couple of dishes. "I did notice that we had a few of Lillian's favorites on the table."

Gabrielle uncorked the wine and poured them each a glass. "Family takes care of family; it's what we do. Like everyone rallied around to help me with the boys that time Eric was away dealing with that situation on Sertjal."

Lillian returned just as Gabrielle spoke. "I don't think I know that story, Aunt Gabrielle." She took in the spread laid out on the table with a bright smile and went over to wrap her arms around Jean. "Thanks, Mom. You're the best."

Jean blushed a little and waved her off. "It's only dinner. No effort at all."

Lillian grabbed a plate and began loading it with a little from each dish. "You were going to tell me about Sertjal, Aunt Gabby?"

Tabitha frowned. "Wasn't that the place with the peace summit that turned out to be a big fat trap?"

Gabrielle pointed her fork at Tabitha. "That's the one. But if Lillian wants to know about that, she can find it in the history books." Her face became serious. "I want to tell you about another war. The war of motherhood."

Tabitha snorted, spraying herself with wine. "How is motherhood a war? Kids aren't terrorists." She took the tissue Jean offered and wiped herself down.

"No," Gabrielle told her solemnly, "they're worse! Terrorists *sleep*, Tabitha."

Jean and Lillian cracked up at that.

"Damn straight," Jean acknowledged, pulling herself together before she woke Merry. She waved an accusing finger at her daughter. "Our Merry sleeps like an angel once you persuade her that she's tired. You, on the other hand, did not sleep through the night until you were almost five years old. Your dad used to have to walk you around the nursery so you would settle, and the slightest noise woke you again."

Gabrielle chuckled. "At least you only had Lillian to contend with. My boys were experts in parental torture from day one."

"That's true. That phase the twins went through of only sleeping one at a time almost broke us all." Jean's expression of horror made them burst out laughing again.

"That's the story I was getting around to telling." Gabrielle took a sip of her wine and leaned in, dropping her voice to a slightly spooky timbre. "It was the Year of Many Ops, and Eric was away more than he'd been home. I was still adjusting to life as a stay-at-home mom, and I was epically exhausted."

"Even with your nanos?" Lillian asked.

"Even with them. The boys were teething, and they hadn't done anything except cry for days. I hadn't slept or washed or even eaten anything nutritious enough to be called food for so long that I was almost functioning as a regular human.

Tabitha leaned over and gave Gabrielle a one-armed hug. "I remember when we came to visit you and the boys. You were pretty ripe, Gabby."

Gabrielle touched her head to Tabitha's. "That was the best bath and nap I ever had in my whole life. You all were my heroes that day."

Jean snickered. "You had that big red mark on your face from where you'd fallen asleep at the kitchen table. I couldn't believe you were wearing the same robe you'd had on the previous time I saw you."

Lillian raised her eyebrows at her always-immaculately-dressed aunt. "That's not like you."

Gabrielle shrugged. "We can't be strong all the time. Not without support. From my perspective, I had two teething infant sons and no husband around to give me a break so I could sleep. Until your Mom, Tabitha, and Bethany Anne stepped in to help out, I almost went quietly crazy."

"*Quietly?*" Jean smirked. "I remember it a little differently, but that's okay. I can admit that there were times I went through the same thing. Whenever your dad was away on an extended mission, Lilly, it was difficult to find the right balance between my work and being there for you." Her eyes became distant as she fell into her memory. "You won't remember this, but I used to cry when I got home from work and you were already asleep. It broke my heart to know I'd missed out on hearing about your day."

"I always knew why you had to be at work, Mom. I never blamed you for any of it." Lillian dropped onto a chair and accepted the glass from Gabrielle. "I worry that Merry might feel differently. I mean, I'm not saving the Empire like you were." She sighed as she picked through the food on her plate, her normally cool and collected demeanor wavering for once. "I don't feel like I have any balance at all right now, Mom. The business is taking all of my time, and I'm barely ever home for Merry."

"Your business needs your attention," Jean reminded her. "You're putting the time in now to make that business a success. Once it's established and you can provide for your daughter, your time will become more your own again."

Lillian smiled thinly. "I hope so. Practically, though, there are always going to be times like this—especially when we're approaching a product launch. Time goes out the window, and as far as I can tell? There's nothing I can do about it."

Gabrielle nodded. "There are times in life when we have to buckle down and work like hell itself is driving you. Those who truly love you will not only understand, they'll be there to help and support you through it."

Tabitha held a hand over her mouth while she spoke with it full. "What Gabrielle said. We're all here for you, Lillian."

Jean reached over and covered Lillian's hand with her

own. "You're never alone. Just like we weren't when each of us went through the same thing."

Lillian frowned for a microsecond before her mask of impassivity dropped back into place. "Yeah, but there's one difference between my situation and yours. Dad and Uncle Eric came back."

CHAPTER TWELVE

System of the Six, Planet Vietania, Plomerilia, Palace

There was a slight delay at the palace gates when the guards questioned the crew's claim to an audience. They were suspicious that the appointment hadn't been there until the day before, and had been waiting to see who was so important that they could circumvent protocol like that.

John, who was wearing his sword and cape today, stepped in to diffuse the situation. His princely manner appeared to trigger obedience in the guards, since five minutes after he ushered them inside the gatehouse they were heading across the extensive palace grounds toward the castle.

They walked up the wide stone avenue that led from the gates directly to the palace steps. Nickie actually kind of liked the landscaping of the grounds. She'd expected it all to be perfectly manicured and micromanaged but instead, she spied trailing vines and stands of trees that hid summerhouses and pergolas along winding paths. The sound of running water gave away the water features as they passed along the tree-lined carriageway.

The first view of the palace drew a gasp from them all. It was grand—all columns, stained glass windows, and spires like something from a gothic fairy tale.

"It's…" Adelaide's voice trailed off, lost for words.

"It's beautiful," Grim managed.

Use your comm, Nickie reminded them. *Mere, can you hack anything to give us an advantage?*

Meredith sniffed her disapproval. *I can hack anything on this planet with the potential to be hacked.*

I hope you're not tech-shaming them, Meredith? Nickie teased. *We can't all be shit-hot advanced EIs.*

Meredith was mollified. *I wasn't kidding, Nickie. The palace is relatively low-tech. They haven't got anything that can keep me out.*

Nickie tilted her head to look at the palace from close up. Every stone looked to be hand-carved. The windows had the same hand-crafted look. *Shit, this place must have cost a few fortunes to build. Do* not *break a thing.*

Everyone murmured their agreement as they ascended the steps.

They went under the portcullis and into the grand atrium, where they were shown to an anteroom by an aide and told to wait to be called for their audience with the queen.

A short time later, a tall, thin man entered the anteroom from a door opposite the one they'd entered by. "Her Majesty will see you now. This way, if you will." He held up a hand when they all rose to follow. "Just the captain and one other. The rest will have to wait here."

Queen-in-waiting Cynthia McLeod was a vision in black lace. Her mourning garments were haute couture from the heart of the Federation. The queen did not acknowledge them at first. She lounged across her throne with her feet dangling over the wide armrest.

The young queen continued what she was doing on her datapad until Nickie coughed pointedly. Then she looked up, which the aide took as his cue to announce Nickie and John.

He waved Nickie forward. "Your Majesty, this is Captain Meredith Dakkar and Marius Regis from the Silver Line Trading Company."

The queen was unimpressed. "What do they want?" she asked the aide. She glanced in Nickie's direction. "They don't look like they're any fun. Can't you take care of it?"

Meredith, I've changed my mind. We'll take this one out instead.

Nickie...

Joking, Mere. I'm joking. Sort of.

The aide was clearly used to handling the petulant queen. "Unfortunately not, my queen. This matter requires your attention."

Cynthia pouted. "What's the point of you if I have to deal with boring stuff?" She reluctantly sat up and waved dismissively at Nickie and John. "Very well, get on with it then."

Nickie didn't get a chance to start. The door to the side of the throne opened and a woman breezed through, her attention on the datapad she was reading. Cynthia's guards didn't react to her presence.

That's Jolie, John told her.

What is she doing here? Nickie frowned. *And why aren't the guards bothered? I thought they were rivals?*

Things got even more surreal a moment later when Cynthia turned to see who had entered the throne room. "Jolie! Good! Now that you're here, you can deal with these traders."

She got up and hooked an arm through one of her guard's. "Come on, boys. I'm done here. Jolie is much better at all this boring stuff, don't you think?"

The guards covered their discomfort with her flirtation as she led them away.

Jolie gave the crew an apologetic smile. "My apologies for this. My sister will hear you in just a moment." She ran after Cynthia to stop her from leaving the throne room.

They heard Jolie speak a moment later. "Cynthia, we talked about this."

"But I don't *want* to!" the queen whined. "I have a party to get ready for."

Jolie put a hand on Cynthia's shoulder and turned the younger woman back to face Nickie. "Just listen to what they have to say. I'll be around if you need me, but you know I have no authority to approve any trade agreement."

"Fiiiine." Cynthia flounced back to the throne and sat down huffily.

Jolie nodded. "I'll be in the blue room."

Nickie didn't trust herself to keep the dislike out of her tone, so she nudged John forward. *You should take this. Be princely or some shit.*

Aren't you technically royalty as well? he complained.

Nickie raised an eyebrow at him. *You've met my uncle, right? Do we act like fucking royalty? Get in there and do whatever you need to do to get her interested enough to keep us around. I want to talk to the sister.*

John took a hesitant step toward the queen. *You owe me one for this.*

Nuh-uh, Nickie corrected. *You insisted you could be useful, and this is you being useful. Suck it up, sweetheart.*

John sighed and made his way to the throne. Cynthia was much happier to deal with a handsome man than she had been to listen to Nickie. She simpered while John laid the compliments on as thick as butter.

The aide sighed as Jolie swept past, a beacon of efficiency who was there one minute and gone through the door behind the throne the next.

Nickie leaned in to whisper to the aide, "Is this how things work around here?"

"Unfortunately, yes." He looked down, red-faced. "I shouldn't speak so freely."

Nickie patted the man's bony shoulder. "Whatever. I'm not judging."

The aide sighed as Cynthia let out a high-pitched giggle at something John said. "If you want to get anything done around here you have to go through Jolie. It's going to be hell once the mourning period ends and she's crowned. That's as much as I'm willing to admit."

"So they're rivals in public, but in private Jolie runs everything."

"Not just here. She's responsible for the health care reforms, the education reforms, and the favorable trade deals we're going into the Federation with. The people have filed a petition asking for Cynthia to abdicate in favor of Jolie, but Cynthia was raised by her mother to hold onto the crown by whatever means." He sighed again. "It's sad, really. She doesn't enjoy the role."

Nickie saw exactly what tactics Cynthia employed. She held court with John and her male guards, flirting at an expert level that had all of them hanging on her every word. John flicked a glance Nickie's way, and she glared at him to remind him of the reason they were there.

He grimaced an apology and turned back to Cynthia. He said something and Cynthia looked at Nickie with barely concealed impatience.

She stood and waved at the door Jolie had disappeared through. "Let's get this over with. Jolie should have the room ready by now."

Jolie was just arranging a tray with drinks when they entered the meeting room.

Cynthia flounced in and dropped into the chair at the head of the table. She fluttered her eyelashes at John and patted the seat next to hers. "Marius, you can sit by me."

Nickie snickered when John obeyed. She took the seat at the other end of the table so she could get a read on both sisters without being seen to stare.

Cynthia continued to flirt outrageously with John, who was doing an excellent job of looking like he was enjoying the attention.

Jolie gave them a glance and turned to Nickie. "You have some mining technology we might be interested in."

Nickie was grateful for a reason to look away. She nodded. "Post-Empire ore extractors."

Jolie was interested. "Post-Empire? You mean Federation?"

"I said what I meant." Nickie smirked at Jolie's confused look. "This tech bolts onto the existing machinery you have and is guaranteed to improve efficiency by a minimum of thirty percent. A little more if the machine was Empire-made."

Jolie's eyebrows went up. "That's a huge increase in yield. It could make a huge difference to our economy if what you say is true. Can you back these claims up?"

"Of course," Nickie replied. She appreciated Jolie's straightforward approach. "We can set up a demo at your convenience."

"What about cost?" Jolie looked Nickie straight in the eye. "If it's going to be prohibitive, save us both the time now."

Nickie shrugged. "I have to make a living, but my price will be fair."

Jolie gave Cynthia an impatient glance. "Cynthia, are you listening to this?"

Cynthia affected a yawn. "Yes, but I'm *bored*. Can we just buy the technology from them and go to dinner?" She laid a hand on John's arm. "You'll join me for dinner, won't you, Marius?"

John turned bright red. "Oh, um…yeah. Sure."

Jolie sighed. "We can't just buy it without knowing if it works, Cynthia."

Cynthia pouted. "So why do you need me to be here?" She stood and grabbed John by the hand. "Come with me, Marius. I'm going to show you how royalty lives."

Nickie would have been annoyed about not being

invited if she hadn't wanted to speak to Jolie further. She snorted. "Yeah, Marius. Tell me how the other half lives when you get back."

Jolie also stood to leave. "Captain Dakkar, would you like to make arrangements for your demonstration now? I can have someone bring us dinner."

Nickie nodded. "That would be great, thanks, but my crew has been waiting a while."

Jolie put a hand to her mouth. "Oh, I arranged for them to be given a tour of the city at night. They left just after Wilhelm collected you from the anteroom."

Nice of you all to let me know you'd left, she sent over the comm.

Oh, shit! Keen blurted. *To be honest, I plain forgot I had the comm in.*

Holy heck, me too, Adelaide added. *You scared the crap out of me then, boss.*

I'm at the ship, Grim informed her. *My purchases from the markets this morning need to be organized.*

Seeing as you're not sitting in that room, you may as well enjoy the tour. I'm going to hang out here for a bit. I'll see you all back at the ship.

She turned her brightest smile on Jolie. "I'd love to join you for dinner."

System of the Six, Planet Vietania, Plomerilia, Palace

Dinner turned out to be a plate of sandwiches and a flask of coffee shared while Nickie demonstrated the tech she was selling. There wasn't enough to fill Nickie even if she hadn't had the extra calorie requirement that came with her nanocytes. She noticed recently that she'd been a little hungrier, and Meredith had told her it was because she'd found a way to slightly increase the trickle of energy flowing to her power packs.

Nickie was grateful for the effort since the presence of the crew had caused a massive spike in the number of times she found herself in life-threatening situations. She needed a decent meal, though. As soon as she felt she could excuse herself without offending Jolie, she made her way out of the palace to head back to the *Granddaughter*.

John was nowhere to be seen, and he'd deactivated his comm.

"Well, fuck you, too," she mumbled as she left the palace grounds. She flagged down a cab on the main strip outside the palace, which was filled with tourists even at this late hour.

She gave the driver her destination, and as she sat back, her stomach let out a loud growl. Grim had mentioned stocking the galley. She opened a channel to him.

Grim was surprised to hear from her. *What's up? I didn't expect you back for hours.*

John's off living it up at some swanky-ass dinner, and all I got was a few sandwiches. It's not fair. I'm on my way back to the ship. Would you make us something good to eat?

I'll make you a meal John would be jealous of, Grim promised. *I already have some marinades going.*

Nickie grinned. *You're the best, Grim. I'll see you soon.*

System of the Six, Planet Vietania, Plomerilia, Shipyard, Aboard the *Penitent Granddaughter*, Bridge

Nickie was woken by Meredith in the small hours. She almost fell out of her chair.

What the fuck, Meredith?

You asked me to wake you when John returned.

Shit, yeah. Sorry. She rubbed the sleep from her eyes. *Where is he?*

Outside the ship, attempting to call the ramp.

Um...attempting?

Meredith brought up the ship's external camera feed on the viewscreen. John was a little worse for wear. He was clearly inebriated, and his clothes were disordered. He wobbled around beneath the ship, calling to be let in.

Nickie made a face at the scene. "What's he been up to, and why'd he come here instead of going to his own ship? If he thinks he's getting a booty call, he can fuck right off."

Shall I allow him aboard?

Can you hose him off or something first? Sober him up?

Meredith snickered. *Funnily enough, I can.*

Wait, hang on a minute. Nickie reached into the storage compartment in her chair and grabbed the bag of popcorn she'd stashed there for a snacking emergency. Then she sat back and put her feet up. *Okay, ready.*

John was too drunk to avoid the sheet of ice-cold water that sluiced from the *Granddaughter* a minute later. Nickie almost dropped her popcorn, she laughed so hard when Meredith dropped the unexpected shower on him.

John spluttered and shook himself. "What the fuck, Nickie?" he yelled. "Just let me in. I have to tell you something about Cynthia."

He's going to attract attention soon, Meredith warned.

Nickie sighed. *Buzzkill. I suppose you'd better let him aboard.*

John marched onto the bridge a few minutes later, still dripping. "What was that all about?" he demanded.

"Have you seen your state?" Nickie pointed at his untucked shirt, his messy hair, and the haphazard way his cape hung from his shoulders. "Be grateful I let you aboard at all."

"You would have left me out there?"

"In a heartbeat," she told him cheerfully. "But we're in the middle of a mission and your big mouth was about to blow it, so I didn't have much choice."

John looked at her for a minute, lost for words. Then he came to a resolution of some sort, and the gathering storm on his face passed. "The mission. Fine. I agree with Addie, Jolie is the best person to rule this planet. but Cynthia isn't all bad."

Nickie sighed. "It's not what we were sent here to decide. If it turns out that the rightful heir is the worst one for the job, then I don't see how keeping her in power helps the Federation."

"I thought you hated the Federation," John teased.

"I hate the Federation. I don't hate the people who live in it. And I don't hate these people, even if a fuck-load of them are self-obsessed assholes."

John had nothing to add to that. "So which sister do we make queen?"

"I don't know yet," Nickie admitted. "Do we leave someone inept in charge? Or manipulate the situation to do what's right for these people, whatever the cost?" She got up to pace the bridge.

Nickie? Your heart rate has gone up. Are you okay?

I'm fine, Mere, but I should have known better than to get involved with any of the Federation's fucking business. This shit's getting more complicated by the minute.

Well, yes. Politics are rarely direct.

Nickie snorted. *You can say that again. Killing Skaines was a hell of a lot easier.*

I could, but I'd rather point out that you have grown beyond that.

"Are you talking to Meredith?" John asked.

"She was giving me her version of a pep talk."

It was a great pep talk, Meredith countered. I was about to tell you that the next entry in your aunt's diary has become available, but now I don't think I will bother.

In the middle of the night?

John frowned. "What, the unshakable Nickie Grimes needs a pep talk? These people are going to break into civil war without your intervention. They need someone like you to step in. And if not you, then it will be some mercenary who doesn't give a shit."

Nickie rubbed her tired eyes. "Surely there must be someone in the Federation."

"Didn't your uncle say there was a problem with them interfering? It had to be someone on the outside. That's a very short list of people. There's only you, Nickie."

Nickie pointed at John. "And you."

John shook his head. "I'm heading back to my planet once this mission is complete, but I don't imagine for a second that this is the last of the problems that the Federation will need solved."

"Work for the Federation from outside it? Yeah, no."

Nickie held up a finger. "Don't even think about suggesting that this will be an ongoing thing. You dragged me into this shit, and as soon as we solve this issue, I'll be getting on my ship and getting the fuck out of here."

She stopped her pacing. "Fuck this. I don't care what the Federation wants. I'm going to do the right thing."

"Which is?" John pressed.

Nickie grinned. "A vigilante has got to do what a vigilante has got to do. We're going to make sure Jolie is the one crowned queen."

John looked a little doubtful. "And how are we going to do that?"

"We start by having you lure Cynthia to your ship so we can grab her." She stood and yawned. "The plan can wait until tomorrow."

John nodded. "It *is* late. I'd better get back to my ship."

Nickie waved him off. "Yeah, you'd better." She left him to see himself out and dashed back to her quarters.

Once inside with the door locked, she dropped onto her bed and closed her eyes. She hoped this entry continued the anecdotes about her and Tabitha's time together when she was tiny. Sleep, again, could wait.

Hit me, Meredith.

CHAPTER THIRTEEN

**<u>Orbiting the QBBS *Meredith Reynolds*, QBS *Achronyx*,
Bridge</u>**

Tabitha paced the bridge while she went through all of the pre-flight checklists with Achronyx.

She wanted to be out of here already.

The last two days had dragged, despite the fact that every minute had been filled with the thousand tasks she had to complete before they could leave for Arista. The Tontos had returned from their retreat in the small hours of the morning, and she was waiting less than patiently for them to arrive at the ship.

"Achronyx, where *are* they?" She pouted. "I've missed them. They should be here by now."

"They only returned from Zaphod a few hours ago. Hirotoshi has just boarded. The others are on their way. I am also anxious to get to Arista, Tabitha."

Tabitha dropped into the captain's chair and huffed. "I know. It's been eating at me ever since Barnabas told me

139

about it." She sighed. "I feel responsible. I should have known what was going on out there. I've let my snitches run too freely recently."

Hirotoshi arrived on the bridge. "Perhaps, Kemosabe, it is time to tighten your grip on them again?"

Tabitha spun her chair around and jumped up, stepping closer and hugging Hirotoshi. "You're back! How was Zaphod? And your contemplation?"

Hirotoshi dropped his bags by his station and opened his arms to envelope Tabitha in a brotherly embrace. "It is good to see you too. Zaphod was much the same as always. The Abbot and Stacy send their regards."

"Stacy's living in the main temple?"

Hirotoshi inclined his head. "She is nearing the end of her days. You may want to make time to say your goodbyes soon."

That saddened Tabitha. She remembered the first time they'd met, how vibrant and full of life her friend had been. "It's difficult to see people age when we just stay the same." She sniffed as the grief hit. "It's like I can't escape loss at the moment. Shin, Todd, and now Stacy is going to die while we just live on forever."

She leaned into his hug and Hirotoshi held her close while she cried.

When she was spent, he handed her a handkerchief he produced from seemingly nowhere to dry her face.

"All things must pass. It is the way life works, Kemosabe. Even for us, eventually."

"Thanks, Hirotoshi." She sniffed. "I guess it just got to me for a minute."

"It is only natural that such news would shake you."

Achronyx interrupted, "Tabitha, the others have arrived onboard the ship. They have gone to unload their gear. We can leave whenever you are ready."

Tabitha scrubbed her face with the handkerchief, then handed it back to Hirotoshi with her Ranger face on. She strode over to the captain's chair and dropped into it resolutely. "I was ready two days ago. Let's get the hell out of here. We have a colony to save."

"As you wish, Ranger Tabitha," Achronyx intoned cheerfully.

Arista System, Planet Terminus, Dark Side of the Fourth Moon, QBS *Achronyx*, Meeting Room

The *Achronyx* Gated in at a safe distance from the main planet. Tabitha wanted to get a closer look at the system before they made a move.

She had Achronyx tuck the cloaked ship into some debris around the massive moon and got to work investigating.

The time was well spent.

While the Tontos were busy preparing to put boots on the ground, Tabitha and Achronyx had gotten themselves acquainted with the spread-out colony before calling the briefing.

Tabitha's armored boots clanked on the floor as she paced in front of the wallscreen where Achronyx had put up an infrared image showing the population center on the main planet. "The people are mostly concentrated on Terminus, which has the most infrastructure."

"What about the other planets?" Hirotoshi asked.

Tabitha twirled her finger. "Next set, Achronyx." Achronyx switched from the overhead view of Terminus to a split view that showed the centers of population on the other planets in the system. "There are smaller outposts on the planets Brinma and Vatu to support the mines and manufacturing facilities they have there. The exoplanet, Eulia, is uninhabitable due to a lack of breathable atmosphere and questionable gravity. But it's made up of mostly of iron and other useful ores, so they claimed it as part of the system."

"What are they manufacturing?" Hirotoshi asked.

Tabitha shrugged. "I'm not sure yet. I think we'll find out when we go planetside. I want to speak to the people who live there. The people of Terminus are shipped out to work the mines and factories, but their families are here on Terminus."

Hirotoshi nodded. "That is a wise course of action. What about our so-called gang's headquarters? Do we have a location?"

Tabitha grinned. "You bet your ass we do. I even have a live feed. Show us the compound, Achronyx."

"There will be a short time delay due to our position," Achronyx told her. "I'm having to route it through the planet's satellites, and they are not anything I would describe as modern."

Tabitha waved her left hand, tapping her right fingers impatiently on the armrest. "That's fine. Just get it onscreen."

The screen switched to an infrared feed of a solid sandstone building on three distinct levels. The L-shaped building was surrounded on all sides by a wide, high wall.

The infrared showed that there were people on all three levels, and more around the courtyard and on the walls.

"We know that our targets are inside this compound, and so are the children." Tabitha scowled at the moving red blobs on the screen. "I think Barnabas was a little off in his description of these dead-fuckfaces-walking as a gang. There's way too much organization here for some two-bit bullies to be running it."

Ryu frowned at the building on the screen. "The operation *does* appear to be much larger than we anticipated. They have taken over the infrastructure. This looks to be the colony's administration center."

"It was," Achronyx confirmed, "until the criminals took control. The main concentration of gang activity appears to be here on Terminus. I'm picking up communications between Terminus and the other three planets, as well."

Tabitha turned back to the screen and glared at the compound, where the infrared showed slow-moving dots at intervals on the walls. There were more people moving around on the first and second floors.

On the top floor, the infrared showed rooms with rows of stationary hotspots that Tabitha could only assume were the children.

Tabitha leaned forward with both hands on the table. "The children are alive for now. Whatever the hell is going on down there, it's not worth risking their lives to go rushing in. We need to get some more information before we act."

Ryu scratched his cheek. "Yes, like what the criminals want the people here for so badly that they're willing to do something this despicable to innocent children."

Tabitha pulled out her chair and sat down. "It doesn't matter why. They're not going to live long enough to explain. I thought the Skaines were bad, but this? This is the lowest thing someone could do."

"It will not stand, Kemosabe," Hirotoshi reassured her. "We are here, and we will put an end to the evil."

"Damn right, we will," Tabitha agreed. She slapped the table. "Okay, enough talking. Here's how we're going to do this. I'm going to Terminus with Hirotoshi to talk to the people and dig around the gang's headquarters. Ryu and Katsu, you guys take a Pod out to the smaller colonies on Brinma and Vatu. Jun and Kouki, you go to Eulia and find out what's happening in the mines out there."

"Would it not be better to remain together?" Jun asked.

Tabitha shook her head. "I would normally say yes, but we need a picture of what's going on out there as well. I don't want to clear out one roach nest only to discover there was system-wide infestation all along."

"That…is actually a sensible plan," Jun agreed, looking at Ryu, who allowed a tiny shrug of his shoulders as he grinned. "Very well."

Kouki looked away from the screen, his eyes clouded with anger. "But when we have all the information we need…"

Tabitha nodded once. "We destroy the gang together — with extreme prejudice. Nobody gets away with this kind of shit on my watch or any of yours." She stood and clapped her hands. "What are you all waiting for? Next stop is the armory."

· · ·

Arista System, Planet Terminus, Colony Outskirts

Tabitha and Hirotoshi stepped out of the Pod and were smacked in the face by a wave of dry heat. The Arista beat down on them like Tabitha liked to beat on the Skaine, and it was difficult to even draw breath without the air scorching their lungs.

Tabitha wiped her forehead with the hem of her cloak and shuddered as a wide rivulet of sweat dripped from her neck down her spine. "Desert. How wonderful." She adjusted her armor's temperature controls to provide some relief from the heat, and shuddered again when they kicked in and the sweat down her back became ice-cold. "Achronyx, cloak the Pod in case any of the locals find it and decide to try to take a joyride. I'd hate to get back here and find a fried colonist." She looked around, noticing the shimmers of heat floating over the ground in a few places. "Although they're probably all as dried-out as jerky anyway, living in this heat."

Hirotoshi adjusted the hood of his cloak to cover his eyes from Arista's glare and set off walking. "The longer we stand around complaining about the heat, the longer we will have to endure it."

Tabitha pulled up her own hood to avoid the burning rays. "All I'm saying is that there are better places to build than in the middle of a desert." She caught up. "Where do they even get their water?"

"There is water here." Hirotoshi nodded to the dark clouds on the horizon and kept trekking through the loose sand and scree. "This is a well-established colony. You can be certain that they have developed systems for dealing with whatever challenges the environment presents."

"True." Tabitha knocked a tumbleweed out of her path. "We're pretty resilient as a species."

They left the box canyon they'd landed in and made their way toward the buildings in the near distance.

"It's pretty grim out here," Tabitha remarked, kicking one of the many small rocks that littered the ground beneath their feet. "I always wonder why people choose to settle so far from home in such harsh environments." She stuck a finger inside the collar of her armor in the vain hope it would provide some relief from the irritation it was causing her. "Why not find somewhere all lovely and lush, where things grow, and the planet doesn't try to turn you into a pot roast inside your armor?"

"It's the desire to push the boundaries, Kemosabe. To be human is to crave individuality even as you close in with your fellow man to fight for survival against the odds. Surely you of all people understand that?"

Tabitha screwed up her nose when she almost tripped on an embedded rock. She was still sweating in her cloak-covered armor despite the temperature controls being set to full. "Yeah, I do. But still, this is not the kind of environment I would choose to live in just so I could express my need for individuality."

Hirotoshi turned his head to look at her. "The Empire is always in need of source materials, and colonies like this supply a great deal of that. That's why they had so much assistance from the Empire in the first place."

Tabitha's eyes lit up. "Do you think they still have the original colony ship? I haven't seen one of those in forever."

Hirotoshi shrugged. "It is likely. We have visited many

places over the years where the colony ship was repurposed as a monument for the colonists to gather at."

Tabitha was in the mood to argue. "Yeah, but there have been more where the colonists stripped their ship down to components and repurposed the whole thing as soon as they began to build."

Hirotoshi nodded. "That is true. I suppose we will find out soon enough."

The buildings ahead soon came into focus, as did the small group of armed colonists standing between Tabitha and Hirotoshi and their goal.

Tabitha waved at them. "Hey there!" She counted two men and four women, two blasters, a shotgun, and a pair of nice-looking pistols of a rough make she assumed was local. *Interesting. They manufacture weapons here. More interesting is, Barnabas didn't know that.*

I noticed, Kemosabe. I think we may have the reason our colony was invaded.

One of the men stepped forward with his blaster raised, wavering between her and Hirotoshi. "Who're you, and what are you doing here, strangers?"

Tabitha shrugged back her cloak and tapped the Ranger badge that hung around her neck. "We're here about your gang issue."

The man primed his blaster, and it began to emit a high-pitched sound. "You ought to turn around and go back to the Empire, Rangers. There's nothing you can do here except get us all killed."

The noise coming from the blaster was like a drill to the brain in Tabitha's enhanced hearing. *Achronyx, can you do anything about that whine?*

Achronyx made a noncommittal noise. *I can't, but I can hack the blaster.*

Tabitha snickered. *I suppose that will have to do.*

The man's blaster fell silent. He looked at it with a puzzled expression and banged the power pack a couple of times with the heel of his hand.

Tabitha shook her head. "Nobody is getting anyone killed. We want to know what's really going on here so we can resolve the situation. You can start by telling us about the gang that is feeding drugs to your children."

A woman looked at her, surprised. "How do you know about that?"

Hirotoshi smiled. "The Rangers find out everything in the end."

"Why should we trust you?" another man called. "For all we know, you've been sent by Brooks to trick us!"

The ghost of a smile touched Hirotoshi's mouth. *We have a name.*

It's a start. Tabitha didn't think it was good enough. She needed to earn these people's trust. "Listen, let's start over. We're here to help. What's your name?"

The man hedged a little, then softened at her warm smile. "Tailor Reid, ma'am."

"Tailor. Good. You can call me Ranger Two." Tabitha walked over and pushed Tailor's impotent blaster down to point at the ground. "You won't be needing that just yet. Maybe later, when we get the kids back."

"How are you going to get them back?" a distraught woman asked. "They'll die if we take them back." She dropped the shotgun she'd been pointing at Tabitha to her side and waved the others down. "Just forget it, Ranger. It's hopeless."

Tabitha's heart hurt. Her face softened just a bit. "What do you mean, they'll die? What is going on here?" She looked from one face to another, seeing if anyone would give her a hint.

Hirotoshi looked up at Arista, which was nearing its peak over the parched sands. The clouds in the distance did not look to be getting any closer, putting an end to any hope of cover from the searing midday heat. "We should discuss this inside."

Tabitha nodded solemnly. "Yeah, preferably somewhere that serves food and cold drinks. It's too *Gott Verdammt* hot out here."

"We can go to the Hub," Tailor told them. He turned and started walking back toward the settlement.

The other colonists went home after they passed through the huge gates on the south side of the perimeter wall, leaving them with just Tailor and Sarah, who turned out to be married.

The husband and wife led Tabitha and Hirotoshi through the busy marketplace, which they stepped straight into as soon as they were through the gate.

The market stretched along the outer wall. There were brightly-colored awnings for as far as Tabitha could see, and the competing voices of thousands of vendors hawking their goods filled the air. She was tempted to stop for a snack at a few of the better-smelling food carts they passed, but they were headed toward food, and more importantly, information.

The market gave way suddenly to the next ring, which

was the outer residential area. The buildings passed quickly, and they turned onto a cross-street that gave them a straight shot to the center of the settlement.

Tabitha took it all in as they walked briskly and in relative silence. The settlement had an air of tension hanging over it, which was evident in the posture of the people they passed. They were defeated, worn out; damn near *resigned* to their lot.

Tabitha's anger rose another notch. She walked along with her fists clenched beneath her cloak. She almost didn't notice that they'd reached the center of the settlement until Hirotoshi caught her arm.

"Would you look at that?" His normally impassive face was split by a wide grin. "It's the colony ship."

The buildings that wrapped around the massive colony ship obscured it at street level, but it rose above the mudbrick constructions, the midday sun reflecting from every dent in the grit-polished panels.

Tabitha spotted a neon bar sign tucked into the shadows beneath the ramp and nodded. "'All Roads?'" She glanced at the scaffolding around the sides of the ship-turned-building as they wove their way around the steady stream of people using the ramp. They skirted the lines and headed for the bar. "What's the ship used for?"

"It's the Hub," Sarah told them as they walked inside. She nodded to various people they passed as she talked to Tabitha. "We began from here and built outward, which is why the settlement is this way. We're constantly refitting it to serve our needs. It's used as a communal area for those who don't want to eat alone. In other parts of the ship we have public services, since we lost the administration center. There's an infirmary on the third deck, but we're stretched to provide proper care because it wasn't in use before we were invaded."

They went through a set of double doors into the bar. A short time later they were all sitting in a secluded corner with their meals and drinks in front of them.

Tabitha placed a device in the center of the table and pressed the little button on top. "Okay, that will prevent anyone from listening in."

The couple looked at the jammer skeptically.

"Really?" Tailor asked. "I heard that tech existed, but I've never seen it."

"Me either," Sarah agreed.

Tabitha smiled brightly and drew an X on her chest. "Cross my heart and hope to kill every motherfucker who has caused harm to one of your children. Tell me how I can save your kids."

Sarah shook her head. "That's what I tried to tell you, Ranger. You can't. They injected our children with a biochemical weapon, or something close to that. If the children don't receive the antidote every twenty-four hours, they die."

Tabitha covered her mouth to speak with it full. "So we get the antidote before we get the kids." She wiped her lips with her napkin. "That's no problem, I've got the facilities aboard my ship to synthesize enough to get you all back to Yoll and get the kids Pod-doc treatment."

"Can you get into an underground vault?" Tailor looked hopeful for the first time. "That's where they store the anti-dote, in the treasury vault. We can get you to the treasury, but we can't get into the vault."

Tabitha shrugged. "Probably. Where is the treasury?"

Sarah paused with her glass halfway to her mouth. "It's in the basement of the administration center."

Tabitha frowned. "The compound where they're keeping the kids?"

"Uh-huh." Tailor sighed. "You see our dilemma?"

"I do." She turned to Hirotoshi. "What do you think?"

Hirotoshi spoke after a moment. "We may have to think of another solution."

"Can we get into a locked vault without blowing the place up?" she asked.

"Or risking the bad guys hurting the children once they realize they are under attack?"

Tabitha thought about it before she answered, "I don't know."

Achronyx spoke up in her mind. *I don't need the antidote. A blood sample from one of the children would suffice. In fact, it would be more useful than the antidote alone since I could begin analyzing the constituent elements of whatever poison they have been given.*

Tabitha liked that idea even better. *That would be a hell of a lot easier than breaking into a vault.* "Apparently all we need to synthesize the cure is a blood sample from one of the children."

Tailor grimaced before he sighed in resignation. "That could prove to be difficult as well."

CHAPTER FOURTEEN

Tabitha and Hirotoshi took turns watching the night guards patrol the walls from a warehouse across from the compound. The Pod was cloaked on the ridged rooftop a short distance behind them, ready for a quick exit once their objective was complete.

Tabitha passed the binoculars to Hirotoshi. *So, all we need to do is get past those guards and the ones patrolling the grounds, then get into the building and get to the top floor where they're keeping the kids.*

All without alerting any of them to our presence, Hirotoshi finished. *We will only have a few minutes to get in and out between guard rotations.*

Piece of cake. Tabitha carefully shuffled to the edge of the warehouse roof and eyed the distance to the ground before she dropped onto the wall below. *Come on, they're about to change shifts.*

Hirotoshi stowed the binoculars in his pack and followed on silent feet.

The two made their way across the top of the wall, sticking to the shadows to avoid being seen. They soon covered the short distance to the administration center.

Tabitha and Hirotoshi waited until the guards left their position, then scrambled up the high wall while the new shift was distracted by getting settled. The wall was easily scaled since the soft stone it was made from was pitted and full of easy handholds thanks to the dry climate and the ever-present desert wind.

They checked that the coast was clear and dashed at vampiric speed down the stairs on the inside and across the open space between the wall and the administration building.

Tabitha pointed to an open window on the second floor. *We can get in there.* She sprinted over to it and jumped, grabbing the wall with the claws she'd formed while she ran.

Hirotoshi was right beside her. They scaled the side of the building and paused just below the open window when they heard voices.

Tabitha scowled. *Our bad guys?*

Most likely, Hirotoshi replied. *Let's listen for a minute.*

The voices were very congratulatory. The men and women within were all extremely pleased that their profits that quarter had been so high, and some bragged that the unrest they had been fanning in another system nearby was about to bring them huge orders when war broke out.

Tabitha saw red.

So did Hirotoshi when her eyes began to glow. *Tabitha, you must contain your emotions.*

Tabitha's lips drew back in a silent snarl, and her teeth were suddenly much sharper than usual. *They've enslaved these people and stolen their children for the sake of profit, Hirotoshi. They're screwing around with other people's lives as we speak to make more, and they're fucking* laughing *about it.* She started to climb again. *Oh, no. I'm going to* really *ruin their day.*

We have time to ruin their whole lives, what little of them remains, Hirotoshi soothed. *However, we need to remember what we came here to do.*

The red glow faded from Tabitha's eyes, and she sighed. *You're right. We need another way in. Let's just concentrate on getting what we came for and head back to the ship so we can get started on the antidote and spirit the kids out of here soonest.*

Hirotoshi glanced at the roof. *We'll find a way in up there.*

They shinnied up and pulled themselves over the lip of the building onto the flat roof.

There. Tabitha pointed out an access door among the building's air conditioning units and solar panels. The door was locked, but a quick twist of Tabitha's wrist solved that issue, and the two vampires slipped into the building.

Once inside, they made their way down the stairs to the top floor. The stairs fed into a dimly lit corridor which had doors on both sides. There was nobody in sight, and the desk at the other end was unmanned.

Hirotoshi indicated the hulking shadows on the other side of the frosted glass doors. *Guards. We should hurry.*

They went the opposite way from the doors and began

checking the rooms along the corridor, looking for one of the rooms containing the colonists' children.

This place smells like a hospital, Tabitha grumped as she shut the door to an empty meeting room.

That can only be a good thing, Hirotoshi assured her. *If they are keeping the place clean, then they must also be taking care of the children.*

Hopefully, Tabitha agreed. She wrinkled her nose when they turned a corner and the disinfectant smell grew stronger. *I think we're getting closer. Come on, let's find them.*

They found what they were looking for in the next room they checked. Tabitha and Hirotoshi paused with the door ajar. The large rectangular room was partitioned into cubicles with hospital screens and there was a nurse inside, snoozing in a rocking chair in the corner of the ward.

Some of the curtains were pulled back, showing them the sleeping children in the beds. Tabitha touched the small box in the pouch on her belt and tiptoed over to the nearest bed. She touched the boy's arm tentatively.

Wow, he's way under.

The boy couldn't have been older than thirteen or fourteen, but his sandy hair and freckled complexion made him look much younger.

She laid a soothing hand on his forehead and looked at Hirotoshi as he closed the curtain around them quietly.

Can you smell that?

Hirotoshi sniffed and made a face. *It smells like...corruption.*

What the hell is it?

He frowned. *It's coming from the child. Take the sample. We will know more when Achronyx has analyzed it.*

Tabitha took the blood collection kit from the pouch on her belt. She opened the box and withdrew the hypodermic needle with shaky hands.

Hirotoshi saw her nerves. *Who would have thought a vampire would have trouble taking blood?*

Tabitha looked at him, wide-eyed. *That was almost a joke, Hirotoshi. Careful, you might break something.*

Hirotoshi smiled as Tabitha bent to take the boy's blood with steady hands.

The boy didn't stir from his medically-induced sleep during the whole process. Tabitha located a vein and filled the three sample vials from the kit one at a time, passing each to Hirotoshi to put in the carry case he had in his pack as she exchanged it for the next.

The nurse began to wake as Tabitha removed the hypodermic, cutting off any chance of obtaining samples from any of the other children. Tabitha passed the last vial to Hirotoshi and cleaned the boy's arm, and they tiptoed out to the corridor and back up the stairs to the roof exit.

They snuck out of the compound much the same way they'd gotten in, managing to avoid detection by the guards without any problems. It was a quick return dash to the warehouse roof where the Pod awaited.

***

Tabitha headed straight for the ship's lab when they returned to the *Achronyx*, while Hirotoshi went to the bridge to check in with the other Tontos.

The lights came on in the lab as Tabitha walked in. She placed the carry case on the table and opened it to remove the three vials and feed the contents into the drawer Achronyx opened in the side of one of the machines.

She did the last one and let out a huge yawn.

You're tired.

Tabitha didn't need Achronyx to tell her that. She stretched to accompany the next yawn that escaped her. *You don't say! I'm going to hit the sack. You've got this without me, right?*

Of course, Achronyx told her. *Get some rest. I'll be done with my analysis by the time you get up.*

Tabitha smiled as she left the lab to head to her quarters. *Thanks, Achronyx. You know, you're not such a pain in my ass.*

Achronyx chuckled. *And I'm sure that if I had an ass, you would not be a pain in mine, either.*

Arista System, Planet Terminus, Dark Side of the Fourth Moon, QBS *Achronyx*, Lab, Four Hours Later

Tabitha strolled into the lab, still in her pajamas, and rubbed her bleary eyes when the bright overhead lights came on. "What have you found?"

Achronyx' tone was serious. "We need to act, and soon. I had speculated as to the likelihood of the children being poisoned, but this is much worse."

Tabitha went over to the console by the machine she'd fed the samples into earlier. "Show me the results." She scrolled through Achronyx' findings, her frown deepening as she read. "What is this? Their brain activity is next to nonexistent."

"The drug the children have been given is an extremely

dangerous neurochemical blocker," Achronyx told her. "This is why we need to act. Without the antidote to inhibit its effect the blocker will shut down the children's brains permanently, killing them."

Tabitha sighed. "Is that why the kid I took blood from was so out of it?"

"Yes," Achronyx replied. "There were also high amounts of sedatives in the child's blood."

Tabitha frowned. "Did you work out how to make the antidote?"

"Yes, but real intervention is needed. As it is, the antidote is only able to hold off the effects as long as the children are sedated, and over time they will need larger and larger doses for it to continue working even in this capacity."

"That will have to do until we can get them something better.

"I have already begun to synthesize the antidote, which will have to be enough to get the children to the *Meredith Reynolds* as we planned. However, there are over two hundred children and their parents—"

"And how are we supposed to transport so many people on the *Achronyx*?" Tabitha finished for him. "I was about to ask you the same thing."

"I don't know," he admitted. "The ship doesn't have the facilities for the medical care the children require.

"Then we will call in someone who does." Tabitha got up and headed for the door. "One step at a time. We'll cross that bridge when we come to it. In the meantime, let's find out how my Tontos did on their fishing expedition."

"Hirotoshi is currently in the galley."

"At this time?" Tabitha headed for the galley, her curiosity well and truly piqued. She found Hirotoshi at the counter prepping ingredients for sandwiches.

She flounced in and pulled a stool out from under the counter to sit on. "You're in here at a weird time."

"As are you, Kemosabe." Hirotoshi poured her a cup of hot coffee. "Achronyx warned me he was waking you earlier than expected. Breakfast and coffee are the best remedies for a rude awakening." He turned back to the griddle and tossed the contents onto two plates.

Tabitha sipped the blessed nectar gratefully. "Thanks. How are the others getting on with their assignments?"

Hirotoshi put a plate in front of Tabitha, then sat opposite her with his own. "They found nothing untoward. The overall conclusion was that taking the children hostage has been enough to keep the colonists in line, so the other planets have been left alone to run as they always have."

"So they're on their way back?"

Hirotoshi nodded.

"Good, because we're going down to the planet as soon as they get back." A cold smile spread over Tabitha's face. "Achronyx, message the Reids and let them know we're coming just as soon as we have enough of the antidote. Tell them to gather the other parents. We've got some Justice to administer, Empress' Ranger style."

Arista System, Terminus, The Hub, All Roads Bar

The bar beneath the ramp was packed with solemn people drinking steadily to repress the kernel of hope they didn't dare allow to germinate.

Nevertheless, they had turned up to hear Tabitha and the Tontos out.

The Reids came to stand with Tabitha by the bar, and Sarah called for quiet. "Thank you all for coming out at this early hour. We called because we have news. The Ranger here has come to help us get our kids back, but she needs our help to do it."

The assembled parents all began talking at once. The Tontos fanned out in front of Tabitha and Sarah in case it turned ugly.

Tabitha couldn't see above the heads and shoulders of the crowd. She sure as hell wasn't going to jump up and down like a teenager at a concert just so she could see, so she climbed up onto the bar to address the crowd from there. "I have judged the organization guilty of enslavement, and a whole shit-load of crimes related to your children. The penalty for those crimes is death. I'm going to wipe those bastards from the face of this planet for what they've done to you."

"What about the antidote?" someone shouted out. "You can't do anything without it."

Tabitha held up a hand. "I have enough of the antidote to get the kids safely to the *Meredith Reynolds* where they can be treated in the Pod-docs. I just need a way to get you all there."

Sarah grinned. "Is that all? Leave that to us." A few of the people chuckled.

Tabitha frowned lightly, wondering what the in-joke was. "Are you sure?"

Sarah chuckled. "Yeah, it won't be an issue. We can take the colony ship."

"What?" Tabitha's tone was one of utter disbelief. "But this thing has sat here for decades. It's surrounded by buildings!"

Sarah winked. "We've been preparing for this opportunity. The ship will fly."

Tabitha grinned and shrugged. "Then I guess there's nothing left to do except get your children back."

The next hour was a flurry of preparation, and all too soon the motley group of Rangers and colonists left the bar and made their way through the settlement under a silver and orange sky.

Tabitha and the Tontos peeled off from the group at the prearranged point while the parents stormed ahead to mob the gate and distract the gang from the true attack.

They were over the wall in a flash, and Tabitha led the Tontos over to the front entrance. She removed the doors with the judicious application of her armored boot—the doors flew in, and the guards behind them flew back.

Tabitha strode into the space vacated by the guards with her JD Specials locked and loaded. "*Whooooop!* Strike!" She stepped over the unconscious guards and looked back at the entrance when she reached the foot of the staircase. "Come on, guys, I think it's safe to say they know we're here."

They pounded up the stairs and split up to clear the offices on the second level where the gang leaders had set up their headquarters. Tabitha shot the first person who came out of the door at the top of the stairs, then caught his falling body and flung it at the three who followed.

Her JD Special bucked in her hand, punctuating their

grunts of surprise with the soft explosion of each headshot. She stepped over the corpses and opened the door they'd come through.

Tabitha shut the door and locked it behind her, hissing happily when she saw where she was. The room beyond was empty of people, and she had hit the jackpot—computer monitors, servers, and controls.

Oh, my. Achronyx chuckled. *This was a lucky find.*

Tabitha stared at the closed-circuit camera feeds of the entire administration center with something approaching rhapsody. *I know, right? The whole building can be controlled from here.*

We can lock this place down and guide the Tontos right to the leaders.

This whole thing just became so much easier that it'll be like shooting fish in a barrel. Her finger hovered over the buttons while she scrutinized the control panel. *Here we go.* She pressed an orange button, and the building went into lockdown.

Kemosabe? Hirotoshi sounded concerned for her.

Tabitha tapped at the console to let them out of the room they were locked in. *Don't worry, I'm the one doing this. I've found their ops center. I'm opening the front gates to let the colonists in, aaaand you should have just received the location of every single scumbag in this building. Don't say I never give you anything.*

That certainly uncomplicates things, Hirotoshi told her.

Kind of the point, she replied airily. *Just keep moving, I'll provide access from here and keep an eye on what's happening with the colonists at the same time.*

You should keep them outside for the moment, he cautioned. *This will not take long.*

It was quick—if rather wet—work. The Tontos swept through the building like deadly whispers. Wherever they were heard, the guilty died. There was no fuss or drama, just the mess they left behind.

When the Tontos were done, Tabitha lifted the lockdown and let the parents in through the front gate. They flooded the entrance, and soon the top floor was heaving with happy parents reunited with their stolen children.

Tabitha searched the rooms for the Reids.

She found them on a bench in a secluded corridor, deep in conversation. Sarah was weeping, and Tailor was doing his best to comfort her despite the grief etched into his own face.

Tabitha hurried over. "What's happened?"

The couple looked at her sadly. "Our son," Tailor told her softly. "The nurse told us that he didn't make it."

Tabitha dropped to her knees beside Sarah and placed a comforting hand on the grieving mother's back. "That's... I'm so sorry." Losing a child had to be the hardest thing anyone could go through. Tabitha couldn't even begin to imagine the depth of the pain they were in right now.

Tabitha didn't know what else to say. She was certain that whatever she said would be the wrong thing. That their son's murderer was also dead would be no consolation in the face of their loss.

Her own experiences of loss recently had taught her that she couldn't fix everything, no matter how hard she tried. Sometimes the only thing left to do was be there to pick up the pieces afterward.

Sarah's shoulders shook, and her sobs echoed in the sterile corridor. They stayed like that for a little while, Sarah and her husband holding hands and Tabitha kneeling by the couple's feet while the three of them wept for their lost child.

CHAPTER FIFTEEN

System of the Six, Planet Vietania, Plomerilia, Palace, Anteroom, One Week Later

Nickie made an effort not to stamp her foot.

For the last week, Meredith had helped her drag out the demonstrations and negotiations for the sale. John worked his charms on Cynthia in an effort to gain her trust enough to persuade her to ditch her guards and visit his ship.

Added to her frustration was the time since she'd received a diary entry from her Aunt Tabitha. She hadn't asked Meredith if there was another because she was still working to process the altered image she was beginning to get of her mother.

It was difficult to bear, knowing that her mom had been so alone. Nickie now saw it hadn't been as cut and dried as she'd always believed. Lillian wasn't a child-neglecting monster, but rather a woman doing her best to raise her daughter despite the grief she'd felt over losing Nickie's father.

At the very least, Nickie now understood that Lillian's absence had been out of necessity and not a desire to avoid her daughter. She couldn't help but wonder how things would have been different if she hadn't fought her mother at every opportunity. Adults had to work to live, and she had punished her mom over and over for her effort to provide for the two of them.

Nickie got it now.

Especially since she had people of her own she was responsible for. Like Prince PITA. The meetings were over for the day, but John was conspicuously absent yet again. It had been getting somewhat awkward when he returned to the ship each night minus Cynthia. The last two nights he had remained at the castle, claiming the festivities had finished too late for him to bother coming all the way to the shipyard to sleep.

Nickie had ceased to be pissed that she hadn't received any invitations, but her bed was feeling awfully big for one at the moment, and John was on her mind.

He finally turned up just as she gave up waiting and crossed into the grand atrium on her way out of the castle. He saw Nickie and hurried to meet her. "Hey, I hoped I'd catch you before you left. I'm not coming back to the ship tonight."

Nickie stopped to wait for him. "Again? You could have told me that over the comm."

John's gaze dropped to his pocket. "Damn, the *comm*. I forgot."

Nickie looked askance at the guitar dangling from a strap on his back while he fished his comm piece out of his pocket and fitted it. "Please tell me you're close to getting her to trust you."

John reddened slightly. "I'm biding my time. We need to be sure she'll come with me when I ask her to. A few more days, I promise."

"Are you kidding me?" She glanced around to make sure they weren't being watched and dragged him into an empty corridor. "What's the holdup? It's been a week already, and she's clearly into you. Just get her down to the ship."

John's voice dropped to a harsh whisper. "So you can *murder* her? Nickie, I can't do it. There has to be another way."

Nickie couldn't believe what she was hearing. "What way?" she hissed. "Please, enlighten me. We have this shit-storm that's about to explode, and the only way to stop it is to take out Cynthia so that Jolie can lead them through it in one fucking piece."

John was adamant. "No. She doesn't deserve to die."

"I don't *want* to kill her." Nickie threw her hands up in frustration. "But would she leave if you asked? She's just one person. Do all of the people in this system deserve to suffer because you have second thoughts now that it's time to get your hands dirty?"

"Is that what you think?" John leaned against the wall. "That's damn unfair, Nickie."

She shrugged. "So what if it is? You heard my uncle. Sometimes the choice is that there *is* no choice. We have to suck it up."

John looked at her as if he were seeing her for the first

time. "You're being a coldhearted bitch about this. Or maybe..." His voice trailed off, and he looked away.

Nickie snorted. "Maybe what?"

He answered with thinly disguised anger, "Maybe you're jealous."

"Of what?" Her voice was low, and calmer than she believed she could manage.

John missed the hint that he was treading on dangerous ground. "Of Cynthia, so you're pushing your own agenda to remove her."

Nickie sneered at the ridiculousness of his suggestion. "What the fuck have you been drinking?"

John narrowed his eyes. "You've turned into such a bitch."

"I was always a bitch," Nickie told him. "You were just too busy trying to bone me to notice." She noted his expression. "Oh, my. Have you two fucked or something? Is that why you're getting a white-knight complex about your target?" She laughed when he turned bright red. "Typical. I bet the only reason you can't complete your mission is that you've gotten attached."

John pushed off the wall. "Cynthia isn't a 'target,' she's a human being."

"Yeah, well, in this case, she's a target. *Our* target, and you've fucked up by thinking of her as anything different. *Fuck*, John! What world do you live in? These people are depending on us whether they know it or not. This is not the time to get cold feet. Welcome to reality."

"What reality is that?" John demanded. "One where you just kill with no compunction? Take out a world leader without a second thought?" He stepped away from Nickie. "I don't know if I want to be around someone like that."

Nickie growled. "That's the fucking definition of vigilantism, you dumbass." She was hurt by his turnaround, but she wasn't going to let him know that. "You're the one who followed me on this fucking mission! I accommodated your princely ass against my better judgment, and now you're screwing it all up with your fucking conscience." She poked him in the chest. "This is the only plan we've got since she isn't letting anyone else near her. You need to stick to it, or every death that happens when everything collapses is on you."

John made as if to argue with Nickie but she stopped him with the finger she'd just poked him with.

"Can you carry *that* on your precious conscience? All those lives, all these planets. Versus one person. Complete your mission, John."

There was a rustle from the direction of the atrium.

John used the distraction to move a little farther away from Nickie. "I need to get back before I'm missed."

Nickie waved him off. "Don't let me keep you." She grabbed John's arm as he passed her. "Just get her to the ship. Don't fuck it up."

He tugged free and scowled at her. "I will, but when this is over, I'm done with you."

"Fine by me. I didn't ask you to tag along in the first place."

Nickie watched him go with mixed feelings. In a way, she was glad to get it over with before she'd invested any feelings in John. He wasn't a keeper anyway. Nickie might have baggage, but he came with a whole planet's worth. On the other hand, she'd be going back to an empty bed again.

Her eyes dropped to his retreating ass. It was a *really* nice one.

John?

He turned back with a strange expression. *What?*

Keep your comm in.

He shook his head and stormed off.

Nickie waited until he was out of sight before falling back against the wall. She breathed in and let it out slowly to ease the thundering of her heart.

Dammit. What the fuck was that?

Nickie, are you okay?

What do you think?

I think you need some time to cool down. How about you go back to the ship? A new diary entry has just unlocked.

Nickie left the palace without looking back. *Sounds like a plan. Fuck this place, and fuck John.*

CHAPTER SIXTEEN

QBBS *Meredith Reynolds*, Rangers' Private Training Area

Tabitha placed the staff she'd been practicing with back on its mount when she heard the hesitant footsteps approaching.

Tabitha had returned to the *Meredith Reynolds* with the colony ship in tow behind the *Achronyx* like a whale guided by a sardine. The rush to get the children taken care of had eaten up the hours, but they were out of the woods and expected to recover in time.

Tabitha's work hadn't ended there. She had also thrown together support for the parents, found them accommodations aboard the *Meredith Reynolds* while the kids were in recovery, put the colony leaders in touch with the appropriate people to deal with selling the weapons they made now they had control of their manufacturing again, and scheduled them for a discussion on planetary defenses with William.

All in all, it had been a hectic few days, and there had

been no time for Tabitha to catch up with Tiera until tonight. She still had a couple of things to straighten out with the arrangements she had begun to make before leaving for the Arista System, but they would wait for now.

She grinned when the top of Tiera's head and her wide eyes appeared around the corner of the door. "Hey, you made it! Come in."

Tiera stepped in and closed the door gingerly behind herself. She looked warily at the weaponry mounted on every available surface in the wide room. "Are you sure it's okay for me to be in here?" she whispered in an awed voice.

Tabitha waved her over. "Of course it is. I invited you. Otherwise, Meredith would have lasered you into ash at the door when you requested entry."

Tiera's eyes widened. "Really?"

Tabitha snickered. "No, but feel free to start the rumor. Did you bring your training gear?"

Tiera shrugged off her backpack. "Is there somewhere I can get changed?"

Tabitha indicated a screened off area in the corner. "Yeah, you can use the cubicle over there. Didn't Sebastian want to come with you today?"

Tiera crossed the mats and went into the cubicle to change. "Oh, he wanted to, but it's a school night. He'll have to wait to visit."

Tabitha felt bad for the kid. The Ranger offices were completely out of bounds ordinarily. Tabitha would have put money on Sebastian being at home stewing instead of studying or sleeping like he should be. "Fair enough. I could have scheduled this earlier in the day if you'd asked."

"It wouldn't have made a difference," Tiera called. "This was the only time I had free all day to do this." She came out wearing her workout gear, and the two women went over to the barre to stretch before they got started.

"Are your hours still sucking?" Tabitha asked.

Tiera snorted. "Sucking? They blow goats. But the bills are paid, and Sebastian has everything he needs. I haven't been in that position for a long time so I can appreciate it even if my body is kicking up a constant protest. Hell, if I get more than five minutes free, we can even afford to go and do some of those fun things he's always talking about."

"If you're happy, then I guess I can't keep complaining." Tabitha gestured for Tiera to join her on the mat. "What have you learned from Maxim so far?"

Tiera listed some of the techniques Maxim had taught her since their lessons had begun. "But mostly it's been about how to use my size to my advantage instead of being afraid to attack because I'm smaller than my opponent." She frowned as she twisted her hair into a quick bun. "I still haven't been able to take him down, though."

Tabitha chuckled. "Oh, *that's* easy. You just go through his legs and up his back, and before he can do a thing about it, you put him in a sleeper hold, and it's night-night, Maxim." She shrugged at Tiera's incredulous look. "Don't judge until you've tried it. We short girls have to make use of every advantage we can."

Tiera giggled as she took her stance. "I know all about that. Just wait and see, you're gonna be surprised!"

Tabitha played completely fair. Which was to say, she pushed Tiera to her limit over the next hour but never beyond.

By the time Tabitha called an end to the punishing session, she was satisfied that Tiera wasn't going to flake if she got caught up in a dangerous situation in the line of duty. "You've improved a lot already."

Tiera shrugged. "I took basic hand-to-hand in school, same as everyone. I just don't enjoy it, that's all." She mopped her face with her towel, then turned to get her water bottle. "I really appreciate you taking the time to do this."

Tabitha waved her off and went to collect her own water bottle. "Don't worry about it. My motivations aren't completely selfless. I want my favorite genius designer in one piece. I just wish you would let me find you a better job than station security."

Tiera threw her towel into her bag with a dark chuckle. "Unless you can pull a job out of your ass that lets me work at my art and pays me more than security, with hours that are reasonable enough that I get to see my son before bedtime, I don't even want to talk about it." She sighed. "Jobs like that don't exist."

"It's just not fair," Tabitha moaned. "You're a good person, who works hard. You shouldn't have to struggle just because you're doing it alone. You deserve to be happy, too."

Tiera smiled wryly. "Those are the sacrifices you make as a single parent. Whatever pays the bills is a good job. Besides, I'm still young. My personal fulfillment can wait. This is my son's time. Sebastian is all that matters right now."

Tabitha admired that attitude greatly. "I've said it

before, and I'll say it again. Moms are heroes, especially single moms."

"And single dads," Tiera reminded her. "I've been to a few support groups, and there are enough of those around, too."

Tabitha nodded her agreement. "All of you. I only have Merry for a few hours here and there, and she wears me out in just that short time. If I had to work a job I hated…" She paused as the implications of parenthood occurred to her for the first time. "Not even just your job. It's like your whole reason for existing has to change, all your effort put into this new person you made."

Tiera raised her eyebrows and nodded sagely. "Yep, pretty much. But look at what you get in return."

"Attitude, rolled eyes, and a constant dull thudding beat wafting along on the wave of stink coming from under their bedroom door?" Tabitha winked. "Although Sebastian isn't exactly the rebellious type."

Tiera laughed. "I know, right? I feel like he needs to act out at least once, but he's so sensible it's almost painful."

"He's a good kid," Tabitha told her. "You should be proud of him, and of yourself for the fantastic job you did holding things together after Jimmy decided that getting his dick wet was a higher priority than his duty to the two of you."

Tiera snorted. "I don't need him; he did me a favor by leaving. Things will get better. They always do." She caught sight of the time and started to grab her things and stuff them into her bag. "Oh, dammit. I need to get back before Sebastian's bedtime."

Tabitha walked her out and then went back through the

Rangers' area to her office. She didn't spend much time in here, so it was pretty bare as a result.

Achronyx, remind me to do something with this room.

Like what? Achronyx asked.

She looked at the bare walls, the spartan desk, and the empty shelves. *I don't know, something to make it look like it's mine?*

What would be the point? You don't use this office, and if the rumors I've been hearing are true, we won't even be here for much longer.

Tabitha poked the cushion on the chair at the desk and took a seat. At least *one* thing had been chosen with care. *We all have the decision to make. Mine is no decision at all: I go where Bethany Anne goes.*

I expected nothing different, Achronyx assured her.

I wonder what everyone else will choose?

Either way, the time of the Empire is drawing to a close, and preparations for the future must begin.

That's what I wanted to talk to you about. Who does ADAM have lined up to take care of his fashion businesses? I know he has someone; it's ADAM.

Why not just ask him? Achronyx inquired.

Because I haven't got a whole plan yet, that's why, Tabitha grumbled.

Or even part of one? Achronyx teased.

I have that much, Tabitha protested. I was going to talk to ADAM when I had all the pieces in place.

What do you need to know? I have time for some research before we leave.

You heard Tiera's wish list. I want to know if that job exists and if it's available. Tabitha replayed Achronyx' last remark. *We're leaving? Since when?*

Since Barnabas messaged me a minute ago. We have an urgent call.

QBBS *Meredith Reynolds*, Rangers' Offices

Tabitha and Hirotoshi arrived at almost exactly the same time.

Barnabas was waiting for them when they got to his office. "Come in, we are pressed for time."

"What's up?" Tabitha asked. "Achronyx told me it was urgent.

Barnabas had the look of a cat who had gotten the cream. "I have a lead on a consignment of the weapons from Arista."

"That's great!" Tabitha paused. "What's the emergency?"

Barnabas pressed his lips together. "I've tracked the weapons from Arista to Omidian."

Hirotoshi groaned. "Oh, that's not good. Are they having another revolution?"

Tabitha made a pained face at the mention of the settlement, a terraformed moonlet on one of the main trade routes just outside Yollin space. It was well-known for its propensity for breaking out into civil unrest every decade or two, and infamous among the Empire's peacekeepers as a place where common sense went to die. "Whereabouts on Omidian?"

Barnabas held up his hands. "I honestly can't say. I only got word of this a few minutes before I called you here. I know the route until the consignment crosses into Yollin space, but that was as much as my informant had."

Tabitha drummed her fingers on the arm of her chair. "Hmmm. Do you have the chain of supply going back?"

Barnabas nodded. "Yes, I have someone on it. I need you to get out to the border and track the consignment from the moment it arrives in-system, then I want you to follow the seller to the buy location and arrest everyone involved. Preferably *before* the weapons end up in the hands of whoever ordered them."

Tabitha nodded. "Okay. What if the culprits are the royal family?"

"Then I trust you to deal with it," Barnabas told her. "If it does turn out that the royals are involved, they get the same treatment as anyone else. It shouldn't be anything too difficult, but still, call for backup if it turns out to be a wider-reaching problem than we are anticipating."

Tabitha nodded. "That we can do. I hope it's not another revolution."

"I *sincerely* hope it is not another revolution." Hirotoshi rubbed his forehead. "I still have a headache from the last one."

"We all do," Barnabas commiserated. "If it weren't for the law, I would happily rid them of their leadership problems and institute a republic. Then there wouldn't be any need to send Rangers in every time their elected leader decides they don't need to be elected anymore." He sighed. "These things are so tiresome."

Tabitha sat up suddenly. "You know who they are? They're the planetary equivalent of that uncle who turns up drunk to every family occasion and starts an argument with himself over who said what thirty years ago. It's embarrassing for them that we need to keep stepping in."

"It is," Barnabas agreed. "However, they are still a relatively young settlement, and there are bound to be teething problems that will settle in a few generations. Perhaps the monarchy will work for them."

Tabitha raised an eyebrow. "What if it takes another fifty years?"

"Then we will continue to monitor the situation." Barnabas shrugged. "They will eventually work out a constitution that pleases everyone, and since Bethany Anne restricted weapons after the last war, there hasn't been a problem. In fact, I would have guessed that they were in recovery since their economy is doing so much better." His eyebrows narrowed. "It *is* a little strange. I have had no news of unrest from my informants. If there had been another incident within the royal court, I would have been informed."

Tabitha frowned in thought. "It doesn't have to be the royals at the center of it. Although with their track record, it was definitely the first thing that came to mind when you mentioned the planet."

"Mine also," Hirotoshi concurred. "There could be an assassination attempt underway. Or a coup. If some of the weapons from Arista are being funneled there, it could get nasty."

"That is my concern precisely." Barnabas nodded toward the door. "The two of you should get going as soon as possible. There's no time for delay."

Tabitha got up to leave. "Already leaving. Keep sending updates as you get them."

Barnabas inclined his head. "Of course."

Barnabas stood abruptly as Tabitha followed Hirotoshi out of the office. "Oh, and Tabitha? I'd like to discuss something when you return."

Tabitha frowned. "Is it important?"

Her mentor's face was grave. His pursed lips relieved a bit of her worry, but not much. "It is, but it will wait for now."

Omidian, High Orbit, QBS *Achronyx*, Bridge

Tabitha and Hirotoshi sat forward in their seats while Achronyx guided the ship through the outer spread of rocks to get to the moonlet where the settlement was based.

The challenge was avoiding the half-frozen spinning chunks of rock that were almost-but-not-quite too large to escape the weak gravity field that remained around the loosely clustered corpse of a broken planet.

Tabitha pounded on the console when the small freighter hung a left and skated across the moonlet's thin upper atmosphere before dropping like a stone into the cloud layer below. "Shit! Where did they go?"

"My guess would be to an out-of-the-way place where they can make the exchange without being seen."

Tabitha thought differently. "Wanna bet? I say they're going to do it somewhere public. Hide in plain sight."

Hirotoshi smirked. "I will take that bet."

The *Achronyx* swooped in, the only clue to the ship's presence the disturbance it caused pushing the clouds before it when they broke through the cloudbank into the lower atmosphere.

Tabitha huffed when the freighter adjusted its course to head east of the shining city in the distance. "Looks like you were right. They're heading for the outlands."

Hirotoshi chuckled dryly. "It was just a lucky guess, but now I am in the position of having you owe me a forfeit since we did not set any stakes beforehand." Hirotoshi didn't exactly sound smug, but Tabitha could tell that he was feeling it. He tapped a finger to his lips in a show of indecision. "Hmmm. What should I do with such an opportunity?"

"Okay, no need to make a big deal out of it." Tabitha got out of the captain's chair and headed toward the door. "We still need to find out who the buyer is." She looked over her shoulder. "Double or nothing?"

Hirotoshi raised an eyebrow. "*Two* unnamed forfeits? I would be a fool to pass up the chance." He chuckled at her surprise. "What are the choices?"

Tabitha considered it while they kept a close eye on their target. "I like this less stuffy side of you. Okay...how about you win if it's the royals, and I win if it's just a garden-variety scumbag?"

Hirotoshi nodded. "Sounds fair. At least that way if I win, my headache will be offset by the victory of you owing me two forfeits."

"And if *I* win, I'm going to combine them into something you'll never, ever forget," Tabitha assured him with a wink. "You're going to regret betting before you know the stakes."

"I want a taste of the action, too," Achronyx complained. "You always forget me."

"I didn't forget you. I didn't think you'd be interested." Tabitha looked at Hirotoshi and shrugged. "Sorry, Achronyx. Who's your bet on? Royals, or criminals?"

"Neither," Achronyx came back promptly. "I'm going for vigilantes."

Tabitha's laughter became chuckles, then they stopped and her lips pressed together. "I hadn't considered that possibility."

Hirotoshi indicated the screen. "The freighter is coming in to land. We will find out soon enough."

Tabitha sat up straight and turned her chair back to the console. "Achronyx, bring us in above them and get the video rolling. As soon as payment changes hands, we'll bust them."

The screen switched to an aerial view of a small gritty shipyard which was surrounded on all sides by dust, dirt, and a whole lot of nothing else. The place had clearly been abandoned years before, yet there were signs of very recent activity all over the property.

"I have a group of people in the main building," Achronyx announced.

"What's their weapons status?" Tabitha asked.

"I'm detecting no weapons," Achronyx replied. "Except the ones aboard the freighter, of course."

Tabitha rolled her eyes. "Of course."

Hirotoshi tensed. "Stop squabbling. Something is happening."

On the screen, the freighter's main hatch began to open,

and a wiry space-suited figure stepped out. The figure looked around without removing their helmet.

The casual way they held the handheld blaster in one gloved fist spoke volumes to Tabitha, as did the way their glance kept returning to the freighter. Her lip curled. "Looks like we have ourselves a gunrunner."

There was a shuffling sound from the speakers, and the doors of the building creaked open.

"Here come the buyers," Hirotoshi murmured.

Tabitha rubbed her hands together. "Come on, show me the criminals. Mama wants her paperwork done for the next decade…"

Hirotoshi glanced at her incredulously. "You would waste a free forfeit on getting your paperwork done?"

Tabitha shrugged without taking her eyes from the screen. "Anyone would think you haven't been paying attention this last century or so. You do remember how I *feel* about paperwork?"

"It is not your favorite thing, Kemosabe," Hirotoshi conceded with a wry smile.

"Not my favorite?" Tabitha snorted. "Give me five hundred years, and I will never tire of your gift for understatement. I need an administrative minion. My old one isn't cutting it anymore."

"What she means," Achronyx sulked, "is that she annoyed me, and now I won't do it for her. She was trying to get Peter to do it for her last week."

Hirotoshi snickered. "I can imagine how that went down."

Tabitha gasped theatrically. "Achronyx! I can't believe you would be so disloyal. Just for that, you should clear my backlog for me." She stopped snickering when the door opened wide and the people sidled out into the shipyard.

"Um…" Tabitha saw the arrivals' nervous edge. They stuck together for protection like a group of meerkats while they walked over to the freighter. "They don't look much like royals. Or scumbags."

They actually looked a little scared. The group of no more than a dozen edged toward the gunrunner, who stood waiting for them with their body language screaming boredom.

Tabitha got up and leaned over her console, balancing on her hands to get a better look. "Turn up the volume, Achronyx."

Achronyx did as Tabitha asked just as the meet began.

"You have what we asked for?" the man at the front of the group asked.

The space-suited figure nodded once. "You have the credit chip?"

The man made a face and pulled out a drawstring bag. "It's not all on one chip. Your services don't come cheaply. We had to pool our resources for this."

The seller took their helmet off, revealing his weaselly-looking face at last.

The man pulled his hand back when Weasel Face reached for the bag. "Show us the guns first. Do we look like we came off the first colony ship?"

"Achronyx had it wrong as well," Tabitha remarked. She rolled her eyes at Hirotoshi's stony expression. "What? I'm just trying to make light of the situation."

"I was closer than either of you," Achronyx retorted. "It

is a shame none of us decided to go for 'angry civilian,' since that is what we have here by the look of things."

Tabitha smirked. "Never mind, I'll find another way to get my paperwork done. The bet is voided. Get ready, we're going down there."

Tabitha and Hirotoshi worked quickly to get their weapons strapped on, then ran for the drop doors in the cargo bay while Achronyx piped the audio from the people on the ground through their comms.

Tabitha snagged a G-bar from the rack on the wall and headed over to the drop doors. She grabbed one of the straps that dangled from the reinforced bar above her head and waited for Achronyx to open the doors.

She checked her grip as Hirotoshi joined her and they leaned out with their feet planted firmly on the lip of the drop.

All the while, the events continued to unfold in the shipyard below. The sale was already looking precarious. It spiraled rapidly into a less-than-fortuitous deal for all involved when the seller demanded an extra payment on top of the already-agreed-upon price and the man lost his temper.

The other buyers had found their courage at that point, their initial nerves at the illicit nature of the meeting offset by the simple mathematics of twelve against one. They all began shouting at the seller, filling Tabitha's audio link with an incomprehensible babble.

Tabitha groaned when she saw the gunrunner's blaster hand twitch. "Aw, shit. We can't let this go down. This asshat is either going to rob these people blind or blow their fool heads off because they spooked him. Light them up and let's go fishing, Achronyx."

Achronyx switched on the ship's floodlights at the same time he released the drones. Tabitha gave the signal, and she and Hirotoshi let go of their straps and plummeted through the open drop doors.

Tabitha heard Achronyx read the people on the ground their rights over the ship's external speakers.

"Citizens of the Etheric Empire. You are under arrest. You have the right to shut the hell up and do as the nice Ranger tells you, in which case you will receive a fair hearing. Or you can resist arrest, and she will be happy to beat some obedience into you and *then* you will receive a fair hearing. Your choice, really."

Tabitha snickered and twisted her G-bar to activate it. *Nice intro.*

You are welcome. Do you realize you've activated the manual control on the G-bar?

Uh-huh. It's only a short drop. Tabitha's hand slipped and caught the control, and the G-bar halted in midair with a sharp jerk. The sudden reintroduction of gravity pulled the breath from Tabitha's lungs and constricted her chest painfully while simultaneously stretching the joints in her arms and shoulders to their limit.

All she could do for a second was hang there treading air.

As Hirotoshi passed the spot where Tabitha hung from the bar, he winked and continued his smooth dive.

Fiiine, she conceded. *Achronyx, take this thing over.*

Achronyx brought them down at the edge of the ship-yard. The drones zipped around in a coordinated sweep, discharging their taser nets into the conflict. The hapless civilians went down immediately, twitching under the nets as they were captured.

The gunrunner tried to flee, which Tabitha counted as resisting arrest. She shot him in the back with a round designed to incapacitate a raging Shrillexian.

She went over and poked the criminal with her toe to turn him over. The man flopped over like a jellyfish and began to snore. "Oops. Probably shouldn't have hit him with that. He'll have a really long nap, right, Achronyx?"

He'll be fine... Well, I think *he will wake up.*

Tabitha didn't think he sounded too hopeful about that. *Net him anyway just to be sure. I don't want to get back here to arrest him and find he escaped.*

Tabitha waited for the drone to appear before she left to find the man she thought was the leader of the people. She scooped her tiny drones out of their pouch on her belt and released them by Weasel Face's ship as she walked past. The drones snapped through the air, working to get scans of whatever was inside the freighter's cargo hold as Tabitha continued on her way.

Tabitha found Hirotoshi with a man. He was awake and struggling in the net that held him despite the electric shocks it gave him each time he strained against the mesh.

Tabitha told Achronyx to turn off the shocks unless anyone tried anything as she walked over. She squatted by the angry man, turning her head sideways to look at him. "Are you in charge of these people?"

The man glowered at her. "Who the fuck are you?"

Tabitha shook her head. "What is it with the lack of

manners these days? My name is Ranger Two. And *you* are?"

"Pissed off!" the man bawled at the top of his lungs. "You let me out of this right fucking now!"

"Jake, don't piss the Ranger off!" A woman with a plaster cast on her foot stormed haphazardly from the building. Tabitha raised an eyebrow as she and Hirotoshi shared a look.

She waved one of her crutches and called as she got closer, "Sorry, Ranger ma'am. He doesn't mean it."

"I damn well *do* mean it!" the man roared, struggling. "Let me go!"

The woman reached Tabitha and poked Jake with her crutch. "Carry on disrespecting the Ranger and I'll ask her to leave you in there overnight, you gobshite. If your da could see you now, he'd tear a stripe from your hide."

Tabitha had to hold back a fit of giggles. "Hopefully that won't be necessary, Mrs…"

The old woman beamed. "Oh, you're a sweet one. The name's Eileen, and you don't need any introduction at all, my dear Ranger. Thank you for your work on Elysium about seventy years ago. You saved my grandfather from a mine collapse, and I'm pretty sure that you just saved my grandson from catching his death due to a sudden case of stupid."

Tabitha smirked and accepted Eileen's hug. "You are welcome, but I can't save him from stupid entirely. Unfortunately, I caught him attempting to buy black market weapons, and that comes with a penalty."

Eileen shook her head sadly. "I understand."

"You can stop talking about me like I'm not even here," Jake complained. "I'm not a child anymore."

"Was it a very adult thing you did today? Who will look after your daughters now?" Eileen shook her fist at her grandson. "Me, that's who. And one of them is addicted to dust, so who will have to keep her under lock and key?" She whacked him with her crutch to punctuate her answer. "Me!"

Jake growled in frustration. "None of us would be here buying illegal guns if anyone had taken us seriously, but *noooo*. They're scared to do anything about the gang that's destroying our families, but they will send in a damned Ranger to arrest us when we grow the balls to do something about it ourselves."

Tabitha folded her arms and listened to the tale unfold while Jake ranted it out. There was a drug problem here; some gang had found a way of producing this "dust" without breaking a single law.

The parents had learned of the problem too late.

Tabitha couldn't believe what she was hearing. "Your children are dying, and this gang is responsible?"

Jake nodded miserably. "That's the short version, yeah."

Tabitha considered the situation. *Achronyx, you won the bet after all. These people need Justice.*

Then aren't they lucky you showed up?

I'm not sure they needed me. They could just send this fierce woman in. Tabitha smirked at Eileen, whose verbal flaying of her grandson contained an enthusiastic rage that reminded her of someone close to her heart.

"Your solution was to buy weapons from a shady dealer and shoot the place up?" Eileen tsked. "You were going to go to Bright's and do *what*, exactly? You wouldn't get past his security, even with guns."

Tabitha walked over to the woman. "I'm going to take care of the gang problem." She looked at Jake. "I haven't decided what to do about your grandson yet."

"He's a good boy, really," Eileen assured her. "They all are. This is a bad situation we're in." She hobbled over to Jake and knelt beside him.

Achronyx, you can drop the nets now, except for the one holding the gunrunner. Tabitha sighed and recalled her drones as Hirotoshi came over. "This is not as cut and dried as I had hoped it would be. The longer we're here, the more the chance I won't make it for Merry's birthday."

Hirotoshi smiled and touched the sword at his hip. "Then we shall endeavor to keep it as simple as possible."

Omidian, Abandoned Shipyard

Hirotoshi freed the other parents from the nets while Tabitha spoke with Eileen and Jake. He had put the gunrunner in a secure cabin, where he would remain under the watchful eye of Achronyx until they were done on Omidian, and now he was overseeing the transfer of the weapons from the freighter to their ship.

Tabitha looked the group over. "You can all thank your lucky stars that I'm not going to arrest you for this. As it is, I get that you're all worried for your children, so I'm letting you off with just a warning—*provided* you go home to your kids and give up the idea of revenge."

She heard one of the women mutter to another that she

was going to wait until the Ranger left and attack the hideout anyway.

Tabitha sighed. This must be how Barnabas felt when she argued every point he was making. Maybe she should do that less in the future. "Anyone I find near the gang's location *will* be arrested. No exceptions. By the time I leave, all that will be left of that gang will be a smoking crater. Now go home. *All of you.*"

She watched them leave the shipyard. A few were still grumbling, but they were drowned out by Eileen's loud appreciation of the pain Tabitha was about to bring down on the gang who had ruined their lives.

Hirotoshi returned from loading the ship in time to hear the tail end of the grandmother's rousing speech. "She has a lot of faith in you."

Tabitha nodded. "Now all I have to do is live up to it."

Tabitha and Hirotoshi left the shipyard and made their way through the settlement. The streets were laid out on a grid, like many of the places humans had colonized. Tabitha found that predictability easy to work with, and soon they were crossing the last few blocks to the gang's lair.

The tone of the neighborhood changed as they got closer to their destination. The cheery front yards and well-kept community areas were replaced within the short space of a few streets by an area that felt to Tabitha like somewhere the people just survived, not lived.

Tabitha and Hirotoshi glanced at each other. They were experienced enough to know that they were getting closer to the cancer at the root of this settlement's problems.

Tabitha stood in the shadow of a tree at the intersection

between the main road and the side street the gang's hideout was on. The target property was a little way down the street, at the end of a row of what had probably been perfect family homes not so long ago.

There were no families around now, and no children playing in the early morning sunshine. The empty houses around the drug den had graffiti-covered metal sheets over the doors and windows. The whole street had an undertone of menace that radiated from the house the gang was holed up in.

Tabitha moved a step closer to the tree when a vehicle approached from the other end of the street. It cruised past the hideout and stopped a few feet away from where Tabitha and Hirotoshi hugged the shadows.

A teenager of around eighteen or nineteen got out of the passenger side. The boy pulled his hood up to cover his face and set off walking with his hands in his pockets. He skulked along the street and up to the front of the house, skirting the piles of junk and garbage in the front yard as he sidled up to the door.

The door opened just a crack, and Tabitha caught a glimpse of a sallow face through the gap. The teenager thrust something, Tabitha assumed the payment, at the person behind the door. A few seconds later, the slump vanished from his shoulders and he practically skipped back to the vehicle.

Tabitha wasn't here to play community safety officer; nevertheless, she had to do something. She covered the few steps to the teenagers' vehicle in a blink and opened the door.

She ducked her head in and snatched the bag of drugs

out of the clueless teenager's hand. "I'll take that."

"Hey! You can't just—" He looked up into Tabitha's red, red eyes, and then behind her at Hirotoshi and his mouth dropped open. "Whaaat?"

The girl in the driver's seat let out an involuntary yip when her eyes alighted on Tabitha's badge. "Kelvin, look. R-r-ranger T-two."

Kelvin's mouth opened and closed, but all that came out was a series of wheezy gasps. He finally squeezed the words out. "We're not breaking the law, Susie. She can't arrest us."

Tabitha toned the eyes down now that the teens were listening to her satisfaction. She held the bag up. "This drug is now illegal by decree of the Empress' Rangers, so yeah, I *can* arrest you." She tossed the bag to Hirotoshi, noticing the way the teens' eyes followed it all the way to Hirotoshi's pocket.

"Are you going to arrest us?" All the color had drained from Suzie's face.

Tabitha almost felt sorry for them. Almost. "Consider this a wakeup call," she told them sternly. "You two have decided to turn over a new leaf, starting right now. Your parents didn't give you life hoping for you to turn out like this." She slammed the door closed. "Go home; they are probably worried sick. And for crying out loud, get a better hobby than taking drugs. What a *Gott Verdammt* waste of your youth!"

Tabitha stood with her hands on her hips and glared at the vehicle as the girl reversed and drove away. She didn't care if she sounded like a stuffy old woman. She hated to see so much potential wasted.

Every one of the teenagers this gang had its claws into had once been an innocent. It might be beyond Tabitha's powers to get that back for them, but she *could* prevent the same theft from happening to any more of these children.

She turned back to the house up the street, catching the movement of the door closing from the corner of her eye. She resisted the urge to shoot the scumbag behind the door outright. "Why dig in somewhere like this? Couldn't they operate out of the docks like the rest of the space rats?"

Hirotoshi walked beside her with stony disapproval etched into his normally impassive features. "Apparently not."

"At least we got confirmation that they're all there." Tabitha's lip curled. "Probably because it's the only place they're welcome."

They passed one empty house after another. There were signs of the previous occupants leaving in a hurry and the squatters who had replaced them all along the street. What appeared to have once been a pleasant neighborhood had been run to ruin by the presence of the gang.

Tabitha glanced into a driveway and saw a small stuffed toy lying abandoned in a dirty puddle by the doorstep. The curtain beyond twitched and then fell.

Her jaw clenched, and her hand dropped to release the extra pouch on her belt. "This ends today." She fished two small boxes and a remote control out of the pouch, and handed one of the boxes to Hirotoshi before putting the other and the remote in her pocket for easy access. "You take the outside, I'll take the inside."

Hirotoshi's eyebrows went up when he opened the box to confirm the contents. "No prisoners?"

"No. No speeches, no excuses, and *no* survivors." Tabitha's face was cold. "I'm not even going to announce myself. I've hit my limit of children being used to make a profit. This whole stinking mess has been the single most disgusting thing I've had to deal with in all my time as a Ranger. Shit. Hell, in all my time as a human being."

Hirotoshi shrugged, and when he spoke his tone was deliberately level. "I'm not against it, Kemosabe. However, you usually reserve skipping the hearing for perpetrators of slavery."

"What is this, if not slavery?" Tabitha raised a hand and swept it around to encompass the street. "*This* is their hearing. They brought the evidence against themselves. They're guilty, and all that's left is to deliver the punishment." She stalked toward the house, throwing a hand into the air to release her drones.

Hirotoshi nodded once. "Then as you say, all that is left is to deliver the punishment." He hesitated as he peeled off to go around to the back of the house. "I would not show these people even a drop of the mercy you are granting them. To die in their sleep is an easy escape considering the pain they have caused."

Tabitha watched Hirotoshi until he was obscured by the side of the house before she approached the front door. *Yeah, well I don't want to waste time on them. This is in, out, and* boom. *Done.*

The front door opened as Tabitha approached and the sallow-faced man came out. Tabitha shot him without pausing and he hit the floor, dead before he'd even registered her presence. *Well, that saved me the effort of kicking the damn door in.*

Are these charges sufficient?

Just make sure you cover all the structural points in the base-ment. Tabitha opened the small box. *Jean told me they have a small blast radius but a hell of a bang, and we've got plenty of them. Remind me to thank her when we get home.*

She darted through the front door and made a lap of the house at vampiric speed, depositing the almost-invisible discs from the box on every available surface as she went. She made sure she paid extra attention to the rooms where she came across sleeping gang members.

A few of the people sprawled around the rooms stirred, but Tabitha made it out of the house without disturbing anyone. She headed for the front of the house, where she found Hirotoshi waiting for her on the street.

Tabitha walked over to Hirotoshi. She took the remote detonator from her pocket and pressed the trigger without a word.

The two stood in silence while the house collapsed like a souffle. The roof caved in and dropped into the top floor, which gave way as the ground floor vanished into the base-ment in a massive cloud of dust and debris.

The mantle of dust settled on the crater where the hideout had been.

There was no movement from the rubble.

Hirotoshi glanced at Tabitha, waiting for her to make a joke as she usually did in these situations. "No zingy one-liner?"

Tabitha turned away from the scene of destruction and walked toward the pickup point, her voice sad as she said, "I told you, no speeches."

CHAPTER SEVENTEEN

System of the Six, Planet Vietania, Plomerilia, Palace Security Office

Jolie watched the news report a second time, and then a third. She put the datapad she was using on the table and pushed it away as though it were hot. The man in the photo was definitely Marius, but the newscaster gave his name as John, crown prince of Zuifra.

Why would a prince pretend to be a common trader?

The whole thing stank of intrigue, and she was going to get to the bottom of it. The name of the planet rang a bell, which made it as good a place as any to start her search. In the meantime, she sent for Simon, her resident hacker, and handed the datapad to him. "Find out if this is true. Cynthia might be in danger."

Simon frowned as he watched the report. "That's not good. Want me to dig into the rest of them as well?"

Jolie nodded. "If they're here for nefarious reasons, then we need to find out what they want before they succeed."

"Got it." He hesitated before leaving. "Shouldn't we tell the queen?"

Jolie shook her head. "Not without evidence. And even *with* evidence, we'll need to get guards so loyal to Cynthia that they'll listen to us when we tell them what's going on."

Jolie got to work the moment he closed the door. The name Zuifra sounded familiar, but she couldn't quite grasp why. She opened her computer and input various spellings until she got a hit.

Zuifra was familiar because she had learned about its founding during her schooling. The planet's founding colony had come from the Six, having chosen exile over living under Vietanian law. Prince John's family had splintered from the Vietanian royal family after a civil war over a broken marriage contract, which at the time had seemed arbitrary to Jolie.

Jolie sighed sadly. How differently she viewed the lesson in hindsight. She saw the parallels between the war generations ago and the one that was sure to erupt at the end of her father's mourning period, no matter which of them took the crown. The population was split between the older generations, the ones who remembered Jolie's mother and saw Jolie stepping into her shoes, and the young and monied who were enchanted by the persona Cynthia presented to the public.

The situation here and now would be laughable to some. It was to her, and she loved Cynthia. However, the dilemma she had always feared facing had come to pass, and her fatuous sister would run the whole system into ruin if she were allowed to rule.

Jolie loved her people too much to allow it.

She scanned through the history, her mind on the upcoming Senate hearing. She had no clue which way the Senate would rule on the petition to force Cynthia to abdicate in her favor. Jolie hadn't encouraged the movement. Her place was on the front lines, not sat behind a wall of courtiers and ministers. Still, if it became her duty, she would uphold it.

In some ways, she preferred that her sister take the crown since it freed Jolie for her work. If only Cynthia were more focused on ruling instead of finding a man to do it for her so she could party!

If only they didn't rely on some romantic and archaic governance system that favored birthright over suitability.

Simon returned, and Jolie was surprised to see a couple of hours had passed while she was reading and thinking. Her hacker handed her the datapad she'd given him earlier with a serious expression on his face. "It's not as bad as you thought, Your Highness, but you were right about the prince."

"I know I was right about the prince. We're probably distantly related." Jolie closed her own research and began to skim through Simon's reports. She hissed in disbelief when she got to the bleary-eyed mug shot of Captain Meredith Dakkar that Simon had dug up from the records of a mining outpost she'd trashed. "This reads like a rap sheet."

Simon lifted a shoulder. "She likes a fight, that's for sure."

"A fight?" Jolie laughed. "That's an understatement. This is more like the aftermath of a hurricane, only the path she ripped goes through all the seediest joints outside the Federation."

"It looks that way." Simon leaned over and swiped a couple of pages. "Here, this is where it gets interesting."

Jolie looked at the page he'd skipped to and read the associated charges. "What the hell? She's *from* the Federation? She's a *Grimes* Grimes?"

Simon shrugged. "I couldn't get confirmation on that, but you should treat her as though she is until we know for certain. You don't want to piss off a Grimes by accident."

"We're not going to aggravate her in any way." Jolie dropped the datapad and rubbed her tired eyes. "Shit. This means that it's not the Federation. The Empress' people are involved. This… This could be even worse than I thought."

Simon was confused by her reaction. "I thought the worst that could happen was that they were assassins?"

Jolie shook her head. "The worst that could happen is that they're here to take over to ensure a smooth transition whether or not we come to a solution." She gathered the papers up. "We have to stop it from happening."

"I don't get it," Simon admitted. "Stop *what* from happening?"

"The marriage, of course," she told him as if it were obvious. "Prince John is here to woo Cynthia and annex Vietania for Zuifra, or at least that's what it looks like to me. Whether it's true or not, they've been spending so much time together if it gets out that he's from the Federation then everything we've been working for could go down the drain. It's an added complication we don't need."

Simon gave her a sympathetic look. "I don't envy you, Your Highness. What are your choices here?"

Jolie snorted and picked up the datapad. "The choice is that I have no choice but to act. If Prince John thinks he's going to steal this planet by seducing my sister, he's got a shock coming."

System of the Six, Planet Vietania, Plomerilia, Palace

John touched his glass to Cynthia's and smiled. "To us."

"To us," Cynthia echoed with a touch of melancholy in her smile. "For as long as we can *be* us. Until reality interrupts." She sighed and placed her glass on the table before turning to gaze at the view from the balcony. "My coronation will be here soon enough, and then my life will never be my own again."

John's heart soared. At last, Cynthia was opening up to him, and he had a chance to save her from Nickie's drastic solution. "You don't like the idea of being queen?"

Cynthia laughed ruefully. "It's not the kind of thing you choose, silly. I was born to be queen. It's what I am, whether I want it or not. And it's *hard*!" Her nose wrinkled in that pretty way John was beginning to find adorable. "I didn't want Daddy to die, but he did, and now I have to deal with everything. I'm the next in line, so I have to step up."

John's dimple winked as he sipped his wine. "Do you?"

Cynthia turned to look at him. "What are you suggesting? Of course, I do."

"I'm not entirely sure since I'm completely drunk and at your mercy, Your Majesty." He took Cynthia's hand and kissed her fingers. "What life would you have if you could choose for yourself?"

The queen-in-waiting giggled. "I don't know. I would still want to be a queen since it's the only thing I know how to do. I always knew that after my coronation I would have to be all serious like Jolie, but I'm a person, too! I want to dance and laugh and love. I want to see the galaxy, or at least some of it."

Cynthia's eyes grew dreamy. "And when I've done all of that, I want to marry someone who loves me for me, not someone who just wants to be king. I want to have a grand romance that spans the ages. One that the people our children's children's children rule will call the greatest love of all time."

John was lost in her daydream. It evoked something in him so similar to the feeling that had driven him to find adventure that he felt her longing as if it were his own. "Then let Jolie rule. Come away with me, and I'll give you all of that."

Cynthia pulled her hand away. "Are you crazy? And let her win?"

John waved a hand. "Let her. What do you care when you're dancing on the *Meredith Reynolds*, or kissing me as we watch the birth of a star on some far away station? You would be a princess or a queen or whatever you wanted to be."

Nickie spoke in his ear. *Easy there, Romeo. Great acting, but you're laying it on a bit thick.*

John almost fell over. *What the hell, Nickie! Have you been listening the whole time?*

Well, yeah. It's kinda the point of having the comm.

He felt all the blood in his body rush to his face.

Cynthia looked at him with mild concern. *Shut up before she notices!*

Just keep up the good work, hot stuff. Seriously, great acting.

John surreptitiously removed his comm bud, deactivated it, and dropped it into his pocket. *I'm not acting.* He returned his attention to Cynthia, who was asking if he was okay.

"I'm fine," he replied. "I just… I'm shaken. I've fallen for you, Cynthia. I didn't expect it, not so soon after meeting you. I want to take you away from all of this. If you will have me." He took her hands again. "Cynthia McLeod, will you elope with me?"

Cynthia stood, pulling John up to his feet. She let go of his hands and looked deep into his eyes, searching for the lie in his love. "I… I barely know you."

John grinned. "Does it matter? This week has been the best of my life. Not because of the dinners or the parties, because I met *you*. Can you honestly say you don't feel the same connection?" He almost didn't dare meet her eyes. This was a huge gamble.

Cynthia looked hard at him, then turned her face to the moonlight. It lit her profile perfectly so that John could see the indecision painted across her features. She sighed. "No. I can't. What if I leave? What does that make me?"

John kissed her. "It would make you happy, and your sister would take care of the people. It would solve the problem I know you care about as much as you pretend not to, and you and I could live our happily ever after."

Cynthia was quiet for a while.

John sat back in his chair and sipped his wine while the woman beside him decided whether the rest of their lives would be spent together. He was being almost completely honest; he *hadn't* expected to fall for Cynthia. His first reaction to her had been less than magnanimous, but the more time he spent with her, the more he realized that she was a product of her upbringing.

She was actually an insightful, intelligent, and caring woman—someone he could see himself spending happy years with. Nickie crossed his mind. There had been potential there too, or so he'd thought. She'd been cold since High Tortuga, which to him was worse than being the focus of her sharp tongue.

John was over that. He was more than a drunken fuck to be dismissed the next day. He might regret not taking her up on her offer, but not so much that he would chase pain to receive another one.

Besides, Nickie would never settle. She was wilder than wild; it would be like trying to catch a storm with only two hands and a fishing net. With Cynthia, he could have a true partnership. She was from his world, and she understood the pressures of royal life. She wanted love as much as he did.

"Cynthia, there are some things you need to know before you agree to run away with me."

Cynthia sat up, suddenly worried. "What is it, Marius?"

John made a face. "That's the first thing. My name isn't Marius, it's—"

"John," Jolie cut in from the balcony doors. She stalked over and handed Cynthia the datapad she was carrying. "*Prince* John, to be exact. He's a fraud."

Cynthia turned to John with a look of disbelief. "Is this true? You're a prince?"

John nodded. "That's what I was about to tell you when your sister interrupted."

"See?" Jolie cried. "He's an impostor. He and his captain are conning us." She pointed at John. "You're not going to marry my sister just to get your hands on this planet."

"I don't want your planet," John told her. "I have enough on my hands preparing to rule my own."

Cynthia looked at John with rapidly-filling eyes. "You lied? After everything I told you?"

John hated the look of betrayal she was giving him. "We're just here to make sure the Six get into the Federation in one piece." He smiled sadly. "I told you I wasn't here to fall in love. When you bared your heart, and it was the same as mine, that was when I knew I loved you. I get it, Cynthia. I might be a prince, but everything else is the truth. The power, the wealth—I don't care about any of that. I'll even renounce my title if it means I get to go to sleep every night with the woman I love. With you."

Cynthia took a step toward John just as the balcony doors swung open again and a troop of guards came out with their weapons raised.

"Arrest him!" Jolie ordered.

The guards advanced on John.

"No!" Cynthia cried. She flung herself in front of John. "You will not touch him!"

The guards paid the queen-in-waiting no attention. They gently scooped her out of the way and took John by the arms. Cynthia screamed at them to release him, but the guards herded John toward the door regardless.

Cynthia rounded on her sister with clenched fists. "You complete *bitch*! You just can't stand to see anyone happy, can you? What did you tell them? Make them let him go *now!*"

"I won't. Cynthia, he's a liar! You're not thinking about anyone except yourself, as usual!" Jolie yelled back. "All you can see is a pretty face and a dick to ride."

John heard Nickie shouting faintly in his pocket. He shook the guards off and turned back to argue with Jolie. "Not true! I might have been here initially to make sure your family drama didn't fuck it up for everyone else, but I love Cynthia." He struggled against the guards when they grabbed him again. "Unhand me!"

"Take him to the dungeons," Jolie ordered. "Don't let him out of your sight."

The guards nodded and dragged John through the balcony doors as the sisters continued to scream at each other.

System of the Six, Planet Vietania, Plomerilia, Palace Dungeon

John sat down on the metal bunk and sighed.

The guards had shoved him in here and left him in darkness. Their footsteps faded, and a single flickering light came on overhead. He fumbled in his pocket for his comm bud and stuck it in his ear to reactivate it.

Slutty fucking bitch-biscuits! Meredith, find him. If they've hurt him, I swear I'll blow a hole in their fucking castle and rip their fucking spleens from their bodies.

John decided that facing Nickie's wrath was a slightly more attractive option than her making good on that threat. *Nickie, I'm here.*

Nickie didn't hear him; she was in full-on war mode. John was almost glad to be in the dungeon, as far from her rage as possible.

He swallowed and raised his mental voice to be heard. *Nickie. I'm* fine.

Nickie stopped cursing. *John? About time. Where did they take you? Are you okay? Next time I tell you to keep your comm in, keep your fucking comm in, you ass.*

John snickered. *I thought you didn't care?* He didn't add that there wouldn't be a next time. *I'm okay. I'm in a cell somewhere on the underground levels.*

Can you get out?

I don't know. He got up to poke around. There was no way to escape as far as he could see. The six-by-six cell was windowless. The ventilation shaft was too narrow even for his arm to fit inside, and the door was bolted and hinged on the outside. He tested the bars on the door's small viewing window, but they held fast. *Damn, this is best-built prison cell I've ever come across.*

Nickie's voice started to get louder again. *I told you not to fuck around. You took too long getting her to trust you. If you'd done all this yesterday, we'd be out of here already.*

John sat down on the cell's metal platform. *Hindsight is all well and good, but it doesn't get me out of this situation.*

There was a scrape at the door.

"Who's there?" he called.

Cynthia's tearstained face appeared, and her pale hands grasped the bars. "It's me."

Who is it? Nickie demanded.

It's Cynthia. John jumped to his feet and ran the few steps to the door.

See if you can get her to let you out.

John ignored Nickie and reached out for Cynthia's hands. "Cynthia, are you okay? I didn't mean for you to find out like that. I wanted to explain."

She looked at him like she didn't know him at all. "Mar…John. That's your name, right?"

John nodded. "Yeah."

"And you're a prince. From Zulfir?"

"Zuifra," he corrected gently. "I'm the crown prince."

She gave him a look. "Really? So you want me to abandon my crown and then put another one on my head that's just as heavy to bear as the one I'm leaving behind?"

John cupped her hands with his. "Cynthia, I wouldn't do that to you. You can be whatever you want to be, even if all you want is to stay here and keep fighting for a crown that will make you miserable. It's not my choice, it's yours. But if it were mine, we would run away and be happy together. I told you I understood the pressures of your life. Well, now you know why."

Cynthia still had doubts. "What about your planet? Your family?"

John shrugged. "I have a sibling. Actually, I have three. My parents must have known I would have itchy feet because they were diligent about the spares."

"Spares?"

John nodded. "Yeah, you know, 'an heir and a spare?' They will cope fine without me if that's what you want."

Cynthia considered John's confession. "I suppose you *do* get it."

Nickie cut in. *Fucking awesome! Finally, we're getting this shitshow resolved. Now just get her to the* Briar Rose *and we can get the fuck out of here, mission accomplished.*

Cynthia extracted her hands from John's. "Okay."

John grinned. "Okay? We're going to do this?"

Cynthia nodded shyly. "Yeah, we are. Be ready. I'll come back for you as soon as Jolie is gone for the night. She hasn't got *all* of the guards in her pocket. I can get the keys, and we can leave." She stood on her tiptoes to kiss him quickly through the bars and left.

John leaned against the door and sighed.

Nearly home, Nickie told him. *Just get her to the ship, and I'll take care of the rest.*

CHAPTER EIGHTEEN

System of the Six, Planet Vietania, Plomerilia, Aboard the *Penitent Granddaughter*

"Get your sorry behinds in gear! We've got a royal pain in the ass to rescue, and another one to kidnap."

Durq cringed a little at Nickie's hoarse yell, but since she'd been stuck at that volume since John had turned his comm off, he wasn't too concerned that it might spill over onto him.

Nickie paced the floor of the cargo hold with her hands behind her back. "Grim, Keen, you're coming with me in case Prince PITA is followed. Adelaide, Durq, you stay here and get the ship ready for a quick exit in case it goes tits-up." Nickie looked at the nervous faces. She grinned and clapped her hands. "Well? Get to it! And don't worry, we'll get John back."

The crew hustled to get ready.

Nickie took the box with her Jean Dukes Specials out of the safe and brought it over to the extra crate Sofia had sent over with the rest of their gear. She still wasn't sure she was ready to open it. The implications of what she'd been gifted with were too huge to deal with while she was in the middle of the mission, so she had stowed the crate in the hold and put it in the back of her mind until now.

The crate contained a smooth lacquered box. Completely smooth. She ran a hand over the lid and then felt around where she thought the join should be.

Maybe she should have done this a little sooner. She considered the puzzle for a second. If Grandma Jean had made this, the locking mechanism was keyed to her DNA.

She smirked and pulled her belt knife. A drop or two would do. She made a short, shallow slice on the heel of her hand and smeared the blood along the place she would have placed a hand on the old-style box before the cut healed over.

There was a click, and the lid lifted fractionally.

Nickie peered into the box. There was a note on top of the packing materials inside.

She picked it up gingerly, hardly daring to see who it was from.

Dearest Nickie,

Bethany Anne instructed me to send you this gift as a token of her recognition of how far you've come. She sends her love, and her hopes that you will be ready to return to the family soon, as do we all.

Your loving uncle,
Barnabas

A small sob escaped Nickie's lips when she removed the layer of foam protecting the treasure beneath.

Grim looked over from where he was adjusting his armor. "What's up, boss?"

Nickie was too choked up to speak. She pointed at the box wordlessly and started stripping down to her underclothes.

"What? What is it?" Grim hurried over and looked into the box. "Oh. Oh, my."

The others came over, and they all stood around the box while a half-undressed Nickie unpacked her armor. It was flat-black, her favorite, and sleek as hell. The plates were thinner than any armor Nickie had seen in a hell of a long time, and there were no visible locking mechanisms for them, which sent a thrill up Nickie's spine. That meant the armor was stuffed with nanotech. She'd missed a lot in the time she'd been away, but she would lay money on this being one of her grandma's latest designs.

Her Aunt Bethany Anne was good like that. If you pissed her off there was nowhere you could hide from the beating she would give you, but if you pleased her? You probably still got a beating come training, but you got cool shit, too. It was almost worth the hassle of the mission ahead just to get to wear it for a while.

Nickie kicked off her boots, almost falling over the overalls around her ankles in her rush to get the armor on. "Grandma Jean really outdid herself. Watch this shit." She got into the armored boots and pressed the lower left leg plates into the ankle of her boot to activate the self-locking mechanism. The two plates merged and locked onto her boot. She grinned. "Guaranteed to be a perfect fit. *Every fucking time.*"

Keen's eyes shone as she held the torso plate up to the light before putting it on. "You don't say. Quite frankly, that armor is the most beautiful thing a grizzled old Space Marine like me has ever seen."

Nickie grinned and held up the backplate. "I know, right? My grandma is the fucking bomb when it comes to this shit. A hand?"

Adelaide took the plate. "It's not sticky like ours. What do I do with it? There are no clips or buckles."

"Just press it to my back," Nickie told her.

Adelaide gasped when the armor's back and sides moved to interlock seamlessly.

"Cool as fuck, huh?" The armor moved with Nickie like a second skin as she twisted from side to side. She held the pieces to her hips to join top and bottom and fitted her JD Specials to the belt.

Addie grabbed Nickie's arm and lifted it to get a better look at the join. "I *need* to know how that works!"

Nickie grinned as she attached her arm plates. "Family secret."

Addie's mouth twitched. "You don't know, do you?"

Nickie laughed. "Not a fucking clue." The last piece clicked into place, and she rolled her shoulders as the armor made the final adjustments. She picked up her coveralls to retrieve her Aunt Tabitha's badge from the pocket and cursed softly.

"You lost something?" Adelaide asked.

Nickie shook her head. "Just left it in my quarters. I won't be long, so be ready." She grabbed her helmet and hurried to leave the cargo bay. The armor felt so fucking *good.*

Nickie reached her quarters and headed for the bathroom, where she'd hung her aunt's badge on the hook before showering that morning. It wasn't like her to leave it lying around, but she'd been in the shower when John was arrested so she would forgive herself just this once.

She dumped her helmet on the sink and unhooked the badge. She caught sight of herself in the mirror as she slipped the chain over her head. Fuck. She looked like… Like a female version of her grandfather. Like she'd just stepped off the *ArchAngel.*

Like a fucking Grimes.

Your brain chemistry is doing some very interesting things right now, Meredith remarked. *Are you feeling okay?*

Nickie stared at her reflection. *I haven't got time for your fluffy psych bullshit now. We have a mission.* She gave her reflection one last disconcerted glance and left the bathroom. *Has Cynthia freed John yet?*

No. The guard still has a little time before the shift change. That gives us a bit to go over the plan again if you need to.

Nickie's doubts bloomed for a brief moment. *Mere, am I doing the right thing?*

Where did that come from? Meredith asked.

She ran a hand down her armored stomach as she walked back to the cargo hold. *I dunno. What if I'm making the wrong choice? Cynthia is the rightful heir, after all. Maybe John was right. Maybe I* am *pushing my own agenda.*

Are you sure it's not something else that's touched a nerve?

Like what?

Maybe the possibility of returning home? Of your uncle being proud of you for doing a good job?

High Tortuga isn't my home, Nickie argued.

But Barnabas is your family. It's only natural that you would want his respect.

Well, he's like me. He can't stand to be constricted by the fucking Federation either.

That could be nice for you. Barnabas was always a father figure to your Aunt Tabitha in Michael's absence.

Nickie screwed up her nose as she pushed the door to the cargo hold open. *I don't think so. I can see myself hanging out with him sometimes. Maybe. But none of that bonding shit. My life is already full with these guys.*

Keen approached her when she entered the hold. "I'm not sure about this. If John gets caught…"

"That's why we're going out there to help him." Nickie could tell that wasn't all he was worried about. "Spit it out, Keen. What's really bothering you?"

Keen shuffled uncomfortably. "It's just… Cynthia. It doesn't feel right, treating her like this. She's just a kid."

Nickie patted his arm awkwardly. "If she were a real leader, she wouldn't leave her people. We're doing them a favor."

Keen's shoulders dropped. "I guess that's true. Only, what does that say about me? I left my people behind to go gallivanting with you."

Nickie frowned. "It's not the same. You left Reynard in charge, and he's going to do just fine. Fuck, you didn't have to give them the rest of your life."

Keen nodded, unconvinced.

She punched his arm lightly, wincing when he stumbled. "Oops, forgot the armor adds a bit of oomph. You've got nothing to feel guilty about, Keen. Now come on, we've got a queen to kidnap."

Keen ambled away, and Nickie carried on with her prep for the extraction. She hadn't considered that the former Marine would struggle with relinquishing his responsibility to the colony. She assumed he would be glad to get his life back, to leave the never-ending responsibility of the top job to someone with the will and energy to do it. If anything, he had done what was best for Themis.

Nickie couldn't pretend to understand what it was to walk away from that kind of responsibility. She had only recently come to accept responsibility for herself, let alone anyone else.

She had no way of empathizing with Keen. Or Cynthia, if she were honest. Maybe the young queen wasn't just avoiding her duty. Maybe she *was* making the ultimate sacrifice, doing what was best for her people by running away from her birthright.

It was a little harder to stay objective when Nickie looked at it in that light.

Well, fuck.

System of the Six, Planet Vietania, Plomerilia, Palace Dungeon

John heard footsteps, then a nervous giggle.

Cynthia was here.

He got up from the unforgiving platform and waited by the door for her. She appeared at the bars a moment later and unlocked the door to John's cell with fumbling fingers.

John hesitated when she pushed the door open. "You came."

"I couldn't leave you down here." Cynthia blushed as she held out a familiar bag. "Your things. I took them from the guardroom when the guards fell asleep."

John opened the bag and was relieved to see that his weapons were still inside. He fastened his pistols to his hips and slung the bag on his back. "Are you sure about this? It's not too late to change your mind."

Cynthia threw herself into John's arms and kissed him thoroughly. "I've made up my mind. I'm getting you out of here, and I'm coming with you." She let go and tugged his hand to get him moving, her eyes bright with mischief. "Quick, we need to hurry. I drugged the guards, but I don't know how long it will last."

They laughed breathlessly as Cynthia directed them through the twists and turns of the passages, running hand-in-hand through the palace underground. John took over when Cynthia began to tire. He pulled her along behind him, his heart thundering in his chest as the feeling of freedom and the excitement of his escape flooded him with adrenaline.

Twice they had to duck into the shadows when they were almost discovered by the palace guards. The second time, John kissed her to stifle their nervous giggles as the guards passed by not ten feet from where they clung to each other in a recess.

As soon as the coast was clear, they ran on again.

They stopped to catch their breath when they reached the door to the ground floor atrium. John looked around to ensure the way was clear. "What's the quickest way out of here? We need to get to my ship."

Cynthia screwed up her nose. "Let me think. The fastest way is straight out of the palace and through the city, but we would get caught in the city. We'll have to go through the tunnels. There's a passage nearby that we can—"

Just then an alarm sounded, and they heard many pairs of boots approaching the atrium.

Cynthia gasped. "Looks like Seamus and Paul woke up. Jolie must know you're not in the dungeon."

John squeezed her hand gently. "Then we'd better get out of here before she finds us. Where is the passage?"

Cynthia looked around wildly for a moment.

John touched her cheek. "Hey, it's okay. We've got this. One step at a time, and we'll be on the *Briar Rose* before you know it."

She nodded. "Follow me." She ducked behind a plinth with a large bust of a bald man on it. "It's this way."

Cynthia dashed to a row of potted plants in front of a huge wall tapestry and waved John over, then pressed one of the slightly discolored stones beside the tapestry. "Under here."

They ducked under the tapestry as the guards trooped into the atrium. The wall slid back silently to reveal a dark and dusty passage and they slipped inside, safe for the moment.

Cynthia indicated John's bag as the wall slid shut behind them. "There are flashlights in there."

John rummaged until he found them. He passed one to Cynthia, and they set off down the passage. "Does your sister know about this?" he asked as they dashed through the hanging cobwebs. He remembered Jolie using the tunnel to the throne room on a few occasions while he'd been at the palace.

"No, it's an escape tunnel." She paused at a split in the passage, then nodded and took the left branch. "Jolie knows about the service tunnels, but not the emergency ones. There are bolt holes and escape tunnels all over the palace. Only the ruling monarch knows about them, though. My great-great-great…a lot of great-grandfathers ago had them built, then had everyone who built them killed to keep the secret safe."

John grimaced. "Nice."

Cynthia shrugged. "It's prevented a few assassination attempts from succeeding over the years. My father and I used to play hide-and-seek down here when I was a child." She became quiet for a moment. "The tunnel to the ship-yard is in his old office."

The passage brought them out in the courtyard in the center of the palace where Cynthia had thrown a party on his second night here. The courtyard was split by topiaries and vine-covered trellises situated around intimate seating nooks and elaborate statues.

It was perfect for entertaining. Perfect for sneaking, except…

John pulled Cynthia under the wraparound walkway and pointed at the guards patrolling the balcony above. She stepped out of sight, and they waited for their chance to dash over behind the nearest trellis. They worked their way across the courtyard in this way, using the dividing features as cover to remain out of sight of the guards on the balcony.

John half-expected Nickie to interrupt at any moment and demand he tell her what was taking so long but his comm was silent. He and Cynthia crept across the courtyard at an agonizingly slow pace, or so it seemed to him.

They paused to wait in the blind spot behind a hideous carved marble statue of a multi-winged beast being slaughtered by an armored figure when they reached the edge of the courtyard. John was surprised to see that the patrolling guards he'd spotted had only made it halfway around the balcony. He and Cynthia had moved a lot faster than he'd thought.

Cynthia dragged John behind the statue when a quartet of guards pounded through the courtyard. She looked at him, her face flushed with exertion and adrenaline. "The entrance to the administration wing is over there." She pointed to an elaborately carved double door at the opposite end of the walkway, then turned and indicated another door, this one was much plainer. "We'll use the service entrance, then we'll get to Daddy's office without alerting Jolie. She'll be in the security office down the hall with her guards."

When the coast was clear, they dashed from behind the statue to cover the open ground between them and the service entrance under the walkway. Cynthia led John through the small door into a long red-carpeted hallway.

They came out in a recess about halfway along the hallway.

John glanced up and down the hall. "Which way now?" he whispered.

Cynthia headed for the righthand door at the end of the hall.

John glanced at the full-sized oil painting of a man in full regalia on the wall opposite the door. "Is that your father?"

Cynthia smiled at the painting. "Yes. Daddy hated this painting. He always said it made him look stuffy." She took his hand. "Come on, we're nearly there now. We have to be careful near the security office. Jolie will be directing the search from there."

John looked back uneasily. "Where next after this tunnel?"

"We get aboard your ship and leave." Cynthia stuck a hand down the front of her top and pulled out a key on a necklace. "The tunnel will take us all the way to the shipyard."

She bent to the ornate doorknob and jiggled the key in the lock. "This silly thing *always* sticks."

John kept watch while Cynthia worked the key around, and there was a soft snick as the mechanism finally engaged. John moved to follow her through the door, but Cynthia froze as the door at the other end of the hall opened and Jolie came into the hallway.

Cynthia's sister dropped the stack of paperwork she was carrying and let out a scream at the sight of John. "Guards!"

John jumped into action. He snatched the key from the lock and bundled Cynthia through the door to her father's former office. He had the door locked behind them before Jolie's guards had even made it out of the security office.

He turned to Cynthia, who was crying a little from the shock. "Hey, are you okay?"

Cynthia sniffed. "I'm scared."

John took her in his arms as the guards began to pound on the door. "I'll ask you again. Are you sure you want to come with me? I can leave, and you can stay here. I would miss you, but I would understand."

Cynthia gazed at him blankly for a moment before pulling herself together. "No, Jolie will rule better than I ever could. She has the passion."

"So do the guards by the sounds of it," John joked as the pounding grew louder. "I think they found something to use as a ram. We need to get going."

Cynthia nodded resolutely. She rushed over to a bookcase by the fireplace and jumped to reach a book on the third shelf, knocking the others off the shelf in her hurry to open the passage.

The bookcase swung inward, and they ran into the passage as the guards broke the door down and rushed into the room with their weapons drawn.

"Don't shoot!" Jolie cried from behind them. "He's got Cynthia!"

Cynthia dragged John behind her. "There's a nexus up ahead. If we get there, we can lose them and head for the shipyard."

"What about Jolie? She thinks I've kidnapped you,"

There was a crash, and light flooded the tunnel behind them.

They looked back over their shoulders, and Cynthia screamed as the guards spilled into the tunnel. "Forget her! Just run!"

John and Cynthia didn't wait to find out if Jolie followed. They pelted along the tunnel until they came to the eight-way intersection Cynthia had described.

"Where now?" John asked.

"One minute." Cynthia pulled the fastenings from her hair and removed her diadem as she headed for the fourth tunnel. She dropped the jeweled headdress a short way from the mouth of the tunnel before doubling back to the second tunnel. "That should throw them off long enough for us to escape."

John followed her into the second tunnel, and they pushed hard to keep their head start on Jolie and the guards.

CHAPTER NINETEEN

System of the Six, Planet Vietania, Plomerilia, Shipyard, Public Docks

Nickie clung to the shadows beneath the *Briar Rose*, waiting for John to arrive with Cynthia.

She was pissed that she'd forgotten to pick her helmet up when she'd left her quarters, but by the time she'd remembered it had been too late to go back for it.

She just had to make sure that nobody tried to shoot her in the head tonight.

Meredith, Keen, any sign of John and Cynthia yet?

Keen was stationed on the royal dock in view of the tunnel entrance, ready to follow the two from a safe distance and back John up if he needed it.

Nothing yet, Keen reported.

Meredith?

I'm still tracking John's comm, Nickie. They're almost at the dock end of the tunnel. Keen should have eyes on them in a few minutes.

Got you, Keen chipped in. *I'll keep them peeled, then.*

Nickie was happy about John's turnaround, but she wasn't too comfortable with the sickly sweetness of his interactions with Cynthia, so she'd had Meredith monitor their escape from the palace. She didn't want to have to listen to the two of them make kissy noises in her ear the whole time.

Still, she felt bad for Cynthia. John had the young queen convinced that he wanted her, but she was in for the rudest awakening when they got to the ship. Now that Nickie had considered what life in Cynthia's shoes might look like, she felt pretty fucking bad that she had to take her out.

Are you having second thoughts?

Nickie sighed and leaned her head against the strut she was using as cover. *I have a mission to complete. I don't have the luxury of second thoughts. Cynthia has to go, or everything goes to shit.*

But does she have to die?

Nickie hit the metal with the heel of her hand. *What do you suggest, Meredith? That I drop her off at the nearest luxury resort world for deposed planetary leaders and go on my merry way?* She looked at the slight dent she'd made in the metal and shook her head. *Barnabas was clear that he expects me to make the hard choice.*

Just keep an open mind, Nickie. Another solution may yet present itself, given a little time.

What *fucking time, Meredith?* Nickie snorted softly. *Where are they now? Did they make it to the dock yet?*

Oh, dear.

What? Are they still in the tunnel?

They're less than five minutes away from the tunnel

entrance, but they've got company. Company with guns.

Thanks for the clarification, I didn't pick that up at all. Nickie set off running for the royal dock, which was over on the other side of the shipyard.

Nickie cut around the sleeping ships in the open part of the shipyard reserved for visiting merchants and traders. She gave it all she had, but even at her top speed, she was going to be cutting it fine.

She vaulted over the wall that separated the public docks from the private ones in one fluid movement and landed in a crouch on the other side.

Meredith, what's the quickest way through here?

Nickie's route appeared in the corner of her vision when Meredith fed it to her internal HUD.

You're not going to make it in time. I can interact with your armor and give you a boost, but it will cost some of the charge you have saved in your power packs.

Go for it. I can't leave Keen alone to deal with whoever is chasing John and Cynthia.

Nickie's lungs burned with the effort of her mad dash.

One minute. Hurry, Nickie.

Fuck it all, why can't things go according to plan just once?

This would have been the ideal time for such a rarity to occur.

I know, right? Nickie opened it up another notch as the armor's assistance kicked in. The tech her grandmother had stuffed into Nickie's gift worked with her body to enhance her already superhuman speed, and she all but flew across the shipyard.

She burst onto the royal dock, scaring Keen almost to death with the suddenness of her arrival. She glanced at him as he scrambled to his feet. "Get your ass in gear, Keen. They're almost here, and they're being chased."

Keen drew his weapons and sighted on the tunnel entrance. "I'm ready."

Incoming, Meredith broadcast over the comm.

Nickie's JD Specials were in her hands and raised to the center of the tunnel mouth before she'd finished turning to face it.

John and Cynthia came stumbling out, panting and exhausted from their escape. They spotted Keen and Nickie on the other side of the dock and forced themselves to keep running. Cynthia half-collapsed against John when they came to a stop beside Nickie.

Nickie gave them half a minute to drag some air into their tortured lungs before she made them start running again.

Cynthia's pace was ridiculously slow. Nickie was tempted to pick the woman up and carry her like a sack of potatoes, but instead, she turned to John. "Do you have any idea how many are chasing you?"

"No," John panted. "Sounded like at least half a dozen, but you know how sound can play tricks on you in tunnels. It could have been anywhere between three and thirty."

Nickie found that no use whatsoever. "Whatever. Let's just get the hell out of here before the guards catch up. Both ships are ready for a quick takeoff." She glanced at Cynthia. "Let's just get there and get this over with."

John gave her a strange look and returned to helping Cynthia along.

Nickie checked that Keen was keeping up okay. The older man's fitness belied his age and put John's to shame.

He trotted briskly behind them, his breathing regular and even as he guarded their rear. "Someone's been working out," Nickie teased.

Keen puffed his chest out as he ran. "Can't be running missions with a desk jockey's body, can I?"

Nickie winked at him. "No, you can't. Keep it up."

The guards appeared just as they came to the huge steel gates at the exit. There would be no easy escape this time. The shipyard was closed for the night, and the gates were secured with heavy chains.

Cynthia wavered when she saw the obstacle to their escape. "How are we going to get out?"

Nickie had jumped the wall to get in, so she hadn't seen the chains. "Don't stress it. I have a skeleton key." She dialed her new JD Special up to seven, then shrugged and gave it another two levels since she had the protection of her armor. "I'm pretty sure my wrist can take it."

I'm not sure about that at all, Meredith cautioned.

Nickie aimed at the middle of the gates where the chain was joined with a huge padlock. *I guess we'll see.*

It could not.

The resulting explosion tore the gate from the surrounding wall and covered Nickie's scream of pain as her wrist shattered inside her armor.

Sonofabitch! That fucking hurt!

I hate to say I told you so, Meredith began.

No, you don't, Nickie snarked. *You fucking love it, and nothing you say will convince me differently.* She gritted her teeth and dialed her JD Special back down to six as the bone began to knit together.

The explosion may have covered Nickie's scream, but it

had given their pursuers a location to home in on. The group made a run for the public shipyard, but the guards had seen them and gave chase into the settling dust at the exit.

Cynthia screamed and ducked behind John when one of the guards opened fire on them. John covered her with his body while Keen dropped the guard who had shot at them.

"Try not to kill them," Nickie ordered. "They're just doing their duty." She fired at the wall over the hole where the door used to be. The bricks collapsed, blocking the exit and cutting the guards off. "That should hold them. Come on."

They darted between the ships, working their way across the shipyard until the *Briar Rose* came into sight.

The ramp descended as they approached and Nickie fell back a few steps to walk behind the others. It was time, and she was fresh out of choices. She sighed and squeezed the grip of her JD Special, resigned to her duty as the only one who understood why this innocent woman had to die.

She didn't have to be happy about it. She just had to do it.

John took Cynthia over to the foot of the ramp and turned his head to find Nickie. He gave her a hard look and wrapped his arm around Cynthia.

"What's wrong?" Cynthia asked.

"It's okay," John told her. "I just need to say goodbye."

Cynthia nodded and kissed him. "Just hurry before Jolie and the guards find us. The sooner we're on our way to Zuifra, the better."

Nickie froze, her gun arm falling limply to her side.

"What is this?"

John smiled at Cynthia. "We're eloping. For real."

Keen patted Nickie on the back. "Would you look at that! Looks like all we had to do was introduce those two. No kidnapping or assassinations necessary after all."

Cynthia's eyes widened at Keen's joke. "What do you mean, assassination?" She turned to John. "What does he mean?"

John shook his head. "Nobody was going to assassinate anyone." He looked pointedly at Nickie. "*Were* they?"

Nickie opened her mouth to argue and decided that fudging the truth would serve her better at this moment. "Well, no. But *eloping*? You've only known each other for five minutes."

John shrugged. "I've only known you for five more. When you know, you know. You know?"

Nickie *didn't* know, but neither did she care. At least she knew the reason for his rapid change of attitude now. "So, what? You two are gonna get married?"

John and Cynthia looked at each other and grinned. "Yes," they said in unison.

Keen stuck out his hand to shake John's. "Congratulations to the two of you." He sniffed a little as he spoke. "Couldn't be happier for you."

Cynthia blushed. "Thank you!"

Nickie considered being a bitch about it, but she realized that not only did she not feel slighted, she was actually happy for John. She certainly didn't want any of the things he and Cynthia were so happy about. "Where next for you two?"

John flashed his dimple at her and squeezed Cynthia to

him. "I'm taking Cynthia back to Zuifra with me. I have to deliver the tech I picked up from High Tortuga. After that, who knows? It solves your problem."

Cynthia snuggled in under John's arm. "I can't be the queen my people need. John helped me see that. I can't keep pretending that I want what my mother wanted for me. It's not fair to Vietania."

Nickie would have torn Cynthia to shreds over that just a few hours ago. However, she now appreciated that the decision was not an easy one to have made. "That's…pretty mature. Good for you."

"What will happen here?" Keen asked.

Cynthia's face was serious. "Jolie will take over, and the Six can join the Federation without a civil war." She broke into a soppy smile as she looked up at John. "Besides, we have to give love a chance when it appears, right?"

John touched his nose to hers. "You've got that right."

Nickie was about to throw up from the gooeyness of it all when they were bathed in blinding white light from somewhere above.

A voice came from the middle of the light.

"Lay down your weapons and step away from the queen."

None of them complied. Nickie glanced around the dark shipyard and made out at least four guard units secreted behind the surrounding ships, possibly five.

Fuck. My. Life. She held back her sigh, then pointed her JD Special at the light and yelled at whoever was flying, "How about you land that thing, and we talk about it like civilized human beings?"

"You get away from my sister!" a new voice yelled. "You

can't get away with kidnapping her. You're surrounded!"

Jolie sounded terrified, which worried Nickie. Fear of losing someone made people do stupid things. She should know. It occurred to Nickie that this whole situation could be down to the lack of communication between the sisters. "Cynthia, did you two ever get along?"

Cynthia looked sad. "Yes. We used to play when we were little, but Jolie changed. She got all serious and stuffy, and all she does is nag me these days. I don't know why things changed between us."

Nickie dropped her gun hand and motioned for John and Keen to do the same. "Fuck it."

Maybe the hammer wasn't the solution here after all, which was fucking annoying since she was dressed to smash. She was a fighter, not a wet nurse. If being a vigilante meant she had to keep doing this chatty emotional shit all the time, maybe she should start charging Barnabas by the hour for it.

The light vanished as suddenly as it had appeared and Jolie landed her hovercraft. The door opened, and Jolie stepped out with a gun in her shaking hand. She aimed the gun at John with hot murder in her eyes. "You're not taking my sister anywhere."

Cynthia threw herself in front of John to protect him. "They're not kidnapping me!" she raged. "I love John, or at least I'm beginning to. I'm leaving with him, and you can't stop me!"

Jolie glared at John, not taking her eyes off him as she pleaded with her sister. "Cynthia, he's brainwashed you. He's from the Federation. I have proof. Look!"

"I already know, Jolie. And I don't care! You love the

Federation, so what's your problem?"

"It's not just that he's from the Federation." Jolie pulled a datapad out of her bag and shoved it roughly at Cynthia. "His people came from here originally, and now he wants to take Vietania over."

Cynthia snorted and pushed it away. "He doesn't want to be king of his *own* planet, let alone this one."

John made a small noise beside her. "Actually, I don't know about that. Things can always change. But whatever the decision I'll include you in it, Cynthia."

Cynthia wrapped an arm around John's waist. "See?" she demanded. "I told you. We're doing this because we want to. Because we're in love!"

Jolie sneered at John. "I don't believe a word you're saying, you lying bastard. I'm arresting you all for treason."

Nickie stepped between them and took the gun out of Jolie's hand. "Take it easy. Nobody is getting shot tonight, and nobody is getting arrested. We didn't come here to take over, Jolie. We're here to help with this situation. To get you and the rest of the Six safely into the Federation. Just listen to Cynthia. It doesn't have to end badly between you two."

Jolie sneered. "Stay out of this. I don't care who you are to the Empress, this is family business."

Nickie smirked. "Don't I know it! But your family business is fucking things up for everyone, so here I am to fix it however is necessary. Luckily for you and your sister, these two have fallen in love or whatever, and they're going to leave you to run shit here. Just accept it and move on or you'll lose her forever."

Jolie gave her a scathing glare. "No. I won't accept it."

Cynthia hadn't yet achieved the level of maturity that Nickie had grown to recently. She stamped her foot and growled with frustration. "Jolie, why can't you ever let me have anything? Just let me go!"

Jolie waved her datapad in Cynthia's face. "He's a fraud!"

Cynthia stamped her foot. "What do you care? All you want is to be queen, and you're getting your wish. You can *have* the crown. I don't want it!"

"It's not about who gets to be queen!" Jolie was almost in tears by this point. "Cynthia, he wants to take you away from me!"

Nickie remained quiet. It was as she'd thought.

The guards milled around, uncomfortable with the whole situation. They had all thought Cynthia was being kidnapped. Apparently, she was just being her usual dramatic self, and more than one of them wondered why they were here in the middle of the night for nothing.

Cynthia clung to John as if letting him go would mean she got dragged back to the place. "Jolie, *please*. Let me go."

Jolie shook her head. "I won't. You're all I have left, even if you do hate me."

Cynthia snorted. "Me, hate you? It's you who hates me!"

The tears ran freely down Jolie's cheeks. "I don't hate you! You're just a pain in my ass."

"Because I don't *want* to be queen!"

Jolie was shaken. "You never said! I thought you just wanted all the power without any of the responsibility."

Cynthia shook her head earnestly. "I don't want any of that. I just want a family and to be loved. I never asked to be queen. I never wanted to take that from you!"

Jolie melted at that. "Oh, Cynthia, why didn't you just say so?"

"Because you were horrible to me! Mother said you were jealous and I believed her."

"I was just frustrated that you wasted all your time on unimportant things. That I was doing your job, and you seemed to just float through life with nothing touching you."

Cynthia let go of John and rushed to wrap her arms around her sister. "I'm so sorry, Jolie. I know I've been a bitch, and I'm sorry. I do love you."

Jolie sobbed as she returned Cynthia's hug. "I'm sorry too. I took my frustration out on you too many times. It wasn't your fault that Father was made to marry your mom instead of mine. I do love you; you have to know that."

Cynthia sniffed and wiped her face on her sleeve. "I love you, too."

Nickie wanted to leave. This was getting too deep—and too close to her own issues. "Listen, can we wrap this up? It's great that you two are talking now, but maybe you could do it at a more suitable time and place? Like not in a shipyard in the middle of the night?"

The sisters chuckled and let go of one another.

Jolie stepped back and nodded. "If you really want to leave, I won't stop you." She narrowed her eyes at John. "But if you hurt my sister then I will bring everything I have down on your head. Do you understand?"

John gave Jolie a cheeky salute. "I promise to treat her like the queen she is for as long as she chooses to be with me. Does that satisfy you?"

Jolie nodded again. "I suppose it will have to."

"Hey," Keen interjected, "if you two are getting married, does that mean the feud between your families is over?"

Jolie snickered. "Seeing as neither family remembered we were feuding in the first place, I think it's safe to say relations between Vietania and Zuifra will improve."

Cynthia glanced up the ramp. "I would *love* that! But we should go."

John nodded his agreement, and the two turned to climb the ramp.

Cynthia turned back as they were about to board the *Briar Rose* and waved to her sister. "Jolie! Goodbye for now. Take care of the people, and good luck!"

With that, she and John went inside, and as soon as Briar had retracted the ramp, they were gone.

Nickie and the others watched the ship fly into the night. Jolie was still crying, although Nickie didn't think the new queen noticed.

Jolie turned to Nickie once the light of the ship had receded into a pinprick in the blanket of stars above. "Now what?"

"What do you mean?" Nickie patted her on the back. "You get crowned, then you rule this planet like you always should have. My work here is done. The conflict is resolved, and the Six can join the Federation."

Jolie looked at her skeptically. "I should still arrest you for interfering."

Nickie smirked. "Well, you could try, but you probably want to stay on my good side. You know, since I just did you the biggest favor?"

With that, she turned and headed across the shipyard to the *Penitent Granddaughter's* dock.

CHAPTER TWENTY

<u>System of the Six, Leaving Vietania, Aboard the *Penitent Granddaughter*, Bridge</u>

Adelaide, Durq, and Grim listened openmouthed as Nickie and Keen recounted the night's adventures.

"So he just ran off with her?" Addie's face was a picture of shock. "After he spent all that time chasing you?"

Nickie shrugged. "It's not a big deal. I wasn't too attached to him anyway. Maybe I'll get a dog when we get back to High Tortuga. Or a cat. Cats are low maintenance, right?"

"A dog would definitely be more loyal than John," Grim grumped. "I thought he was a nice guy."

Nickie snickered. "He is, which is exactly why he's not for me. Can you imagine if I had to put up with him *all* the time?"

Grim chuckled. "I only spent one afternoon alone with him, and I wanted to go AWOL just to get away. I agree—nice, but too much."

"I could have seen you in a crown." Adelaide burst out laughing as she spoke. "Oh, who am I kidding? You're a fighter, not a wifey-type. We don't need any princes to ride to the rescue when we have you around to kick ass."

Nickie didn't know what to say to that. She bent over the console to input the coordinates for High Tortuga.

I could do that.

Not now, Meredith.

Grim sat up suddenly. "Did you just say that we're going back to High Tortuga?"

"Uh-huh."

The crew looked at each other in stunned silence.

Nickie looked up and frowned. "What?"

Grim was first to recover. "You're going there of your own free will?"

Nickie glared at him. "Yeah, what's the problem?"

"I have to say I'm surprised," Addie admitted.

Even Durq put his two credits in. "I think it's good. We are a family, but Nickie has a blood family too, and she needs them."

Nickie gazed blankly at the little Skaine. "You're a shrink now?"

Durq tilted his head. "I hope not, Nickie. I'm already very small."

That brought a laugh from the whole crew, Meredith included.

Durq looked around in puzzlement. "What? What did I say?"

Nickie smiled and got back to plotting their route. "Nothing, it's fine."

Grim and Addie whispered to each other.

"You know I can hear you, right?" Nickie pointed to her ear. "Super hearing, remember?"

"You can't blame us for speculating, boss," Grim told her. "This is the biggest thing that's happened since we joined up."

Nickie raised an eyebrow. It actually was. The enormity of the decision she'd just made without even thinking about it hit her, and she realized she could do with a little time alone to process it all. "Yeah, well, if you all want to gossip like housewives, you can go do it in the galley." She winced at her tone. "Sorry. I'm not mad at you, but I could use some time alone."

Grim nodded. "That's okay. We have dinner to prepare, don't we, Durq?"

Adelaide and Keen got up too.

"We'll see you in the mess later?" Addie asked Nickie hopefully.

Nickie nodded, too choked up to speak.

<hr>

Nickie sat back in her captain's chair and closed her eyes with a huge sigh.

Would you like to talk about it? Meredith asked.

What's with everyone wanting to talk all the damn time? Nickie huffed. *I just want to think, Meredith. When I know how I feel, maybe I'll talk.*

Okay, then I'll leave you to it.

Nickie realized she'd been short with Meredith too. *Sorry, Mere. It's been a long week, and my head is up my ass trying to come to terms with it all.*

I'm proud of you for knowing that you need to take time for your own emotional maintenance.

Stop trying to butter me up, Meredith.

Just call if you change your mind about talking.

I will.

It wasn't so much the twist of John's elopement with Cynthia. She had pushed the two of them together, after all. She wondered if she'd done it accidentally-on-purpose. She'd had plenty of chances to start something with John, and instead, she'd flipped into bitch mode and pushed him away as soon as any possibility of intimacy occurred.

She knew she wasn't ready for a relationship, not the kind someone like John was looking for. She hadn't even mourned her lost love properly. That would be too hard. She couldn't even name him in her memory because it cut her too deeply to even think about it, let alone picture his face.

Maybe a lover would come along in time, but it would be when *she* was ready. The next thought hit her like a freight liner.

What bothered her was that she felt so alone. She missed her mom, dammit. She missed *all* of her family, and she just wanted to go home.

Shit. No, she *wasn't* ready to go home yet, but maybe she was getting a little closer.

Nickie closed the door to her quarters and headed for the shower to wash the stress of the last week away. Grim and Durq had outdone themselves with dinner, and the crew had all enjoyed sharing the meal and the bottle of Yollin whiskey that Grim had been saving for a special occasion.

Now, all Nickie wanted to do was curl up in bed and sleep.

She rolled her eyes at the helmet on her vanity and took it into the bedroom before stripping for her shower.

She emerged from the bathroom twenty minutes later feeling like a new woman.

How are you feeling now? Meredith asked.

I'm okay. Mostly tired, she replied. *Who knew all this self-acceptance shit could be so fucking exhausting?*

Well, it isn't light work you're doing. Would you like to read your aunt's diary entry before you sleep?

There's a new one?

There is, Meredith confirmed fondly.

Nickie moved her helmet to the dresser and dived under the covers. *What are you waiting for?* she asked. *Load it.*

<h1 style="text-align:center">CHAPTER TWENTY-ONE</h1>

QBBS *Meredith Reynolds*, Rangers' Offices

Tabitha dragged her feet down the corridor past the Rangers' training area and into her office. She sat at her desk and opened her computer to begin the reports for the assignments in Arista and Omidian.

Are you sure you don't want to do this for me, Achronyx?

Absolutely, one-hundred-percent certain, Tabitha.

She looked at the blank page for a long moment before typing the date. Then she resumed staring. Her hands hovered over the keyboard while she searched for the words to explain the chain of events leading to her decision to blow up the drug den with the gang still inside it.

Finally, she let out a long, drawn-out sigh and started to type.

What's the problem?

The words came tumbling from her fingers onto the page in rapid bursts with long pauses between as she worked her way through the report. *I failed, Achronyx.*

There were children being exploited, and I didn't know until it was too late for some of them.

You can't be omnipresent, Achronyx chided. What is it with humans taking responsibility for things that they couldn't possibly have prevented?

I could have gotten there sooner.

You did your part, Tabitha. You saved a lot of lives on Omidian, and the people can move on knowing that their children are safe, thanks to you and Hirotoshi.

I know. She sighed again, louder this time. *But people still died. It's messy out at the edges, Achronyx. I expect that. I didn't think it could be like that so close to home.*

There was a knock at the door, and Barnabas came into her office. "I heard you sighing all the way from the break room. What's up?"

Tabitha pushed the keyboard away and dropped her head into her arms on the desk. "Everything, Barnabas. I'm trying to write my reports, but all I can see are the faces of the people who died."

Barnabas glided across the office and perched on the edge of her desk. "Ah. There isn't really anything I can say to fix that, except that you should also remember the faces of those you saved. They will far outnumber the faces of the dead, and perhaps you will learn to find some solace in that."

Tabitha lifted her head and looked at Barnabas. "That's...pretty clever, actually."

Barnabas rolled his eyes. "Well, accumulated wisdom is a thing." He sighed and laid a hand on her shoulder. "You do not have to go through this in silence. I am here whenever you want to talk."

Tabitha waved off Barnabas' concern. "I'm not going to pretend to be okay about it. Besides, when have you ever known me to stay quiet about anything? I'm talking about it right now," she eyed him, "with you."

Barnabas got up from the desk, massaging the small of his back. "We can continue the conversation in my office. I at least have enough seats for us both."

Tabitha grinned. "I thought about decorating, but there's probably not much point now, right?" She shrugged and got up to leave. "I'll make the next place a bit homier."

"The next place?" Barnabas narrowed his eyes as he followed her into the corridor. "What on earth has Achronyx been telling you?"

Tabitha wasn't sure how much Barnabas knew. She held out for this being one of the incredibly rare occasions where she had more information than her mentor. "Have you been to Devon yet?"

Barnabas frowned, then nodded when he finally caught her meaning. "Baba Yaga was very taken with the place, and that can only be because Bethany Anne has bigger plans in mind. Very astute, Tabitha. You and Achronyx have discussed this at length?"

"We've talked about it." Tabitha shrugged. "If Bethany Anne wants to leave, I'm going with her whether she wants me or not. She can't just go off again. Not without me." She stepped aside for Barnabas when they reached his office.

"Bethany Anne wouldn't do that to us again." He frowned. "If only because we won't allow it."

Tabitha nodded, looking down at her feet while Barnabas let them into his office. "Not everyone will choose to follow her. It's going to be hard to say goodbye."

Barnabas went straight to the cubby where he kept a small water heater and a set of jars containing everything he needed to make tea. "That it will. I will also find it difficult, which is surprising to me. It appears that I have formed many relationships aboard the station without realizing it."

Tabitha headed straight for the most comfortable chair and draped herself across it with her legs over one arm. "Are you thinking about Johnny and his mom?"

"Oh, no, I am aware of my fondness for those two." Barnabas smiled. "Johnny has grown into quite the young man. I shall miss him if we are to part ways." He filled the water heater with enough to make two cups and turned to lean on the counter and talk to Tabitha while he waited for it to boil. "What about you? Is there someone in particular on your mind?"

Tabitha scrunched her nose as she was reminded of the situation that was still unresolved. "Well, yeah. But you already know about Tiera and Sebastian. I keep getting called away before I can find a solution to her problems."

Barnabas furrowed his brow in confusion. "I thought she was adamant that her job with station security was sufficient? You had decided not to interfere the last time we discussed it."

"That went out of the window." Tabitha turned around in her seat to sit up. "Her situation is much like Lillian's, except she hasn't got a family around to help her through the hard times. I can't *not* help."

He started preparing the tea. "Are you saying that you feel responsible?"

Tabitha shook her head. "Not exactly. More like…she's

my people, you know? I want to do what I can to ease her burden, one human being to another. I don't want her to work herself to death when there is another way."

"All you have to do is find it." He brought both cups over. "I have faith that you will."

Tabitha smirked. "I don't suppose you would be interested in ditching the robes and updating your look to help Ashley out?"

Barnabas raised an eyebrow. "I most definitely would not." He handed her one of the cups and sat in his chair with the other. "You are right, though. Not all of our family will find it so easy to tear up the roots they have put down here."

Tabitha sipped her tea and contemplated Barnabas' words. "I'm pretty sure that most of the family will choose to stay with Bethany Anne. Or at least, I hope so." A thought hit her hard enough to hurt physically. She dropped her teacup and the hot tea spilled over her, unnoticed.

Barnabas darted forward and caught the cup. "Are you all right?" He put the cup on the table and grabbed the nearest thing, his scarf, and pressed it into her hand. "Your legs, Tabitha."

Tabitha looked at the scarf for a moment before connecting the dots. She wiped up the mess she'd made and handed the scarf back to him. "Barnabas! What if Pete decides he wants to stay?"

Barnabas tilted his head. "Highly unlikely, but what if he did?"

"I... I don't know." Tabitha couldn't even begin to unravel how she would deal with that choice.

Their relationship was the happiest thing Tabitha had been part of. They gave each other zero stress since they'd skipped the awkward "getting to know you" phase and slipped straight into the easy comfort that only came of spending years together.

He was still the same Peter she had known for almost her whole life, but she didn't need to talk about it to know that they had grown into something more since that night they had turned to one another for comfort in their grief. They'd just been enjoying the moments so much that they hadn't even discussed the future.

Who needed to when life was no longer restricted to a mad eighty-year rush?

Facing the consideration that waking up next to him might become all but impossible was not something she felt equipped to deal with.

Barnabas interrupted her chain of thought. "I am certain that Peter will choose to be wherever you are, since that will be where Bethany Anne is."

Tabitha resolved to find out one way or another when she saw Peter on Merry's birthday. Life would go on, and if they were meant to be, they would make it wherever they ended up.

"I know. Now all I need to do is help Tiera and Ashley find security before life as we know it gets forever rearranged into something that looks completely…different." A slow smile spread across Tabitha's face. "Oh, Barnabas! I might have figured out the solution to Tiera and Ashley's problems!"

Barnabas beamed and sat forward. "I knew you would. I always find that the solution to a tricky problem only occurs if you think about something else. Would you care to enlighten me?"

Tabitha grinned. "Well, if the Empire is going to go through changes, you can bet that one of those will be a change of uniform for everyone. I wonder if the plans for that have been made yet?"

"Knowing Bethany Anne, yes." He patted Tabitha's hand. "But I'm guessing it won't be high on her list of priorities. I would bet she's just waiting for the details to fall into place, and that she doesn't know you have the people she needs to make it happen."

Tabitha squealed with happiness. "Barnabas, you're a genius!" She leapt to her feet and pounded out of the office with her coat flying behind her.

Barnabas wiggled a finger in his ear to try to stop the ringing. "Let me know how it turns out," he said calmly to the closed door.

CHAPTER TWENTY-TWO

QBBS *Meredith Reynolds*, Tabitha's Quarters

Tabitha stood at the vanity in her bathroom with her hair scrunched in her hands. "Up or down. Hmmm… down." She let it go and massaged her scalp with her fingertips to return the body to it. "I don't know why I feel so nervous."

Neither do I, Achronyx teased. Merry will like her gift, and if she doesn't, it's not exactly galaxy-ending. It is unlikely she will even remember this day unless Meredith records it for her.

She walked into the bedroom and picked up the gift-wrapped box containing Merry's coat, then glanced at the closet where she'd hung the coat Ashley had made her to match. *It's a big deal for me! I want her to love it.*

And it's nothing to do with anything else that's happening today?

You got me. I am nervous about what Pete will say. She hugged the box to her chest. *But Ashley was over the moon with ADAM's offer.*

She has been making waves. The new premises are almost up and running already, and I have been helping her interview prospective workers.

Tabitha grinned, warmed to her toes by the speed at which things were falling into place for the two women now that a resolution had been found. *I can't wait to see Tiera's reaction to the surprise. Did she get back to you about meeting me later?*

She did. She will be there, and she promised to bring Sebastian.

Oh, goody!

You have company, Achronyx announced.

Tabitha put the box down and went to answer the door. "Let me guess, it's Peter."

She heard him groan as she approached the door.

"Tabbie, open up and let me in before my arms drop off!"

She opened the door and there he was, completely loaded down by the stack of boxes in his arms, which were straining under the weight of the bags he had hanging from them.

Tabitha's mouth dropped open. "What's all this?"

Peter tilted his body to show her the logo from Ashley's old store on the bags. "I ran into your friend. She gave me all this and told me to tell you she'll be back with the rest in a few days." His voice was muffled by the stack of boot boxes balanced on his outstretched arms. "She was in a hurry, so I offered."

Tabitha recovered from her shock at the sheer volume of the gifts Ashley had sent and smiled at Peter. "That's because you're a good man. Come on, let's get all this inside."

She led him into the living area and piled the bags on the dining table before taking the boot boxes from him. She stood back once he had dropped his bags on the table next to the others. "Wow! Ashley said she had some stock in my size, but shit! And she said there's *more?*"

She started opening the boxes.

"So many decades and yet I feel a need to ask." He looked at her. "Why do women need so many clothes?"

Tabitha looked up from the nest of tissue paper she was carefully removing. "Huh?" She hadn't caught his question. "Never mind the clothing, get a load of these boots!" She held up the current pair. "I'm going to need a closet as big as Bethany Anne's!"

"*Nobody* needs a closet as big as Bethany Anne's." He grinned and rubbed his forearms vigorously to get the feeling back. "I dunno, though. A bigger closet might not cut it. You might want to think about getting a bigger place."

Tabitha's eyes began to tingle. "I just didn't expect all this. I helped because Tiera and Ashley are good people and I hated to see their talents go to waste."

"Ashley knows that." Peter wrapped his arms around Tabitha and kissed her tears away. "You did her and Tiera a huge kindness. I know you didn't do it for a reward, but when someone is grateful for your help, it's only natural they would want to show it." His kisses changed to nibbles that tickled Tabitha's jaw. "What would she do with this stuff anyway? It all looks like it was made for you."

Tabitha snickered. "You always know the right thing to

say. I'm just happy that we found a solution. You know, being a Ranger isn't always about big fights and taking down interplanetary crime syndicates." She leaned her head on his shoulder. "Sometimes it's about fixing something at home. Like finding a place for Tiera. It took a while, but we got there in the end."

Peter smiled. "I know. *And* you averted a crisis in two separate systems this month. Tonight you get a well-earned break."

Tabitha lifted her head. "Maybe you're right about getting a bigger place."

Peter was thrown by the sudden change in topic. "Huh?"

"What will your choice be?"

Peter didn't answer immediately. He hadn't gotten to either this age or this stage in his relationship with the fieriest woman in the whole Empire bar Bethany Anne by answering such a softly-spoken question without first *carefully* considering whether even the nuances of his words could be taken out of context. "My choice about what?"

Tabitha did not explode, so Peter knew he hadn't forgotten some important—to her—date. She did look at him with pity, however, which meant he'd missed something. "What's going on, Tabbie?"

Tabitha's eyebrows went up in surprise. "Oh, honey. You really don't know? The choice to stay or leave with Bethany Anne when the Empire breaks up."

Peter's jaw dropped. "The Empire is breaking up?" He leaned against the table and crossed his arms, trying to absorb the bombshell. "That's…*huge*. When did you find out?"

Tabitha leaned next to Peter and put her head on his shoulder. "It's not official, not yet. But ADAM let a few things slip to Achronyx, and I had a long chat with Barnabas about it after I got back from Omidian. Are you okay?"

Peter rubbed his chin while he thought. "You know, it's not a total shock. We didn't come to space to rule. We have a bigger duty here, and putting that to the side was a sacrifice we had to make when we found out that the Kurtherians fucked with every species they came across."

Tabitha's lip curled. "Yeah, well, I think that our Empress is preparing to take the fight to them again."

They sat in silence for a few moments. Peter broke it first. "So you think we're going to war?"

Tabitha shrugged. "Eventually. Bethany Anne has been to hell and back recently. I think that when she ran, she caught up with herself. Our give-no-fucks leader is back, and she will loop us in when she's good and ready. We should be prepared when she does."

"Well, fuck. I'm glad you told me." He wiped his face with a hand. "I don't need to ask why you think Bethany Anne will want to leave. I agree that the constraints of ruling have worn her down. I don't blame her for wanting her freedom back."

"We could try to persuade her otherwise." Tabitha snickered. "But we would have more luck trying to catch the wind." She hesitated a moment before asking again. "When the time comes, will you go with her, or will you stay here and find a place in what comes next?"

Peter put his arm around Tabitha and held her close. "I

go where she goes, same as you." He kissed the top of her head as he whispered, "*Ad Aeternitatem.*"

Tabitha snuggled into Peter's chest and sighed happily. "Good. I was half-afraid I would have to drag you away from here cavewoman-style." She poked him in the chest gently. "I've kind of gotten used to this."

Peter smirked. "'This' being…"

She slapped him in the same spot she'd just poked. "*Us,* you ass. I never thought we would work out."

Peter feigned offense. "Why not?"

Tabitha shrugged. "I dunno. We've known each other forever."

"Which is exactly why we're perfect." He cupped her chin and turned her face up to his. "I wouldn't let you leave me either. It took too long for me to realize that we belong together."

Tabitha's heart first stopped, then skipped, and finally pulsed an extra-hard beat. "We do? I mean, *I* knew it. But you think so, too?"

"How could I not?" Peter squeezed Tabitha and laid his head on hers. "We know everything there is to know about each other. Who better to fall in love with than one of your oldest friends?" He kissed Tabitha's head once more and released her to go and rummage in the fridge.

Tabitha walked over and leaned on the counter where she had a better view of Peter's ass bobbing around while he raided her fridge. "Using that logic, you would be just as happy hooking up with…Meredith."

Peter heard the undertone of jealousy, and it pleased his Were nature *immensely.* "Nah. Meredith doesn't have your heart or the badonkadonk to end all badonkadonks." He turned around with the cooked chicken he'd snagged. "What else have you got to eat?" he asked through a mouthful of chicken.

"You're eating it," she replied. She took a plate from the cupboard and put it on the counter, then hopped onto a stool at the breakfast bar while Peter loaded it.

He opened a cupboard and grimaced at its bareness. "For someone who loves food as much as I do, you never have any in your kitchen."

"Maybe because I've got a problem with a hungry Pricolici who keeps coming over and eating everything?" Tabitha raised an eyebrow at Peter's continuation of his search. "You *do* know there's going to be food at the party?"

Peter shrugged. He put the half-eaten chicken on the plate and stood on his tiptoes to search the overhead cupboard where Tabitha usually kept the good snacks. "Yeah, but I'm hungry now. Besides," he emerged from the cupboard with a package of jerky, "it will all be little-kid food."

Tabitha slipped into the space between Peter and the counter and looked pointedly at his selection. "And that's grown-ass man food?"

Peter puffed his chest out. "I'm a grown-ass man, and that's my food. So, yeah." He pouted when Tabitha burst out laughing. "What? I need meat. It's like a basic requirement."

Tabitha grabbed him around the waist and pulled him toward her. "Funny you should say that. I was just thinking almost exactly the same thing."

. . .

QBBS *Meredith Reynolds*, All Guns Blazing, Private Function Rooms

Tabitha dragged Peter through the corridor that ran along the outside of the main bar toward the sounds of music and children's laughter. "C'mon, Pete! We're late!"

Peter chuckled and allowed her to pull him along. "We're not late, look." He pointed out a couple of little kids in party clothes arriving with their gift-laden parents in tow.

Tabitha stopped dead in her tracks. "Merry's gift! I left it on the dresser! This is what I get for letting you distract me."

Peter shook the shiny bag he had in his free hand. "Good thing I noticed and picked it up, then. I put it in with mine, so you're golden."

She looked at the bag blankly for a second, then shook her head. "I didn't even see you had that. Thanks for being so thoughtful."

"No worries, babe." Peter winked and flashed a grin. "*That's* what you get for letting me distract you."

Tabitha returned his grin and walked through the doors into the party.

The room beyond was decorated with balloons and streamers. Children's party songs played in the background while Merry and her guests ran around their parents' legs with all the energy that twenty boisterous sugar-filled children were capable of.

Tabitha pointed out the food laid out on the tables along one wall. "I told you there would be food."

Peter nodded at Jean, who was sitting by the table with her eyes peeled for anyone who was thinking of raiding the buffet before she had given the go-ahead. "Yeah, and it's guarded by a fearsome warrior." He turned to whisper, "I'd like my hands to remain attached to my body, thanks."

Jean waved Tabitha and Peter over. "Good to see you both. Gifts go there, and Merry is with Lillian in the back."

Tabitha and Peter left their gifts on the table with the others and made their way over to give a harried Lillian some help herding Merry and her friends in the spaceship-shaped bounce house.

The noise coming from the bounce house was incredible. The children's happy screams filled the room and echoed from the high ceiling.

It was so loud that Tabitha wasn't surprised the birthday girl hadn't noticed their arrival. She was too busy bouncing around in the spaceship with a bunch of other kids her age while Lillian watched from the side.

Lillian smiled and pushed back the wisps of hair that had fallen into her face. "You made it! Merry will be delighted. Why don't you go in and surprise her?"

Tabitha removed her shoes and ducked inside the net at the bounce house's entrance. "I'll just say a quick hi and leave her to play with her friends."

Tabitha's "quick hi" turned into her and Peter being mobbed by the children, then the pair of them were pulled into the kids' games until Jean called time to eat.

The children left as one, swarming over to the adults. The only one still in the bounce-house was Merry.

"Time to eat, Twinkle," Lillian called.

"Don't want to!" Merry yelled.

Tabitha and Lillian exchanged a glance, hearing her muttering to Meredith.

Lillian moved to retrieve her, but Tabitha winked and told her to take a break. "I've got her." She climbed back inside the bounce house and found little Merry scrunched up at the back. Her niece was trying to hide the fact that she was crying.

Tabitha scrambled over and sat beside her. "Merry, what's the matter?"

Merry sniffed, and a bubble of snot popped at the end of her nose. She wiped her face on her dress, staining it with tears. "I don't want to have a party anymore."

Tabitha held out her arm, and Merry scooted over to tuck herself under it. "It's okay, *mi pequeña patita*, we can just hide out in here until you feel like joining in again."

"Okay." Merry's voice was barely a whisper. "Aunt Tabbie?"

Tabitha knew that look. "Would you like me to get you some food?"

Merry looked up at Tabitha with such love in her eyes that Tabitha almost started to cry as well. "Yes, please."

Tabitha crawled out of the netting and went over to the table to grab a couple of plates for her and Merry. She returned Peter's wink when he turned from his conversation with John to acknowledge her and got to loading the plates with Merry's favorites from the cold buffet.

Lillian left the table where the children were eating. "Is she okay?"

Tabitha nodded. "She's a little bit tired."

Lillian looked at the party guests and chuckled. "They all are. It's a hard life, being a three-year-old."

Tabitha took the two plates back to the bounce house

and climbed back in, being careful not to spill the food. She was met by a tiny snore.

"Oh, Merry," she murmured, backing out of the bounce house to leave the plates to the side while she collected Merry.

Merry didn't stir when Tabitha picked her up gently and carried her to Lillian, totally exhausted by the energy she'd expended.

A few of the other children were beginning to get sleepy too. Little hands rubbed tired eyes, and the yawns and rosy-cheeked faces of the children were enough to tell their parents that the party was almost over.

Lillian stood by the door with Merry fast asleep in her arms and thanked them all for coming as they left, promising to send them video of Merry opening their gifts when she woke up.

"That was a bit of a letdown," John remarked as he closed the door behind the last parent. "We didn't even get around to the cake before they all started to fall asleep."

Jean shrugged and smiled. "It's how these things go when the kids are so young. I think they did great." She smiled and patted her daughter's back. "You too, Lilly. These things are a royal PITA to do for under-fives."

Lillian chuckled. "You're not wrong." Merry stirred in her arms. "Looks like my Twinkle is waking up."

Merry opened her eyes and blinked at everyone surrounding her. "Is it still my party?"

Lillian dropped a kiss on Merry's forehead. "It's the part that's just us and Grandma and Granddad and your aunts and uncles now."

Merry squirmed to be put down. "Can I eat? I'm hungry!"

Lillian lowered her daughter to the floor. "Of course you can, sweetie. Your plate that Aunt Tabitha fixed for you is here, see?" She picked up the plate and placed it on the table for Merry. "Tuck in, Twinkle. When you're done eating, we can open your gifts. Does that sound good?"

Merry half-grinned and half-yawned. "Sounds perfect, Mommy!" She sat at the table and began tearing into her food.

Peter came up behind Tabitha and wrapped his arms around her waist, resting his head on her shoulder. "She's a cutie. Trouble, but cute."

Tabitha sighed. "I hope she will cope with the move when it happens."

"What move?" Lillian asked. "Who's moving?"

Jean's eyes widened. "Oh, um…"

"Looks like the cat's out of the bag," John told her. "You didn't expect it to stay secret for long, did you?"

Lillian rounded on her parents. "What haven't you told me?" she hissed.

Jean put a finger to her lips when Merry looked up. "Keep your voice down, Lillian." Her eyes unfocused for a brief second. "There, Meredith is filtering for us. Don't get your panties in a twist, daughter mine. There are changes coming. Big ones."

"What kinds of changes?" Lillian demanded. "And *who* is moving?"

John spoke softly to offset Jean's irritation at their daughter's overreaction. "Bethany Anne will be stepping down as Empress as soon as she finds a way to do so without causing upheaval. She plans to leave the Empire behind, and we're going with her."

Lillian looked to all of them before she sighed and collapsed into a chair. "You're *leaving*?"

John nodded. "We are. You too, if it's what you want."

"Of course I want to come with you! Why the hell would I want to be without my family?" Lillian buried her face in her hands. "But...I *can't*. What about the business? I'm having some success at last. If we move it to wherever Aunt Bethany Anne decides to settle, I'll have to start over from scratch. And Merry's schooling? If I take her away from here, she's going to miss out on so much." Her head turned towards the door the kids just left through. "Her friends..."

Tabitha frowned. "I don't envy you your position, but I get it. You have to do what's best for Merry." She glanced at her niece, who was crunching her way through her apple slices without a care in the world. "I'm going to miss you both, especially Merry."

The child in question was done with her food. She pushed her plate away and ran over to the adults. She jumped up and down, clinging to Lillian's leg. "Can I open my gifts now, Mommy? *Pleeeease?*"

Lillian smiled at her daughter and held out a hand. "I suppose now would be a great time to get started."

There was a timid knock on the door. Tabitha turned to see Tiera hovering near the entrance looking a lot less nervous than she had the last time Tabitha had seen her. "I'll be back in a minute," she told the others.

Tabitha walked over to Tiera with a wide grin that she couldn't suppress even if she wanted to. She had thought to reveal the news later, but she decided she couldn't wait to share it after all.

Tiera held out a small gift wrapped package. "Hi, Tabitha. I know we were due to meet later, but I wanted to drop this off. It's an addition to your gift for Merry."

Tabitha took the package. "What is it?"

Tiera winked. "A surprise, of course."

Tabitha grinned as she accepted the package. "I have a surprise for you as well. Have you talked to Ashley in the last few days?"

Tiera shook her head ruefully. "I haven't spoken to anyone except drunks and thieves for days." She made a face. "I think I'm coming around to the idea of letting you help."

Tabitha smirked. "Funny you should say that."

Tiera narrowed her eyes in suspicion. "Why?"

Tabitha looked away guiltily. "Because...I might have already done something to help."

Tiera's eyebrows drew in. "Like what?"

"Like I got in touch with the right people and landed Ashley the biggest commission I could find. She has enough work now to employ a whole staff, not just you. You should go and speak to her. She'll be at her new premises."

"Really? That's... I..." Tiera's face worked through all the emotions that hit her, starting with anger and ending with relief. She took a couple of deep breaths to steady herself and then flung her arms around Tabitha. "Thank you. You're a true friend, Tabitha."

Tabitha returned the hug with feeling. "You're welcome. I'm so pleased for you and Sebastian!"

Tiera smirked. "*I'm* pleased I can hand that uniform back in and thank my bosses for giving me a chance."

"I think Rickie will be pleased to hear it," Tabitha teased. "He worried you weren't tough enough for the job. Pretty sure you set him straight, though."

"Damn right I did," Tiera shot back. "But I'm due home, so I'd better get going. Thank you for helping, despite my pride."

Tabitha turned the package Tiera had given her over in her hands. The shape of the contents was familiar enough to bring a smile to Tabitha's face.

"Aunt Tabbie! Aunt Tabbie!"

Tabitha turned to Merry, who was brandishing a new set of toy Jean Dukes pistols. "Cool beans! What do they hold?"

Merry pulled the triggers, and Tabitha learned that this set fired sticky darts. She tugged the darts from her stomach and chest and grinned. "Look at you! You're gonna be the most fearsome Ranger when you grow up."

Merry squealed with delight. "Just like you, Aunt Tabbie!"

Tabitha caught her and swung her around in a circle. "*Just* like me. Oh, I almost forgot! Your gift, Merry." She went over to the table and hunted down Peter's gift.

She took the shiny gift-wrapped box out and gave it to Merry. "Happy birthday, Merry-love."

"Thank you, Aunt Tabbie!" Merry sat down cross-legged and fumbled at the wrapping paper until she managed to get a corner loose. "What is it?" she asked breathlessly.

"Open it and find out!" Tabitha urged.

Merry lost her patience and tore into the paper. She opened the box and flung handfuls of the protective tissue everywhere in her hurry to get a glimpse of her surprise.

Suddenly, Merry jumped up and let out a high-pitched scream.

Lillian jumped up. "What is it, baby? Are you hurt?"

Merry continued to jump up and down. "Mommy, *Mommy*! Ranger...*coat*!"

Tabitha let out the breath she hadn't realized she'd been holding. "So, you like it?"

"*Yeah!*" Merry was busy trying to get her arms into the coat. Her struggle with the floor-length duster was mostly to do with the fact that she was *still* bouncing around like a frog on acid and kept missing the sleeves.

"Let me help," Tabitha told her. She took the coat and held it out so Merry could slide her arms in.

Merry ran to get her new pistols from the table where she'd left them. She ran back over to Tabitha via the other adults, whom she peppered with sticky darts, and looked up with wide, earnest eyes. "Aunt Tabbie? Am I a Ranger now?"

Tabitha put a finger to her lips while she pretended to consider. "Hmmm. I think you're still missing something." She passed Merry the package that Tiera had dropped off. "Here, let's see if this is what you need."

Merry tore into the wrapping paper and tugged out the badge. "I have a *Ranger badge*?" She held the toy badge up to inspect it. "I have a Ranger badge! I'm a real Ranger now! What does it say?"

Tabitha pointed each word out as she read it. "Empress' Ranger at the top there, see? That's your name in the middle. M-E-R-R-Y. And at the bottom, it says *Ad Aeter-nitatem.*"

"What's 'and a-turney-tatum?'" Merry asked.

"Ad Aeternitatem," Tabitha repeated. "It's a special promise. It means 'For eternity,' which means all the time that there will ever be."

Merry put the badge around her neck and held her arms out for Tabitha to pick her up. "Like how long I love you for, Aunt Tabbie?"

Tabitha touched her nose to Merry's. "Exactly that long, my precious girl."

CHAPTER TWENTY-THREE

<u>Open Space, Aboard the *Penitent Granddaughter*, Nickie's Training Room, the Next Day</u>

Nickie heard the grunts coming from her repurposed cargo hold and couldn't resist investigating.

She quietly slipped inside the door and stood in the shadows while she watched Keen and Grim hard at work training Addie and Durq in fighting techniques. Someone had procured a few mats from somewhere and laid them out in the middle of the hold. She was pleased to see that Grim was participating. He spent too much time hiding in the galley these days.

It was a little strange to watch him teaching Durq, suspiciously in much the same way her grandfather had trained her; the same way her Aunt Bethany Anne trained everyone. It was a hard way to learn, but the little Skaine didn't complain once when he was taken down again and again by the highly-trained Yollin.

Keen paused the set he was running Addie through to

watch a particularly intricate throw that Grim was struggling to remember.

"I haven't done this for a while," he apologized.

Nickie grinned and stepped out of the doorway. "Let me remind you."

Grim sighed. "Oh, shit. This is going to hurt, isn't it?"

Nickie came over to the mat. "You can bet it will, Grimmie. How else are you supposed to remember the lesson?"

Adelaide smiled nervously. "You don't mind that we're in here, do you?"

"Not even a little bit," Nickie replied brightly. "In fact, I love what you've done with the place. It feels homey."

Durq frowned. "You find the training area homey?"

Nickie and Grim snickered.

"If you'd grown up anywhere near my family, you'd know that it's the place I feel *most* at home," Nickie told him. She bowed to Grim. "Ready?"

Grim nodded resignedly. "Yes, but you will be helping me make dinner if you break me too badly. Let's just get it over with."

Nickie spent the next hour running through various techniques she knew for the benefit of the crew. After that, she and Grim left the others to practice while she helped him to the galley.

"That last lock was murder on my poor back," Grim complained as she led him to a stool at the counter.

"Quit your bitching," Nickie told him. "We should talk about how you know all my grandfather's moves, cook o' mine."

Grim winced as he shrugged and irritated his newly-set shoulder. "I've lived a long life, Nickie. Once I fought, and now I cook. There's nothing else to it." He indicated a cupboard. "You can start in there. You need…" He got up with a groan when Nickie began piling ingredients on the counter. "Noooo, all my organization!"

Nickie stepped away and held up her hands. "You can make dinner by yourself if you like?"

Grim sat down again gingerly. "No, you earned it."

Nickie's mouth twitched.

Soon enough she had a pan of something that didn't smell like it would kill them simmering, and the two of them sat at the counter with a glass of cooking sherry each.

Nickie took a sip and made a face. "Ugh, what the fuck is this? It's so *sweet*!" She pushed the glass away and went to the pantry to search for the wine she knew he kept for cooking instead.

Grim knocked his back in one, then snagged hers and polished that off as well. "Pain relief," he told Nickie. "You dented me a little."

Nickie came back with her objective in hand and stopped to look him over. "I can't see any damage to your carapace. Besides, I went easy on you."

Grim snorted, spraying sherry everywhere. "You wouldn't appreciate me telling you that you sounded just like your grandfather just then, but I remember him saying exactly the same thing to me."

Nickie narrowed her eyes at her friend. "So you *were* trained by him. I fucking *knew* it!"

Grim grimaced. "Yeah, well. Adolescent me was all fight and no brain. I was lucky that John didn't kill me on the spot the first time we met."

"You kept this quiet, Grim."

"Would you have believed that I joined you because I wanted to if I'd told you the whole truth back then?"

Nickie shrugged. "We were a bit busy stealing a ship. I probably would have shot you, if I'm honest."

Grim reached for the sherry bottle but stopped and wrapped his arm around his middle with a groan. "So you agree it would have been detrimental to my continued ability to breathe?"

Nickie poured him a shot to save him the pain from his sore ribs. "When you put it that way…"

"I *am* putting it that way," Grim told her. "Although if today were the first day we met, I would tell you everything."

"Really?" Nickie was surprised.

"Really," Grim assured her. "You were completely fucking terrifying when we met, but I recognized you as a kindred spirit." He swallowed his drink. "Deep down, at least."

"Love you too, Grim," Nickie teased.

"I don't doubt it," Grim agreed. "So…High Tortuga. Want to tell me why we're going back there now that the mission is complete?"

She sat and sipped her wine. "I'm coming to the end of my thinking time. I have a decision to make about whether to go back or not."

Grim gave her a sympathetic look. "It looks like you've already made it."

Nickie shrugged. "Not really. I'm not sure I'm ready. I mean, this mission was a little fucked up, but it felt good to do something for others."

"It always does."

"Yeah, but…"

"But what?"

"I dunno, just… It's hard to go back and face all the pain I caused everyone."

Grim shifted in his seat. "*Gott Verdammt*, that hurts. I suppose the bigger question is not whether you are ready but whether you believe you will be welcomed back into the fold when you return."

Nickie thought about that for a minute. "I think I will be. I know that my uncle, at least, does more than tolerate me."

"Well, Barnabas has always marched to the beat of his own drum. He probably sees a kindred spirit in you as well. But Nickie, you *do* realize that you are much more than just tolerable?"

Nickie shrugged. "No, but I never cared what anyone *thought* before. I just decided, fuck them if they didn't like it. This is different. It's not a comfortable thing to know that all my issues with my mom weren't what I thought and that most of it was my fault."

"I'm sure it wasn't either of your faults," Grim assured her.

Nickie shrugged. "It doesn't matter anyway. I don't know if we can fix things between us."

Grim considered that. "Do you want to go home?"

Another shrug. "Maybe. I'm not sure if it's the right thing to do. Some broken things can't be mended."

Grim waved a finger at the sherry for a refill. "Sounds like you need to look at the bigger picture. What do you want from your life? Do you want to keep doing what we're doing?"

Nickie nodded. "I liked the gray area we worked in for this last mission. I am glad that John solved the problem, but I would have been okay with it if I'd had to take Cynthia out. The vigilante thing is maybe something I could get used to."

"So *that's* why we're going back to High Tortuga." Grim eased himself off his stool and went to check on the pan. He stirred it and tasted Nickie's sauce. "This isn't half bad! Needs a little something, though."

Nickie mock-scowled at her friend. "Well, you put the fighter in the kitchen, and this is what you get."

He added a pinch of something to the sauce. "It's a great first attempt."

"I *have* cooked, Grim. I just don't want to waste time when I can grab whatever is around. It's only fuel, at the end of the day."

Grim clutched a hand to his heart. "How can you say that about my food?"

Nickie laughed. "Not *your* food, Grim. Your dinners are the best."

Nickie hadn't known that Yollins could blush.

High Tortuga, Northern Continent, Space Fleet Base

The *Penitent Granddaughter* returned to High Tortuga, where the crew was met once again by Barnabas.

They piled down the ramp, Durq included this time.

Barnabas nodded to them all. "No Prince PITA?" he asked Nickie with a slight smirk.

Nickie tilted her head. "Uncle Barnabas, why ask when you already know the answer?"

"Politeness, dear Nickie. Besides, I want to hear your report. Did you succeed in ensuring a smooth succession to the Vietanian throne?"

Nickie smirked. "You could say that. It did get a bit fucked up, though."

"These things often do." Barnabas smiled. "Walk with me. You can tell me about it when we get to the Pit for a proper debrief. Your crew may take some well-deserved leisure time while we take care of business."

Adelaide chuckled nervously. "The Pit?"

Barnabas waved her off. "Nothing to worry about, Addie. It's not actually a pit. It is the base's security area."

Adelaide's eyes widened at Barnabas' casual use of her nickname. "Oh, okay then."

They left the others at the rec area, and Nickie followed Barnabas through the base to the underground level where the Pit was situated.

Nickie didn't recognize anyone in the bustling command center.

A woman at one of the larger stations looked up as they entered. "Hey, Barnabas. Who's your friend?"

Barnabas smiled at the woman. "Hello yourself, Jennifer. This is my niece, Nickie."

Jennifer looked Nickie over with a smile. "Ah, the infamous Captain Grimes. You caused quite a stir on your last visit."

Nickie grinned. "Yeah, it's a bit of a thing with me."

Barnabas motioned for Nickie to follow him. "We'll use the smaller meeting room. Are you hungry?"

"Always," Nickie told him.

Barnabas chuckled. "You are *definitely* Tabitha's niece."

Nickie grinned, thinking about the last diary entry. "You bet. Hey, Uncle B, is there somewhere I can get a new coat? I feel like a change from overalls all the time."

Barnabas winked. "There are plenty of stores that have what you're thinking of. Leather is a somewhat popular thing around these parts."

Nickie gave him a look. "I thought you weren't reading my mind?"

Barnabas pushed open the door to the meeting room with a chuckle. "Just a peek, my dear. How else would I know what you need? I promise I haven't looked any deeper. It would be rude. We can shop if you are staying long enough."

She would have argued, but she saw the sense in what her uncle said. "We'll see how this debrief goes. Then I'll decide if I'm going to stick around."

Nickie made herself comfortable at the table while Barnabas stuck his head into the fridge and returned with two Cokes.

He handed Nickie hers and sat across from her. "So, what happened on Vietania?"

Nickie made a face. "Ugh, I hate Coke. Is there at least some rum to mix it with?"

Barnabas waved at a cabinet next to the fridge. "Help yourself."

Nickie fixed her drink and sat back down. "So, um… We left the eldest sister in charge."

Barnabas frowned. "You assassinated the rightful heir?"

Nickie shook her head. "No. No assassinations were necessary." She took a sip of her drink and gave her uncle a pointed look. "You didn't exactly have accurate information. We got there and there was a conflict, but it was mostly between the people. The sisters were just mad at each other because they were jealous and frustrated, and the whole system was suffering because of it. The older sister, the illegitimate one—she was the best choice to rule, so I made a decision."

"And the younger sister?"

"She eloped with Prince PITA. It was all sickeningly romantic."

Barnabas smiled. "Slightly unconventional, but if it worked as a solution, who am I to argue with it?"

Nickie pointed at him. "Exactly. It got the job done."

Barnabas gave her a searching look. "And what would you have done if this solution hadn't presented itself?"

Nickie shrugged. "I would have taken the queen out so her sister could rule."

"Hmmmm."

Nickie glared at him. "What? You said, and I quote, 'by any means necessary.' I can get Meredith to play the conversation back if you'd like?"

Barnabas waved her off. "No need, my dear. I was just considering how similar we are. Do you think you could see yourself doing this sort of work for a while?"

Nickie shrugged. "I guess so. It's not the worst."

Barnabas chuckled. "No, it is not." He paused for a second. "How would you feel about sticking around for a few days? I have something to take care of, but I think it would be an excellent time for you to reacquaint yourself with the people who have missed you."

Nickie frowned. "Like who?"

"Well, Sofia, for one. And who knows who else will turn up while you're here?" He folded his hands together on the table. "Things are a little different than when you left. They have…evolved, you might say."

"I thought you wanted me to go out there and do vigilante shit and all that?"

Barnabas inclined his head a touch. "Well, if you are already walking the walk, then you may as well talk it, too.

But I have to admit I'm a little concerned as to whether you understand where the line is for people like us. I want to be sure before I send you out there again."

"What do you mean?"

Barnabas paused to think. "We *could* talk endlessly about this, but what it really comes down to is ethics."

"I have ethics," Nickie grumbled. "It doesn't matter if they don't fit with everyone else's. Except maybe yours."

Barnabas nodded. "I'm sure you do, and that is what I would like to learn about you. Why do you think I became a vigilante when the Rangers were disbanded?"

Nickie grinned. "Because you couldn't live for one minute without fucking things up for whatever assholes decide they can take what isn't theirs?"

Barnabas looked a little guilty.

Nickie clapped her hands in delight. "*HA*! I'm right, aren't I?"

Barnabas sighed. "That is a rather crude way of putting it, but yes. I have lived a long life, Nickie. My rage has been tempered by time." He steepled his hands on the table and adopted a serious expression. "My concern is whether you understand your own motivations and how they affect your decisions."

"You mean, do I know the difference between right and wrong?"

Barnabas nodded. "What you did on Vietania, making the choice to act as a queenmaker? It was not a light thing. The implications of interfering with a planet's constitution are far-reaching, Nickie."

Nickie slumped a little in her seat. "I know, but what was the alternative?"

Barnabas smiled. "That is a very good question, my dear, and one that the Federation is restricted from answering. One that most vigilantes don't bother to consider. But one that I believe you would benefit from thinking about."

"I thought hard about it before making the decision to put Jolie on the throne. It wasn't a snap reaction, Uncle B. And it was the right choice."

Barnabas nodded sagely. "Tell me how you came to the conclusion that the rightful heir was not the right ruler."

Nickie twisted her glass between her hands. She sure as hell wished the alcohol in the rum wasn't being scrubbed from her system as soon as she drank it. This was some heavy shit to deal with. "When we got there the situation was sort of like the brief, but it turned out to be much more complicated than any report could cover."

"In what way?" Barnabas asked.

Nickie thought carefully before she answered. "Well, for a start, there wasn't really a feud between the sisters. It was more like your usual sibling rivalry."

Barnabas frowned as though he hadn't known any of what she was telling him. "What do you mean?"

"They were both a little bitter toward each other. Cynthia, the heir, was forced into being queen, and the firstborn had been sidelined because of some fucking ridiculous law about legitimacy. Cynthia had no leadership skills at all, just wanted to be a socialite. Then we had the older sister, Jolie, who did all the work to run things and had the most public support. If I had removed Jolie as planned, the only way the Six were getting into the Federation would have been as part of the relief efforts after the civil war ended."

Barnabas' frown deepened. "I was unaware that the situation was so severe. I can only apologize for sending you in underprepared."

Nickie shrugged and looked down at her drink. "It's cool. We dealt."

"You did indeed." Barnabas was quiet for a moment. "My final question: what gave you the right to make that decision for a whole planet?"

Nickie's head snapped up.

"That was not an accusation, Nickie. I would like you to tell me why you believe you had the authority to countermand your orders."

Nickie snorted. "Because my orders were stupid, that's why. I did what was right, and if Cynthia hadn't run away with John, I would have taken her out—no problem whatsoever. I had the right because I was there to do whatever those people needed me to do to make sure they carried on living in their humdrum bliss." She paused as a realization hit her. "Ohhhh. Fuck me sideways, Uncle B. This is one of those things where I say I'm sacrificing myself for the cause or some shit, right?"

"Or some shit," Barnabas agreed. He got up from his seat. "I am impressed, Nickie. I am also glad that fate intervened to save you from the burden of killing an innocent. You were faced with difficult decisions, and you made the right choice at each juncture. You should be proud of yourself."

Nickie got up, looking away to hide the burning in her cheeks. "I don't know about that."

Barnabas patted her shoulder. "I do. You did well, and I expect you will do well with your next challenge also."

Nickie narrowed her eyes. "What challenge?"

Barnabas smiled sagely. "All in good time, my dear. Now, I believe you wished to go shopping?"

CHAPTER TWENTY-FIVE

<u>Undisclosed Location, QBS *Shinigami*, Bridge, One Week Later</u>

Barnabas and Shinigami sat together over their usual game of chess, which was to say their usual game of attempting to cheat one another out of a victory.

"It's *my* move," Shinigami protested. Today her avatar wore Tabitha's face, simply because she knew it put Barnabas off kilter much more than Bethany Anne's or Baba Yaga's. She was on an eight-game losing streak, and any advantage she could get against Barnabas was fair as far as she was concerned.

"I distinctly remember you making the last move before Nickie arrived," Barnabas reminded his companion.

Shinigami snickered. "Sucks to be an old man with memory loss."

"Memory loss?" Barnabas snorted. "I'll give you memory loss. Right after I give you a master reset for resorting to such boring tactics and rudeness." Barnabas made his move and winked at her. "*Now* it is your move."

Shinigami stuck out her tongue at him.

Barnabas laughed. "My, my, aren't we petulant today?"

"I would be in a fine mood if I could work out how you are cheating," she grumped. "But it will have to wait. You have a call."

"Oh, yes?"

Without warning, General Lance Reynolds appeared on the viewscreen.

"Barnabas, how the devil are you doing?"

Barnabas smiled at his old friend. "Very well, thank you, Lance. It's been a very productive couple of weeks."

A small voice piped up. "Who is it, Daddy? Is it Bethany Anne? She promised to call me!"

Lance lifted his son Kevin onto his lap. "I'm the one who's making the call, sweetheart. Look, it's your Uncle Barnabas."

"Hi, Unca Barnabas," Kevin trilled. "Thank you for my spaceship!"

"You are very welcome, Kevin," Barnabas replied with a warm smile. The boy was growing up, although not as quickly as Alexis and Gabriel, thank goodness.

"Byeeee!" Kevin waved, then jumped down from Lance's lap and ran off making pew-pew noises.

Barnabas watched him go fondly. "He's an angel."

Lance grinned. "He's a chip off the old block, that's for sure."

"He is that." Barnabas chuckled. "So, what can I do for you? I'm guessing that this isn't a social call."

Lance grinned. "You guessed right. I've had an unexpected contact from the Six. They've resolved their issues and are ready to sign the agreements. However, the monarch of Vietania is not the person I was expecting."

Barnabas was pleasantly surprised. "That was fast. I believe that Queen Jolie's confirmation was a resounding success."

Lance narrowed his eyes. "Yes. I can't help but wonder what you had to do with that, although after suffering through a meeting with the other queen I have to say I'm somewhat grateful for the change."

Barnabas touched the side of his nose. "A vigilante never tells, Lance. You should know that by now."

Lance regarded him skeptically. "I know for a fact that you haven't left High Tortuga, and yet you look like the cat that got the cream. Come on, spill. How did you resolve it? You *did* resolve it, right?"

Barnabas lifted a shoulder. "In a manner of speaking. I outsourced it."

Thank Yous

Massive thanks as always goes out to MA, aka Yoda. Can you believe it's been 18 months and that nickname still STICKS!

Had I known… yeah, I still would have said it.

<EDIT MICHAEL: DAMN YOU *CLAR-RRRRRRRRKKKKKEEEEE!*>

Tee hee.

Thanks Yoda for your continued support and jousting.

Despite the shit I give you, you've still been super helpful in my new solo projects… even though there is a risk my solo books will knock yours out of your regular number #1 slots. (Not that *I'm* competitive… Just giving you something to joust against. You're welcome.)

<Edit Mike: Challenge Accepted. Frankly though, IF I'm going to get kicked out, at least it will be by a friend!>

Seriously though, even though it's not in your best interests commercially, I really appreciate the help you've given in reading the first few chapters, and helping tweak the covers to give them the best chance possible.

I don't for one minute suspect you might be secretly sabotaging me either... ;)

<Edit Mike: I'm not devious enough to fool you ;-) >

Massive, uber thanks also go out to our JIT team and Zen-Steve for all their hard work in making sure the words are consistent with the KU and reach you in tip top condition. Thank you so much for all the care and attention you put into the process. Without you... well, we'd probably be crying in a corner every time we needed to get a release out!

Reviewers

Massive thanks also goes out to our hoard of Amazon reviewers. It's because of you that we get to do this full time. Without your five-star reviews and thoughtful words on Amazon we simply wouldn't have enough folks reading these space shenanigans to be able to write full time.

You are the reason these stories exist and you have no idea how frikkin' grateful I am to you.

Truly, thank you.

Readers and FB page supporters

Last, and certainly by no means least, I'd like to thank you for reading this book. Your enthusiasm for the world, and the characters, is heart-warming. Your words of encouragement, and demands for the next episode are the things that often stay in my mind as I flick from checking the Facebook page to the scrivener file when I start each writing session.

Thank you for being here, for the giggles and interaction, for reading, and reviewing. You rock, and without you, there really would be no reason to write these stories.

Thank you.

E x

Mossad 101

Ok, so it's rare that I start author notes off by saying – OMGyouhavetoseethis!

But – OMGyouhavetoseethis!

As you know, I'm a bit of a Netflix binger. It's my way of relaxing... and also unleashing my creative brain to come up with new stories to tell. I'll see something in Mission Impossible and a variation on it may just appear in a heart to heart conversation between two characters for instance. (Oh yeah, there is no direct pulling from other stories – it's all about it triggering ideas or moral arguments, or set ups that I decide I want to explore while mindlessly watching other things going on on screen! And don't tell me you're not the same ;P)

Anyway, I digress.

Recently, since I've been healing from the adrenal failure, I've had more focus and energy. Enough energy to watch things like The West Wing. (OMG how awesome is it?? I have favourite episodes. I know... super geeky).

But recently I found a show called Mossad 101.

Now anyone who has seen any NCIS will know about their super cool Mossad Agent, Ziva David. She's an inspiration. Bad ass. Cute. Israeli. Multi-lingual. Oh yeah, and she kicks everyone's ass without breaking a sweat.

So when I saw this show, I figured it was going to be lots of badassery and clever stuff going down.

And it didn't fail to impress. Within thirty seconds I was hooked. If you do TV (and I know a lot of you guys don't, because you prefer reading... and that's cool) but if you're ever looking for something cool on TV – check it out: Mossad 101.

Now, I have to tell you, it has subtitles, because it's mostly in Hebrew. I say mostly because when there is a French agent and conversation, they speak French. In an Arabic setting, they speak Arabic. And so it goes... just like in real life. Another reason why it is EPIC.

The subtitles are always in English though.

But it means you have to keep up with reading, and it's no good if you're tired coz it moves fast and it's also got layers of things you might miss if you just miss one screen. (It took me a while to figure this out because I've become so used to wandering off with my headphones on and not looking at the screen to see what's happening. One can do this with NCIS. Not with Mossad!).

Anyway – the text messages are also in Hebrew! IT'S. SO. COOL!

So cool in fact that I've been inspired to learn Hebrew.

I kid you not. (Check Patreon, I've been posting screen-shots of my app in there! This is happening.)

I'm currently on Module 4, of the Pimsleur course, and have just about learned the alphabet. Or aleph-bet as they call it. I'm inspired. I feel like may I knew this in a past life. It seems to be fairly straight forward to pick up and retain. Way more so than my efforts at Arabic or Icelandic.

Anyway – if you're feeling like you want something

about spy training, in Israel, and exposure to a new culture and language (don't you just love that buzz?) then Mossad 101 is your show.

Hit me up if you decide to watch it. I'd love to know what you think...

Nomading

Kind of related to learning Hebrew are my nomading plans.

For my visa I need to leave the US and then come back in. I guess it's a way of immigration keeping track of us aliens. Anyway, I had been toying with the idea of hanging in Paris for a little while. (I miss art museums, and it would serve two purposes). But then, I'm still recovering and lots of travel and jetlag is really the last thing I need just as I'm finding my feet again.

But then, leaning Hebrew and watching Mossad, I started to wonder if maybe it would be sensible to put some new language skills to the test and head out to Tel Aviv. It's been somewhere I've always wanted to go, but when I was nomading the area was still pretty volatile. Anyway, after careful consideration about the border issues here in the US, I decided it was probably more sensible to go to a less volatile and less controversial place for the visa trip.

I'm probably going to head back to Iceland. And probably only for a few days to try and limit the jetlag.

I'm sure I'll get to Israel at some point though.

Bentley is coming (FINALLY!)

As you've heard me harp on about on and off for several months (actually, nearly a year), I have a new series in the works. One that I've been working on without MA. Although it got off to a rocky start, it looks like we're going to be ready to hit publish before the end of the year. I'm hoping within the next month or two.

Jeff has been working on the covers... as you may have seen on the videos we've been sharing on fb and Patreon. As of the time of writing, I'm waiting to see what he comes back with on the big ass space ship that he was working on. He's off on vacay now, so it may have to wait until he gets back.

JIT are also working their way through the first piece of the book to make sure it is on target and compelling enough for us to want to put it in your hands.

Anyway, let me tell you a little about Bentley.

This is basically Firefly meets King Arthur... but he's a chick. So Bentley is a girl. And a badass one at that.

It's sci fi – but sci fi with a twist.

It's also funny (I hope!), sassy and packed with rip roaring adventure. Actually, everything you've come to expect from the Molly series – but with a new crew.

And what a crew.

Imagine, three gods (or lwa – voodoo spirits) being kicked out of the unseen world, and being forced to live out their eternity in the frontiers of space, with only their wits and swords to protect them.

Sure, they have a ship.

And yes, they've found ways to adapt the technology in ways appropriate to ex-gods. But in their fall from grace, they've had to resort to being mercenaries and vagabonds, taking whatever jobs they can, and walking a fine line of morality until they can earn their way back.

And of course, there is a bigger danger they'll need to face long before that ever happens.

Thankfully they're spared the mundanity of most of the ship's maintenance by their onboard android – Jelly Bean. (Android users, you'll get the reference!)

If this is something you think you might enjoy, make sure you get yourself on to our mailing list (with Oz, our in-house AI), so we can give you a heads-up when it hits the Zon.

www.ellleighclarke.com

I'm so excited about this series. It's always nerve-wracking releasing something new… I REALLY hope you like it, coz I'm just a little bit in love with it.

<Edit Mike: Just a little bit??>

And want to be writing about Bentley for a long time to come!

MA's Smack Down

This on Slack the other week, ahead of an MA call:

MA: Might be 3 minutes late
MA: up to
MA: Ok, I'm here.
MA: Oh, and on time!
MA: SMACKIE DOWN

Smackie down???!
He said Smackie down!!!

Hahahhahahaha.

MA and Health

Ellie: is that water you're drinking?

MA: yes! I've been cutting down on all the shit I put into my body. Including the ibuprofen and coke.

Ellie: How come?

MA: It's your fault.

Ellie: Huh?

MA: I'm paying attention to it because of all the stuff you go on about. Not because my body is collapsing…

Ellie: …or you're getting old?

MA: Grrr.

MA and Shakespearian Word-invention

If you've been following these author notes from the beginning of the Molly series you'll know that conflating things has become something of a running joke. It started when I conflated 20booksto50k (MA's pride and joy – a Facebook group for indie authors with over a bazillion members) to 50books. Yes, I got it the wrong way round (somewhat deliberately).

And yes, his ego was kinda miffed, coz it turns the whole concept around… meaning you have to write a shit tonne more books for a lot less money.

It was part of the joke. <Edit Mike: I'm calling bullshit. She just fucked it up and now wants to rewrite history that it was on purpose!>

Now, whenever there is an opportunity to flippantly conflate two things, I take it.

Anyway, for some reason MA asked me something and I felt it was appropriate to use the term: fuckawesome.

I seem to recall he was asking why he should be interested in something, and I was trying to express that it was fucking-awesome. Hence the term fuckawesome was coined.

You heard it here first kids. Go forth and use it to annoy anyone who doesn't like conflation of terms and concepts!

You have my blessing :)

Working Together

In amongst shooting the breeze somehow we got onto the idea of what MA calls "working together, separately."

Ellie: Oh, that's what Amy and I do when we go to the café.

MA: No, that's not quite what I meant.

Ellie: you mean because we sit gossiping and laughing the entire time?

MA: Yes. But no.

Ellie: (looks quizzically)

MA: So working together, separately means you just work on your own thing but you're around strangers. When I want to do that I go to the Aria, just to have bodies around me.

Ellie: (Slowly putting it together) You make it sound like the Aria is just a brothel you use.

(Ridiculous laughter)

MA: No, no. The Aria is just a casino here in Vegas. I just…

Ellie: It's ok. No point explaining. Now I just have an image of you trying to work with a bunch of prostitutes around you as you type.

MA: *Sigh*.

<Edit Mike – This IS the shit I go through.>

MA and Insignificance

MA's computer was running slowly.

MA: dammit. Word is frozen.

Ellie: Is that a mac you're on. (Knowing full well it was a mac he was using… since this is an ongoing 'discussion' we have).

MA: yes. It is a mac.

Ellie: there's your problem.

MA: it doesn't normally do this. Normally it's fine… it's only when I go on the internet when we're on zoom that it freezes.

Ellie: maybe it's caught something from those porn sites you were looking at.

MA: I asn't looking at porn sites. Like I would. I have a 15" screen. Why would I want to feel insignificant by looking at that on a 15" screen!

Ellie: (snigger snigger.)

MA: (blushes, then changes the subject.)

<Edit Mike: Totally slipped on a banana peel of stupidity there…>

Thank You to Our Growing Patreon Family

Last and by no means least I'd like to say a huge thank you to our growing Patreon family.

Allan MacBain, Amy Teegan, Brian Roberts, Cynthia MacLeod, Darrell Heckler, David Pollard, James Burrett, John DeBlanc, Jolie Brackett, Judith Wiseman, Kendra Gilmore, Lester Nye, Mary Morris, Russell Peake, and Sandra Chapman.

You may have noticed that there were two interesting names in this book: Cynthia and Jolie - the two princesses. These were named after two more of our supporters over in Patreon.

John Deblanc's character started in the last book, and James Burrett will make an appearance in the new Jayne Austin series (Book 2) which will be hitting your kindles in the next several weeks.

If you'd like to get a character named after you, and to continue the back stage shenanigans, feel free to join us over at: www.Patreon.com/ellleighclarke .

I'll look forward to hanging out with you over there – either through the Author Shenanigan videos, or on one of our live streams. We've already done a movie day, and believe it or not, I think they got me doing a live baking thing.

(As you may imagine, I'm no baker, so this is going to be interesting. With Thanksgiving just around the corner there is talk of me making pumpkin pie!)

Until then...

Ellie x

Thank Yous

Thank you to everyone who not only read this book, but read Ellie's author notes and decided they were good, but came here to read the MASTER's author notes, as well.

<Insert Ellie's comment Here...>

Apparently, my notes that I wrote from our last Zoom Call are all safe and sound back in my Texas house while I'm here in Frankfurt, Germany. WAY past the ability for me to fly home at a moments notice.

<Insert Ellie's comment about men and their inability to keep their shit together. Seriously, why do I admit to these things and make it easier for her?>

So, I would like to say 'Thank You' to my collaborator as she has made this series happen. Without her prodding, I'd be sitting on my <redacted> not getting this series built in a timely fashion and you wouldn't be reading them.

<<Actual Ellie Edit: so if you're the Master, how is it

that after 16(?) books, you've started copying the format of *my* author notes?>>

STORY... FINALLY we are getting Nickie reintegrated back into the family... kind of. While I don't see Nickie quite all cozy with the family, I believe we will see her understand the issues between what really happened, and what she 'saw' happen as a little girl, with no idea of the challenges her mom faced at the time.

And how Grandpa 'John' wasn't the big baddie she has always made him out to be.

Other Stories!

We (Ellie and I) have two additional story series not set in the Kurtherian Gambit in production. Perhaps not heavily into production... but moving along! Further she mentioned her own series as a take off of Firefly and King Arthur.

All of these stories will likely hit within a few months, with some much closer than others.

It takes 45 minutes...

So, Ellie and I recorded the author notes for the MOLLY Series (The Ascension Myth – Book 01 (on Amazon.com here: My Book) for books 7 and 8 the other day and it took us two hours.

TWO HOURS.

Now, part of the reason was I failed to get the notes

together to share with Ellie ahead of time. A small amount can be blamed on making sure the technology worked.

The OTHER part of the blame I'm dropping at Ellie's feet. Why?

I'm gladded you asked.

Here is a secret. Ellie can't stay on script. Not ONE. DAMNED. BIT.

(it's fun mind you, but she was telling me she had a hard stop. So, I'm stressing and she's chin wagging the whole time.)

<<Ellie Edit: Omg you're learning the appropriate British terminology!>>

Case in point. We have just finished her author notes where we couldn't go sixty seconds I don't think and stay on script. We get to mine, where I think I have a bit more control...since...you know... THEY ARE MY AUTHOR NOTES.

What I learned is I have no control, only the perception of control until even that is taken away from me.

<<Ellie Edit: this is indeed a truth we discover en route to enlightenment.>>

I didn't get the first paragraph recorded before she interrupted me, talking about how we would have interruptions and shit.

I knew right then I was not in control. I would like to say I put a brave face forward and did a yeoman's job of working to hit her timeline and we did.

We finished 9 minutes early.

Just enough time to discuss a few other things before she did have to jump off the call. I guess I can't complain too much, she had moved the meeting up three hours to help me out.

But then, if I wasn't complaining, Ellie wouldn't have an opportunity to take the piss out of me, eh?

;-)

Ad Aeternitatem,
Michael Anderle